Strangers
on a Skein

Books by Anne Canadeo

Black Sheep Knitting Mysteries

While My Pretty One Knits

Knit, Purl, Die

A Stitch Before Dying

Till Death Do Us Purl

The Silence of the Llamas

A Dark and Stormy Knit

The Postman Always Purls Twice

Murder in Mohair

Black Sheep & Company Mysteries

Knit to Kill

Purls and Poison

Hounds of the Basket Stitch

Strangers
on a Skein

Anne Canadeo

KENSINGTON
PUBLISHING CORP.

www.kensingtonbooks.com

KENSINGTON BOOKS are published by

Kensington Publishing Corp.
119 West 40th Street
New York, NY 10018

All Kensington titles, imprints, and distributed lines are available at special quantity discounts for bulk purchases for sales promotion, premiums, fund-raising, educational, or institutional use. Special book excerpts or customized printings can also be created to fit specific needs. For details, write or phone the office of the Kensington Special Sales Manager: Attn. Special Sales Department. Kensington Publishing Corp, 119 West 40th Street, New York, NY 10018. Phone: 1-800-221-2647.

Library of Congress Card Catalogue Number: 2021938937

The K logo is a trademark of Kensington Publishing Corp.

ISBN-13: 978-1-4967-3238-5
ISBN-10: 1-4967-3238-3
First Kensington Hardcover Edition: November 2021

ISBN-13: 978-1-4967-3240-8 (ebook)
ISBN-10: 1-4967-3240-5 (ebook)

10 9 8 7 6 5 4 3 2 1

Printed in the United States of America

For my daughter, Kate, who inspires me every day

"The human face is, after all, nothing more nor less than a mask."

—Agatha Christie

Chapter 1

"Maggie—I'm scared. Correction . . . make that *totally terrified*." Phoebe's voice was low, her dark eyes large and luminous. "I can't do it. No way. What was I thinking?"

Maggie had just arrived at the shop a few minutes before her customary eight o'clock appearance. She found the wide front porch covered with boxes and the front door ajar. As she stepped around the cardboard obstacle course, Phoebe appeared, another load balanced in her arms.

The poor girl looked as if she hadn't slept a wink and was about to burst into tears. Maggie took the cartons from her hold and gave her assistant manager—and dear young friend—a reassuring hug.

"What's this? You were over the moon about the news last night."

"That was then. This is now?"

Maggie shook her head and smiled. "Chin up. A big change like this would make anyone nervous. You know what Eleanor Roosevelt always said—"

Well versed in Maggie's favorite maxims, Phoebe cut her short with an eye roll. " 'We have nothing to fear but fear itself.' "

"That was Franklin, dear. Still applies. I meant, 'You must do the thing which you think you *cannot* do.'" When Phoebe looked unmoved Maggie said, "I felt the same when I opened this shop. Honestly."

How many years ago was that? Seven, at least. Not long after her husband, Bill, had passed away from a sudden heart attack. The impulse to act on her "someday" dream of owning her own knitting shop seemed the only path out of her deep grief.

But not a clear path. Not clear at all. There were many sleepless nights, when she felt sure that she was about to run her predictable, carefully planned life right off the rails. And toss away the better part of her savings, too.

She'd taken the leap despite those fears—perhaps Bill's spirit had gently nudged?—and quickly discovered she'd made the right choice. The perfect choice for her. This was the right choice for Phoebe, too.

"How about, 'Just do it!'? That's the slogan in the sneaker ads, right?"

Phoebe smiled back. A small but hopeful sign. "If you say so."

"I do. And I'm dying for some coffee. I'll start a pot and we'll talk more." Maggie stepped inside, where she dropped her purse, knitting bag, and the day's edition of the local newspaper on the front counter.

She continued to the back of the shop, to the storeroom which had once been a kitchen, before the little Victorian had been turned into retail space. She'd left most of the cabinets and appliances intact, which made it easy to keep a steady flow of coffee, tea, and tasty treats set out for customers and serve savory meals to her knitting group, who met at the shop every week.

Maggie wanted the Black Sheep & Company to be a comfortable place where knitters of every age and skill level could retreat and relax, as if visiting a good friend.

She'd met that bar well, she thought. Her customers seemed to think so.

Maggie set up the coffee maker, while Phoebe stood at a big oak table in the back room, sorting through a carton of her knitted creations. Mostly, amazing and unique sock designs, hence the name of her brand, Socks By Phoebe. Phoebe had started with footwear, but offered much more now and had been selling the items at Maggie's shop, at flea markets, and online for over two years. Her ultimate goal was to open her own shop one day in the not so distant future.

Maggie found her paralyzing bout of doubt surprising, considering Phoebe's elation when she'd gotten word last night that a stall at Plum Harbor Farmers' and Crafts Market was suddenly vacant and her name was next on a long list of waiting vendors.

It seemed to Maggie that the reality of running her own business—not quite a real retail store, but a training-wheels version?—had hit home during the night, and now Phoebe was afflicted by a classic case of "watch out what your wish for." An observation Maggie held to herself.

The call had come a few minutes after six on Tuesday night. Maggie had just flipped the sign on the shop's door to SORRY, WE'RE RESTING OUR NEEDLES. COME BACK SOON! She'd set about her usual nightly fiddling—clearing the register and straightening a display that had seen a lot of customer action—light and airy summer yarns, in refreshing Popsicle colors.

Phoebe had already gone up to her apartment on the second floor, but Maggie soon heard footsteps flying down the wooden staircase. "Mag? Are you still here? Wait! I have to tell you something . . ."

Maggie ran back to meet her, expecting the typical emergency—a leaky pipe, or a blown circuit breaker. Another field mouse? Phoebe had barricaded herself in the bathroom during that crisis, leaving her one-eared, adopted alley cat, Van Gogh, to deal with the intruder.

This news was a different kind entirely. "I can't believe it! There are, like, a zillion people waiting for a stall. And I got it! Isn't that not awesomely lucky?"

Maybe not a zillion, but a fair number, Maggie knew. Local artists and craftspeople, and farmers, too, were all vying for sales space at the busy village market. It was already late July and Phoebe had given up hope of a spot this summer. The turn of events was definitely lucky.

Not so lucky for me, Maggie reflected, though she quickly put her feelings aside. "That's great news. When do you start?"

"I just have to sign some papers and pay the fee. The stalls are mostly canvas, with a wooden floor, but there's a flap with a lock if you need to leave stuff inside. The guy who runs the market, Warren Braeburn, said I can open tomorrow."

Maggie knew Warren a little. More like, knew of him. He was a local farmer who managed the market in Plum Harbor and another like it out in Rockport. It was a second job for him and very taxing, she imagined, on top of running his own farm. So many farmers struggled to make ends meet. There was something noble in the way they pursued their calling. How else could you describe coaxing things to grow from the rocky New England soil?

"Tomorrow? Goodness. Can you manage to set up by then?"

"That's way too soon, even for me. But maybe by Thursday? I'll go down in the morning—if you don't mind?—and check it out. A ton of tourists are coming through the village lately, and I've missed so much time already."

"Very true. The weather this weekend will be perfect."

Setting up in time to catch the weekend's high tide of summer tourists showed good business sense. Plum Harbor was not exactly a vacation destination, not nearly as popular or well known as Cape Cod or Martha's Vineyard. But the classic New England coastal village attracted its fair share of visitors: those who preferred a spot off the beaten track, and weekend sailors who tied up at the village dock and strolled around visiting shops, cafes, and the large Farmers' and Crafts Market that was set up near the village green from June through October.

The out-of-towners certainly helped business, but a large part of Maggie wished the charms of her hometown could remain a well-kept secret. Lately, it seemed the secret was out.

"Thursday still sounds tight to me," Maggie said. "Can you manage it?"

Phoebe offered her trademark impish smile. "With a little help from my friends?"

She meant their close circle of pals—Lucy, Suzanne, and Dana—who met every Thursday night to knit, share good food, and ponder life's mysteries. And put their wits and needles together to solve any mysteries around town, too.

"Of course we'll help you. That goes without saying." Maggie was already figuring out when and how she'd close the shop a few hours to help. "How large is the stall? Do you know?"

"Not that big, eight by twelve, I think. But mine is in a busy aisle, right near the food trucks," Phoebe reported happily.

"That is a good spot. And your friend Robbie is nearby, right? Isn't he working on a truck this summer?"

"The Mighty Green Taco," Phoebe replied. "I doubt I'll see him much. He's crazy busy most of the time." She paused, her smile fading. "Harry's aunt Adele has the stall right across from mine, This & That. She's always been really nice to me. It's Harry I'm worried about. If he drops by to see her, I figure I can hide somewhere?"

Maggie was focused on packing her knitting bag for the evening. She wasn't sure what to say. The possibility of Phoebe running into her former beau Harry McSweeney was not good news. Their breakup a few weeks ago had hurt Phoebe deeply. She'd been so downhearted, and was just coming back to her spunky little self.

"I doubt you'll see much of him. Best not worry about things that might not even happen, right?"

"Absolutely." Phoebe, who knew she had that tendency, looked grateful for the reminder.

Maggie did think a young man like Harry had better things to do than hang around a stall of kitschy garage treasures and piles of costume jewelry. Maggie knew that Adele had always liked Phoebe and was sorry to see the young people break up, so there would be no friction from that quarter.

"You're right. I have more important things to think about than stupid Harry," Phoebe declared as she'd headed back up the stairs. "I have to pull out my entire inventory and figure out what to sell."

Maggie was cheered to hear that plan and headed home, feeling happy for her protégé. But wistful, too. Phoebe had come into her life initially as a customer, armed with basic stitching know-how and eager to learn more. But her startling aptitude and creative flare was unmistakable and she was soon coaching other students in the classes Maggie taught. And dropping in during her spare time for more tips and stitching comradery.

During her years teaching art in the local high school, Maggie had met many students like Phoebe, brimming with talent and potential, but very much in need of support and encouragement from a caring adult. Maggie had been happy to take Phoebe under her wing, and when Phoebe started looking for a new apartment and part-time job that fit her college schedule, the solution felt like synchronicity. Maggie hired her as an assistant and offered the apartment on the second floor at a bargain rent. Phoebe very quickly became essential to the Black Sheep Knitting Shop, and a very dear friend.

More than a friend, Maggie thought. Phoebe had lost her mother when she was only nine or ten. Her father had quickly remarried and started a new family. They lived in Arizona and Phoebe rarely visited. She'd always felt like an outsider in her stepfamily and left home right after she'd graduated high school. She was close to her older brother, but he'd made a career in the military and she rarely saw him.

With so few family ties or maternal guidance, Phoebe had become a daughter to Maggie, in a way. Her Knitting Daughter, she might say.

Maggie had a *real* daughter she loved dearly. Julia had settled in Chicago after college and didn't come east nearly enough. But they were always in touch with phone calls and text messages, and ever close in spirit.

Maggie's relationship with Phoebe was different, but just as lovely and important to her. Without question, she wanted to see Phoebe succeed. Even if it meant leaving the Black Sheep & Company Knitting Shop behind.

Phoebe's cold feet about her new venture were the last thing that Maggie had expected this morning.

She emerged from the storeroom and handed Phoebe a mug of coffee—light, with two sugars, just the way she liked it. Then held out her own mug in a salute.

"We'll have a proper toast soon. With everybody," she said, meaning their close circle. "Until then, I'm wishing you great success. Best of luck with your new business. Though I'm sure you don't need it."

"Thanks, Mag. I hope you're right." Phoebe smiled as they clinked mugs. She sipped, then set her coffee down, her expression suddenly serious. "Something else spooked me last night. I called Warren back with a few questions and asked him why the stall was suddenly vacant. He said the person who was renting it just died. A farmer, Jimmy Hooper. He's been there for years, selling fruit and vegetables. It really creeped me out. I mean, I used to buy stuff from him all the time."

"Jimmy Hooper? I know him, too. Not very well, but his wife was an accomplished knitter. I would run into her all the time." Before she had opened her own shop, Maggie meant. "I buy a lot of produce from him, too. *Bought* a lot, I mean." Maggie corrected herself, adjusting to the past tense of Jimmy. She was surprised to hear this sad news. "When did he die? I didn't hear a word about it."

"Over the weekend. I'm not sure of the exact day." Phoebe paused a moment, then said, "He committed suicide. That's what Warren said." She shivered, hugging the hot coffee in both hands. "It's weird enough to take his space. But you know what they say about people who die in sudden accidents, or off themselves, and all that?"

Maggie didn't like where this was going. She knew some people believed that the spirit of a person who passed away in unexpected or unhappy circumstances got confused about where they belonged, and might linger in a familiar place. Some people used the word *linger*, others said *haunt*.

Either way, it struck her as a silly, superstitious notion. Phoebe, with her active imagination and sensitive nature, was susceptible to such theories.

"I know what you're going to say, Mag. *It's just plain silly and superstitious to worry about such a thing.*"

Maggie had to laugh. "You're a mind reader, as well as a talented mimic. I understand why you feel uneasy. It would be callous not to give the poor man a thought." Maggie sipped her coffee. "I have to admit, I'm shocked to hear it. Jimmy kept to himself after his wife died, but he was an easygoing, cheerful man. Always very friendly and talkative at his stall."

"He always chatted me up, too. He seemed like some happy farmer in a kid's show." An odd analogy, Maggie thought, but it fit Jimmy perfectly. "I'd never take him for the type to commit suicide."

"I wouldn't, either," Maggie agreed. "I suppose we'll learn the reason for his despair at some point." Plum Harbor was a small town. Even the most private information went viral. "He'll certainly be missed. I wonder if there will be a memorial for him."

"I'd like to pay my respects," Phoebe said. "Especially since I got his stall."

"I'll let you know what I hear. It's kind of you to be concerned, Phoebe. But I think that Jimmy would have thoroughly approved of you inheriting his market space. He was an unconventional man. Plowed to his own drummer, you might say?" Phoebe winced at her wordplay. "Just like you knit to yours," Maggie added. "Someone has to take over. I'd say you were the perfect choice."

Phoebe tilted her head, considering Maggie's words. "I never thought of it that way. That makes me feel better."

"Good." Maggie set her empty mug on the table. "We both better get rolling. Throngs of customers will be beating down the door any minute."

An exaggeration, they both knew. Summer was a slow time, but Maggie still found a way to bring in customers. Kids Knit, Too was a popular class, where Maggie taught children a simple hand-knitting technique and they even made a toy. Her class for expectant mothers, and grandmothers, What to Knit When You're Expecting, was sold out year-round.

At ten this morning, she would meet with a small but dedicated group who had signed up for Summer Knitcation. For this eclectic group at different skill levels and interests, her role was more coach than teacher.

Like the famous fable, these knitters were Maggie's worker ants. While the grasshopper knitters put aside their needles in the spring and played in the sun, the worker ants stitched on. Turning out ponchos, baby hats with animals ears, scarves with team colors, and mittens to match. Lap shawls, felted totes, and sweaters of all shapes, styles, and sizes. By the time the holidays arrived, their projects would be snipped, blocked, and gift ready.

She loved her worker-ant knitters. They kept her in business this time of year, that was for sure.

Phoebe headed up to her apartment. "I'd better see what else needs to go. Robbie is going to help me bring everything down to the stall. He'll be here in a little while." Maggie nodded. Robbie was not only Phoebe's "he's just a friend" male pal, but also Harry's roommate. So far, everyone seemed to be navigating the complication well.

Halfway up the stairs, Phoebe turned. "Sorry to cut out on such short notice. I can check out the stall later if you need me here?"

The offer was tempting but Maggie shook her head. "I have to get used to this sea change, too. The sooner the better."

She offered Phoebe a cheerful smile, though it did feel as if she'd been tossed in the deep end. At least Phoebe wasn't abandoning her in the fall or winter. *Best to look on the bright side, if you can find one,* Maggie reflected as she headed back out to the porch.

As she stood among the cartons overflowing with Phoebe's colorful and unique hand-knit socks, hats, hair bands, sweaters, scarves, bikinis, and who knew what else, her thoughts turned back to Jimmy Hooper.

Suicide? She could hardly believe it. Phoebe hadn't said if the police had signed off on that conclusion. The market manager, who had passed along the news, may not have known for sure, either. Maggie knew that when a person died alone, even if the cause appeared to be accidental, a thorough investigation was required under law, including a medical examiner's close inspection of the body and an autopsy. She'd be interested to know if that inquiry was concluded or still ongoing.

Maggie heard a familiar voice call her and looked up to find her friend Lucy coming up the walk. Lucy's dogs, both rescues—Tink, a scraggly golden retriever; and Wally, a three-legged chocolate Lab mix—tugged her along at a swift pace. Lucy walked them into town almost every morning and the dynamic trio stopped at the shop on their way home.

Back in the spring, she and her fiancé, Charles adopted a dog of their own, an adorable Labrador and Portuguese water hound mix, a brown ball of fluff that they'd named Daisy. Ever since, Maggie had noticed she was not only more tolerant of Lucy's panting four-footed companions, she also found their antics rather cute.

The happy hounds bounded up the porch steps, knowing they'd be rewarded with biscuits and cold water while they waited out the visit. But Lucy looked miffed. As miffed as the good-natured blonde ever got. More of a befuddled expression, Maggie decided.

"Why didn't you tell me you're having a yard sale? We have a ton of junk to unload." She followed the dogs up to the porch and tied the dog leashes to the railing. "Can I leave these guys a few minutes and grab some stuff from my garage?"

Maggie laughed. "You can if you like. But I'm not having a sale. This is all Phoebe's. She's opening a stall at the farmers' market. She heard last night that a spot is free."

Lucy's expression melted into her usual sunny smile. "Wow, that's great. She's been waiting all summer for that call. She must be ecstatic."

"She was at first. Until a bout of nerves and superstition set in. I think she'll be fine once she's down there." Maggie shoved some cartons aside with her foot, to clear a path to the wicker love seat and chairs. "It's a sad story actually. Do you know Jimmy Hooper? Hooper's Organic Farm, out near the Piper Nursery?"

"Sure, I know that place. He grows the juiciest tomatoes. I always stop at his stall when I go to the market. He's such a sweet man."

"Was a sweet man. He died this past weekend. Suicide, Phoebe heard. That part rattled her. You know how she buys into those silly ideas about wandering spirits. This is the first I've heard about his passing, too. I was just going to check the *Plum Harbor Times* for some mention of him."

"That's so sad. He hardly seemed the type."

"That was my reaction, too." Maggie considered voicing her suspicions. Not suspicions, exactly, but her curiosity to know if the police had found any evidence of foul play. But she decided not to get on that track with Lucy. Though the question did tug at her.

"Is there a type? Who can really say?" Maggie finally replied.

"I suppose. Was he married?"

"Yes, to his high school sweetheart. They had a son and a daughter, though I'm not sure where the children live now. His wife, Penelope, had a long battle with multiple sclerosis. I know they struggled. There were fundraisers in town for her medical bills. After she died, he socialized a lot less. Maybe even started drinking more than he should have?"

"It's hard enough to make a decent profit from a farm,

without medical bills piled on top. That might drive any-one to drown their troubles."

"True enough," Maggie said, considering the sometimes-slim profits from her own business. "They do say men find it hard to seek help when they feel overwhelmed. That 'strong, silent' macho thing. It's unfortunate."

Lucy sighed. "You can see a person every day but you never know what they might be dealing with privately."

Maggie agreed. Which was why she tried to be kind, or at least patient, with everyone she encountered. Sometimes a challenge, she had to admit.

Lucy pulled a few biscuits from her pocket and tossed them to her dogs. They crunched the treats midair, re-minding Maggie of furry crocodiles. Friendly crocodiles, she'd have to say.

Maggie leaned closer to Lucy, though there was no chance of Phoebe overhearing. "I hope Phoebe doesn't let these eerie ideas about Jimmy rattle her. Other vendors at the market are bound to be talking about his passing."

"There's always gossip when it's suicide," Lucy whis-pered back, "and all kinds of theories about foul play."

"I've been thinking the same thing. I certainly don't want to speculate in front of Phoebe, but I have an eerie feeling there's more to this story. Who knows what the po-lice might discover. Or have discovered already?"

Chapter 2

Before Maggie could say more, the up-and-coming knitwear designer pushed through the screen door.

"Hey, Lucy! Hey, doggos." Phoebe greeted her tail-wagging fans and rubbed their ears in a special way that made the dogs instantly limp with adoration.

Lucy stepped over and hugged her. "I just heard your news, Pheebs. Congratulations. I'm so excited for you."

"Thanks, I'm excited, too. When I'm not being so nutty and nervous." Phoebe turned, gazing out at the street. "Here's Suzanne. I hope she doesn't block the driveway."

Luckily, the big white SUV pulled up to the curb in front of the shop. Suzanne hopped out and waved as she headed their way. Dressed for a busy day at her realty office, she was a picture of style in a linen shift, a bright shade of tangerine. High-wedge sandals, designer sunglasses, and a tan leather tote completed the outfit. Classic Suzanne, Maggie mused.

She stopped at the bottom of the porch steps and stared at Maggie, dumbfounded. "How dare you hold a yard sale without telling me?! I have a basement full of sports equipment to unload. I'll cut you in, ten percent on every sale."

Maggie tried to answer but Suzanne interrupted. "Okay, fifteen. But that's my final offer."

Suzanne's brood—twin boys in middle school, and a high school–age daughter—each played a sport or two for every season. Her business meetings and appointments were carefully scheduled around carpools, team practices, music lessons, scout groups, test reviews, and their many other activities.

Suzanne somehow thrived on the frantic schedule, juggling family responsibilities with her demanding career. Her husband Kevin's flexible schedule as a builder and contractor helped her stay ahead of the curve, but just barely. Especially since she'd opened her own business.

She'd worked many years as a salesperson for Prestige Properties, but when a coworker was murdered last fall, the police pinned Suzanne as the prime suspect. By the time the real killer was apprehended, the firm had unraveled and Suzanne found herself both jobless and notorious around town.

In her usual style, she swiftly made the best of a bad situation. "When life hands you a bowl of lemons, whip up some lemon soufflé!"

Following her own advice, she accelerated her five-year plan of earning a broker's license to five months, and opened her own realty office. So far, Cavanaugh Fine Homes was quite successful and Suzanne had taken a leap in confidence as well.

She was definitely another mentor and role model for Phoebe and often offered tips and experience that were beyond Maggie's territory. Maggie knew Suzanne would be excited to hear Phoebe's news and waited for Phoebe to explain.

"For goodness' sake, it's not a yard sale. I finally got a stall at the market."

"Your own stall at the market? Our baby bird is leaving the nest?" Suzanne hovered between joy and tears. "This is big! I'm absolutely and completely thrilled!"

She swooped up Phoebe's petite form, squeezing her like a tube of toothpaste. "Need some help hauling this stuff downtown? We can just throw it in the Escalade."

"Thanks. Got it covered. Robbie should be here any minute."

Maggie was relieved that the boxes would be moved soon. She planned to hold the morning group outside. It was a fair day, not hot at all for late July. The flower beds that lined the white picket fence and bordered the brick walk were in full bloom, bursting with colorful perennials, and the window boxes that hung from the porch rail were also filled with flowers and trailing vines. The porch was one of Maggie's happy places and an ideal spot for knitting.

"How is Robbie? We haven't seen him around lately." Lucy tossed Tink a bonus biscuit. Wally, who was older, was fast asleep and lightly snoring.

Phoebe shrugged, dashing notes on the carton tops with a fat black marker. She didn't notice the look that passed between Lucy, Maggie, and Suzanne.

"He's working a lot this summer. His girlfriend, Mia, moved down to New York for a really cool job at a children's museum, and he took an extra job. Besides the taco truck, I mean. He has a ton of student loans to pay off . . . don't we all?" Phoebe paused and rolled her eyes.

"Long-distance relationship? That can get old fast. Especially when you're young." Suzanne's tone was goading. She obviously hoped Robbie and Mia wouldn't last.

Phoebe glanced at her. "I probably shouldn't tell you this, but you got that right. Mia met someone new and they broke up last week."

"Poor guy. That's rough." Suzanne's tone dripped with sympathy, but Maggie knew she felt just the opposite, hoping that now Phoebe and Robbie would get together.

As if it was anyone's business but their own. Though, Maggie also couldn't help but speculate about Phoebe's love life. Unlike Suzanne, she kept those speculations to herself, most of the time.

Robbie, Mia, and Phoebe had met during their student days studying art at the local community college, along with Harry, a ceramics artist, whom the knitting circle had nicknamed Harry the Potter. Unlike the boy wonder wizard, Phoebe's Harry had turned out to be a clod and a cad. He'd cheated with another girl and had broken Phoebe's heart. She was such a loyal, trusting soul.

Maggie sometimes got the feeling that Phoebe was not entirely over charming Harry. Like this morning. Her panic over seeing him seemed to indicate she was still hooked.

She just needed more time. The distraction of the market and her own mini business was just the thing.

Seeing her freshly showered and dressed for the work ahead, one would never guess how frazzled Phoebe had looked an hour ago. She wore black spandex shorts and high-top sneakers with a camouflage design, along with a purple tank top that revealed two small, tasteful tattoos on her bicep and lower arm—a row of small blue birds in flight along her forearm and a lotus flower on her bicep along with the word *Namaste* in curly script.

Her long dark hair, streaked with azure blue these days, was clipped in a high ponytail, with a yellow and red bandana twisted and tied as a head band. The curve of one ear was studded with small earrings, along with a tiny piercing in her nostril that Maggie hardly noticed anymore.

No matter the outfit, Phoebe's small, slim frame always brought to Maggie's mind the image of a delicate bird with colorful plumage. Delicate but strong, Maggie amended, as Phoebe hefted two cartons and carried them down the wooden steps.

"I'll help you move the boxes." Lucy sprang up from her seat.

Phoebe balanced her load on one shoulder and made a muscle with her other arm. "We can do it," she said, striking a Rosie the Riveter pose.

"Yes, we can. No need to wait for a man, ladies." Inspired by Phoebe's rallying cry, Maggie helped, too.

By the time the big box truck pulled into the drive, the porch was cleared. Painted lime green, the vehicle looked like a Day-Glo ice cream truck. Once it had parked Maggie could read the sign on the side. THE MIGHTY GREEN TACO—FRESH! ORGANIC! AUTHENTIC! Right next to the slogan, a smiling taco shouted, "Mios Bueno!" in a cartoon balloon.

Robbie hopped out of the driver's side. His bright green T-shirt mirrored the vehicle with the company name and smiling taco on the back. He greeted everyone cheerfully, looking pleased to see Phoebe's friends again.

Or perhaps he just wanted to please Phoebe, acting so friendly toward a group of middle-aged women? Either way, the young man was very warm and likable. He had good social skills, she'd noticed, which could get a person far in life.

The dogs loved Robbie and strained on their leashes to greet him. Dogs were good judges of character, Maggie thought. Or might it have been the scent of food on his clothing? She was sure Tink and Wally liked that about him, too.

Maggie, Lucy, and Suzanne helped the young people load the boxes. The cartons were piled high and deep, but many were left on the drive, as well as the folding tables Phoebe had dragged outside.

"Throw the rest in my hatch. I'll get it to you before the morning meeting, no worries," Suzanne said.

"I'll bring the dogs home, then help you unpack and set up," Lucy offered.

"I can help, too. I'll close for an hour or so at noon," Maggie offered. "You can probably use another table and more baskets?"

Phoebe had looked overwhelmed but smiled again. "That would be great. Thank you. As usual, it takes a village."

A *village of good friends*, Maggie thought as Phoebe waved and jumped into the truck. Robbie climbed behind the wheel and they were off.

Phoebe liked riding in the taco truck. It was so colorful and silly, she felt as if she was gliding down Main Street on a parade float. She often felt like waving and tossing candy to people on the sidewalk. There was also a jingly bell above the windshield. Robbie let her ring it just for fun once in a while.

The air-conditioning was totally lame, but both sides up front were open where doors should have been, and she liked the way the breeze rushed in. She lifted her ponytail off the back of her neck and caught Robbie watching her.

"Ready for the market?"

"Ready or not, it's happening. I'm just setting up today. My friends will help."

Robbie smiled. "Sounds like they can't wait. I thought one or two were about to jump in here with us."

Phoebe laughed. "I did, too. They can get a little intense."

"They can. Now that you mention it. It's sweet to see. Like having four extra moms, or something."

"A little," Phoebe agreed. Which wasn't a bad thing for her. She'd barely had a real mom. "I think of them more like fairy godmothers," she admitted. "Like in *Cinderella*?"

He smiled and caught her eye. "I can see that. Maybe one day they'll turn this truck into a coach and four white horses."

Phoebe smiled at his joke, meanwhile calculating that would make him Prince Charming? Robbie was cute, in his way. But he'd need more than a few taps from a magic wand for her to buy that transformation.

But he was definitely a cool guy, and a nice guy, too. And a good pal, for sure. And now that they were both unattached and the summer wasn't over yet, who knew where their relationship would go? Especially when they were seeing each other almost every day at the market.

Maggie found the sudden quiet and the cool shade an instant relief. Her friends had settled into chairs and she sat on the love seat and set up her yarn swift. She'd just received a carton of fiber made from recycled plastic, and wanted to make a new display.

"Once again, Robbie Walsh saves the day." Suzanne was scrolling through messages on her phone. "We ought to call him Mighty Taco Man."

"He definitely has the mild-mannered, Clark Kent side going for him. Including the black-frame glasses. Very much in style now," Lucy noted. "He just needs to pump up those biceps a bit to pull off the cape and tights."

Maggie opened the first skein and fit it on the swift. "Phoebe doesn't like the muscle man type. She's told me that a few times."

Robbie reminded Maggie more of a friendly scarecrow than a superhero, but she didn't want to admit that aloud. He was attractive in his way, with a wide, infectious grin that lit up his thin face and bright blue eyes. Eyes that got crinkly at the corners when he laughed, which was often. His baggy T-shirts and shorts hung on his tall, lanky build, and his shock of dirty blond hair always seemed to be standing on end. Or was that a hair style? Constructed with hair gel or some such?

"I like him because he's always calm and cheerful," Maggie said. "He balances out Phoebe's highs and lows. Which is infinitely more important than a man's fitness level."

"Smiles or muscles, or none of the above, Phoebe's just not into him," Suzanne reminded them. "She pretends not to notice, but he's totally crazy about her."

"Maybe it's easier for her to act oblivious," Lucy said. "As long he's content with the just-friends status."

Suzanne waved her hand, dismissing the idea. "Men and women can't *really* be friends. Straight men and women, I mean. There's always some subtext, some subtle tension. Even if only one person is feeling it."

Lucy laughed. "Suzanne, that's so old-fashioned. And sexist and antiquated thinking, besides. Men and women can definitely be friends. It happens all the time." Lucy turned to Maggie. "Right, Maggie?"

Maggie wasn't sure how to answer. "I see the logic on both sides," she said finally. "Though in my experience, the question is rarely determined by logic."

"See? Maggie agrees with me. The opposite of logic is chemistry and sexual attraction. Everyone knows that." Suzanne waved her phone, like a judge, closing the case.

"That's not what I meant. Not entirely," Maggie clarified. "Too bad Dana isn't here. I'm sure there's been some research on the subject."

Their good friend and fellow knitter, Dana Haeger, was a psychologist. With an office only a few blocks down Main Street, she always found time to drop by the shop in the morning, or in between clients, claiming that knitting was her own therapy. Maggie decided to text her later with the news about Phoebe. She didn't want to leave Dana out of the loop.

"Getting back to Robbie," Maggie added, "he just broke up with his girlfriend last week. Maybe he isn't ready for a new relationship."

"Are you kidding? I bet he was thrilled when his girl-friend dumped him. Totally saved him from being the bad guy. He's wild about our little fiber goddess. Anyone can see that." Suzanne's tone precluded any argument. "He's sweet and smart. And Phoebe says he's very creative and talented. Just her type. What does he do again? Besides the food truck?"

"Textile design," Maggie replied. "He has a degree in computer art. He had a job in Boston but the company downsized and he was laid off. He came back to Plum Harbor in the spring, and has taken on a few jobs to keep up with student loans."

"He's not only a nice kid, he's responsible and enterpris-ing," Suzanne said. "I like that. Now that the girlfriend-schmirl-friend is out of the way, he should just declare his devotion to Phoebe."

"I don't think it's that simple. Aside from it not being any of our business," Maggie reminded her. "I don't think Phoebe is ready to date anyone. Breaking up with Harry hit her hard. You know how sensitive she is."

"She's well rid of that lug. Harry is such a poser. He thinks he such a big *artiste*. He's a big phony, if you ask me. I wish she'd realize that by now." Suzanne pulled a water container from her bag and took a sip. Bright pink, a tiny gold crown was stamped above words that read, IT'S GOOD TO BE QUEEN.

"Harry had his charms," Lucy recalled. "Now, there's a guy who could do justice to a pair of tights and a cape."

Suzanne laughed. "Agreed. But he was more of a Sven-gali than a superhero. Phoebe was totally under his spell. She nearly broke her neck taking those silly bird photos for him when we were in Maine, remember?"

"He needed them as a reference for his sculptures," Maggie recalled.

"Those photos helped us catch a murderer," Lucy reminded them. "As for the brooding artist thing, Phoebe loved that about him. What was that she used to say?"

Maggie sighed. " 'Harry has such soulful hands.' Whatever that means."

Lucy laughed. "I think we *all* know what *that* means, Mag."

Maggie felt herself blush and quickly turned her attention back to rolling the new yarn; soft and pliable, it offered just the right amount of stretch.

"Don't remind me." Suzanne shook her head. "Harry the Potter was bad news. I just hope our little Phoebe won't miss out on the perfect guy to help her forget Harry's hands and everything else attached to that rat. She doesn't have to date Robbie forever. Just until she gets her mojo back. I'm seeing this as more of a transitional relationship."

Maggie gave Suzanne a look. "If the real estate biz doesn't work out, you can definitely change the sign to 'Relationship Counseling.' "

Maggie had been joking but Suzanne hadn't noticed. "Believe me, these skills come in handy. You have no idea how many couples practically come to blows buying or selling property."

"I trust Phoebe to figure out what to do without our advice. Or matchmaking," Lucy said. "I think it's good for a woman to spend time on her own, free of any relationship. I loved being single. Until I met Matt, I mean."

Practically newlyweds, Lucy and Matt had married just a year ago. They'd both been married before and were in their late thirties. Maggie and the rest of Lucy's friends thought it was time for a little stepsister or stepbrother for Matt's nine-year-old daughter, Dara to appear on the scene.

Though no one but Suzanne dared to nudge Lucy about that question.

"Phoebe has to focus on her new business. Another reason she doesn't need a new relationship," Lucy said. "And she'll still be working here, too. Right, Mag?"

"That's the plan. Monday, Tuesday, Wednesday at the shop. Thursday through Sunday at the market. I'm closed on Sunday in the summer, so it's almost equal time in each spot."

That schedule change had only started last year, after Maggie and Charles got engaged and began living together.

Business was slow in the summer, as much as she hated to admit it. And once Charles came into her life, she had so much more to do than work. She wanted to spend Sundays with him, digging in their garden, sailing, or taking a drive somewhere. This summer, they had to plan their wedding, though they hadn't gotten very far.

"I worry about her working so many hours. Charles, in his sweet, helpful way, offered to step in here, if needed." Maggie smiled. "He doesn't know one end of a knitting needle from the other. But I said, sure. I didn't want to hurt his feelings."

"Charles is a quick study. I bet he'd be a big help," Lucy said.

Suzanne put her phone aside to comment. "I'm not saying he wouldn't be, but don't you think it might be weird to be waited on by a man in a knitting shop? It's more of a female domain. Even more than a hair or nail salon, I think."

"Now, that *is* sexist, Suzanne," Maggie scolded. "For a long time, only men were allowed to knit and belong to elite medieval guilds. Plenty of men knit right now. Even movie stars."

"We all know the illustrious history of knitting by now,

Mag. Funny how women weren't allowed to get their hands on yarn or needles until the prestige and pay grade dropped."

Suzanne's mangled interpretation of the history was in fact, mostly true. Women didn't start knitting until the craft was relegated to a domestic art. Once the mechanical loom was invented, hand-knit garments were only for the lower classes.

Lucy laughed and shook her head. "I love these morning debates and history lessons. But I need to head home if I'm going to help Phoebe. Don't worry about the shop, Maggie. I don't have any big deadlines now and I can jump in here if you need a hand."

Lucy was a graphic artist who ran a business from home. Her schedule allowed for loads of free time, but only because she was willing to tie herself to her computer around the clock when necessary.

"I know it's a big step for Phoebe. But this is big for you, too," Lucy added. "Losing your right hand after all these years?"

Maggie forced a smile. "It will be a change, that's for sure. But only for a few months. The market closes in October."

Then again, once Phoebe had a taste of running her own enterprise, would she return? If her friends had guessed what she was thinking, no one commented. And it was far too soon to speculate.

"Right now, I just want to do all I can to help make this opportunity a huge success."

Suzanne beamed. "That's big of you, Mag. I feel the same about our girl."

"Me too," Lucy said as she stood up and untied the dogs' leashes. "We should definitely meet there tomorrow, for her grand opening. We can make the stall look busy. It will attract other shoppers."

Suzanne took one last gulp from her fancy water bottle,

then fished around her huge purse for car keys. "Good idea. We can have our weekly meeting at the stall."

"I like that, Suzanne. Someone let Dana know, too." Lucy had already untied her dogs and headed down the porch steps ahead of Suzanne. "I'll text you later, and let you know how it's going."

"Please do. I hope to get there sometime around noon. Let me know if Phoebe needs anything."

Once her friends were gone, Maggie finished preparing for the Knit-cation Stitchers. She set up a tray with lemonade, ice tea, and ice water, along with fresh berries and cookies.

With a few minutes to spare, Maggie opened the *Plum Harbor Times* and scanned the headlines. There was the usual argument about the power company possibly raising rates and an upbeat article featuring an Eagle Scout who'd collected a mountain of food for a local pantry.

She finally found a short article about Jimmy Hooper a few pages back. JAMES QUENTIN HOOPER—LOCAL PIONEER OF ORGANIC FARMING, the headline read.

The brief report did not offer much more than Maggie already knew. Jimmy was in his early seventies and had been farming his property for decades. He was among the very first in the area to work the land without pesticides or chemical fertilizers, a path considered very woo-woo, and even ridiculed, when he'd just started out in the late sixties.

Maggie recalled his wife, Penelope. She had long, auburn hair she wore parted down the middle to frame her oval face. Some might have called her plain, but Maggie recalled her wide smile and warm brown eyes. She always seemed peaceful and happy, even after her long, debilitating illness had set in. A great hardship for Jimmy, Maggie knew, since Penelope had helped so much on the farm. But Maggie had never heard him complain or sound bitter about the challenges life had dealt him.

Jimmy and Penelope were genuine hippies, back in the day. Unlike so many others who played the part—with scraggly hair, and tie-dyed shirts—Jimmy and Penelope never outgrew the dream, and never abandoned it to become lawyers or office workers. Or, in her own case, a high school art teacher. She didn't know them well, but had admired them from afar for staying true to their values and the ideals of their youth.

The article commented on Penelope's long battle with MS and her death, about ten years ago. "The farmer was found hanging by the neck from a beam in his barn, an apparent suicide," the article stated. "But a police investigation is ongoing to confirm the cause of death."

Maggie's gaze lingered on the stock statement. She wondered when the reporter's story had been filed. Sunday night perhaps? Or even Saturday? A lot more could be known by now.

There were no plans for a memorial noted, but she did find mention of the Hooper children. His daughter, Carrie, an executive in the insurance industry who lived near Hartford, and his son, Brad an accountant, who had settled in Tucson, Arizona. Maggie guessed that one, if not both, were in Plum Harbor by now to sort through Jimmy's affairs. There was usually so much to do when a person died unexpectedly, especially if they ran a business. Maggie didn't envy their task.

Two women strolled up the path, deep in conversation with each other. Both in summer dresses and sandals, with knitting totes swinging from their arms, they were the first to arrive for the workshop. Maggie set the newspaper aside and slipped on her bright shopkeeper smile.

If Phoebe was here, right about now they'd exchange a glance and one would whisper, "Heads up—it's show-time!"

Maggie felt a wistful pang. An observation of Albert Einstein's came to mind: *The measure of intelligence is the ability to change.*

"Heads up, Al," Maggie murmured as she rose to greet her customers. "I'm about to test one of your theories."

Chapter 3

"I think it's down this aisle, near the end." Maggie had met up with Dana, Suzanne, and Lucy at the village green on Thursday morning, and they walked through the market together, looking for Phoebe's stall.

It was just past ten but the spot was already humming. One or more of her friends kept drifting off to shop, drawn by the attractive displays and tantalizing scents, which made the walk even longer. Maggie felt as if she was herding a group of cats.

"Do you know where Lucy ended up?" she asked Dana.

"She spotted a wheel of brie and popped into Say Cheese!" Dana glanced over her shoulder. "Don't worry. She's catching up. But we've lost Suzanne again."

"At least she warned me. She's checking out Yankee Chowder for takeout possibilities."

"Good plan. I might do that, too. There are so many choices here." Dana deftly sidestepped a mom pushing a double baby stroller.

Lucy ran up to them, waving a white paper bag. "Double-cream Brie, imported from France. Matt's going to love it. I got some goat cheese, too."

"That's my weakness. With a fresh, crusty baguette. I'll

have to circle back here later." Maggie could hardly blame her friends for the shopping frenzy. The market was as enticing as a bazaar in some exotic port that one might visit on vacation.

Along with fresh produce, there were booths that sold baked goods, soup, and chocolate in every possible shape and form. Jellies, jams, and relish, of course. Especially cranberries, New England's favorite fruit. Other aisles featured candles and soap, handmade clothing and jewelry. Most of the vendors sold organic products, which did make some of the items more expensive, though that didn't seem to discourage customers.

"Phoebe did land in the busiest spot," Dana noted as they drew closer to her booth and the aisle grew even more crowded.

"Location, location, location," Suzanne said, stepping up beside them.

Lucy laughed. "I was waiting for you to say that."

"Me too." Dana also smiled at Suzanne's predictable response. "Phoebe can learn a lot about running a business here. Not that she hasn't learned a great deal from you already, Maggie."

"I know what you mean, and I agree." Though many of the lessons would not be easy ones, Maggie could have added. There was a big difference between being an employee—even an involved, assistant manager, like Phoebe—and running your own shop.

But she didn't want to say anything negative. Not this morning. Today was a celebration.

Along with their knitting bags, Dana cradled a big bouquet of sunflowers in one arm and Suzanne held a plastic container with a bow on top and some home-baked goodies packed inside, Maggie had no doubt.

Maggie had brought along a few hand spindles and a large bag of roving. If the stall got slow, a spinning demonstration never failed to draw attention and customers, and the hand-spun yarn fetched a good price, too.

"Ta-da! There is it. Sox by Phoebe & More!" Suzanne stopped a few feet from the stall and read the sign in an awestruck tone. "Let's pretend we're customers and act all excited. Everyone will want to see what she's selling."

Dana smiled but looked embarrassed by the idea. "I'll be excited, playing myself. I don't need to perform street theater right now, thanks."

Suzanne looked disappointed but didn't reply.

"I'll act excited with you," Maggie offered. "It won't be hard. She's done a great job."

The theme of the stall was a snowy day. An inspiration, Maggie thought. How else could Phoebe sell knitwear in the middle of the steaming hot summer?

Murals, painted on rolls of paper, covered three walls of stall with a snow scene: rolling white hills dotted with pine trees and skiers, set against a pale blue sky. Intricate snowflakes, made of white paper cutouts, hung from the ceiling. There was a row of mannequins, posed in clever attitudes, donned in Phoebe's creation from head to toe, along with cardboard stand-up penguins and polar bears, who also looked very stylish in Phoebe's hats and scarves. Long tables on each wall held baskets and racks of more hand-knit items.

As Maggie stepped inside and gazed around the winter wonderland, she felt the temperature drop. The power of suggestion was amazing.

Folding chairs where customers could sit and knit were set up in the middle of the stall, and there were already two women seated with Phoebe and busily stitching.

"Isn't it great? Phoebe made all the decorations. I just helped her hang stuff yesterday." Lucy picked up a cellophane package secured by a length of yarn. "And we put together these cute sock-making kits, for knitters who want to follow in her footsteps, so to speak," Lucy added in a quiet tone. "She's already sold three."

Maggie felt quietly proud of her protégé. "Bravo, Phoebe. You're off to a great start."

"Not so bad. For the first half hour," Phoebe greeted them.

"It's wonderful, Phoebe. I'm so impressed." Dana gave Phoebe a hug and handed her the sunflowers.

Suzanne hugged Phoebe, too. "You're doing great, kid. To mark this milestone, here's your own batch of Seriously Chocolate Brownies."

"All for me? Really?" Phoebe's face lit up as if she'd just won an award.

"I guess you can put some out for your customers, if you really want. But—and this is a pro tip—working in sales, you will need a little chocolate rush now and then."

"I was too nervous for breakfast. I might have one now." Phoebe was about to dive into the chocolate indulgence when her happy expression melted.

Dana stepped forward. "What is it, honey? Are you okay?"

Phoebe shook her head. "It's Harry! He's not supposed to be here. What happened to Aunt Adele? And This & That?"

Maggie followed Phoebe's terrified gaze. "I don't know about Adele. But *that* is definitely Harry McSweeney."

"Harry the Potter, up to his old tricks." Suzanne's confirmation held an angry edge.

"He's setting up a display of his pottery," Phoebe said. "He moved in his portable wheel."

Maggie glanced across the aisle. The stall across from Phoebe's had been closed when they'd arrived, but the canvas flap was now open. She saw tables of pottery—vases, bowls, plates and jugs, even some animal shapes—

formed in Harry's distinctive style. Which Maggie would call anti-form? But most of the pieces were lovely and unusual. The glazes he used were unique as well. Whatever else one might say, she thought he was quite talented.

And handsome as ever, she noticed, in worn jeans and a black T-shirt, muscles bulging as he carried a large, plastic sack filled with dark red clay.

"Give me a break." Phoebe took a shaky breath. "How am I going to hang out here all day if he's hanging out right over there?"

Dana slipped her arm around Phoebe's shoulder. "Take a few deep breaths. No need to panic."

"Really? Seems like the perfect time to me," Phoebe mumbled.

Maggie's heart went out to her. What a thing to happen and of all days. But Dana was taking the right approach. Phoebe needed to calm down and get some perspective.

Lucy placed her hands on Phoebe's shoulders and stared into her eyes. "What happened to the We Can Do It girl? Are you going to let some man—one who deceived and disrespected you—ruin your big opportunity? Are you going to let him ruin your opening day?"

"Lucy's right," Suzanne stepped closer, too. "You were here first. He needs to peddle those wacky sculptures somewhere else. They look like rotten pieces of fruit to me. Petrified fruit, I mean." Suzanne's interpretation was muddled, but made sense in a certain way. "Who buys that stuff anyway?"

"You can ask him yourself," Lucy said. "He's walking this way."

"He is?" Phoebe cringed. "Hide me, please . . . Oh no . . . he saw me. He's waving. What should I do?"

"No help for it now. Check your hair and makeup, pronto." Suzanne grabbed a hand mirror from a hat display and whipped out a cosmetics pouch from her tote.

"Time to channel your inner Beyoncé. You're the prize, kid. He's the biggest loser."

Maggie often thought Suzanne overacted in situations like this, but this time, she was right. What was the first thing a woman worried about when facing a former lover who had done her dirt? How she looked. She wanted to look good enough to cause him deep regret. Everyone knew that.

The down-to-earth advice snapped Phoebe to attention. She swiped on a dash of lip gloss, checked her eye make-up, then set the mirror back on the table. "I don't want to look like I'm trying too hard."

"You look perfect. Perfectly Phoebe," Dana reminded her. "He'll be sorry he ever let you get away."

"I'm sure he is already," Maggie chimed in.

Harry had wound his way through the aisle full of shoppers and stood near the front of Phoebe's stall. He gazed inside, then raised one of his soulful hands in a tentative greeting.

He certainly didn't look like a cruel, arrogant heartbreaker. He seemed as rattled to see Phoebe as she was to see him. Was that an act, to win her trust? Maggie didn't know him well enough to say.

Phoebe waved back. "Now what?" she whispered.

"Get out there, and toss it. Pretend that your life is so amazing, you can barely remember his name," Suzanne coached.

"That last bit might be going overboard. But the rest is fine," Dana added.

Lucy gave Phoebe a gentle nudge. "Go get 'em, honey."

Phoebe's friends watched from a distance as the former sweethearts met just outside her stall for the first conversation since their breakup. Not a word could be heard above the noise from the crowd, but the body language was interesting.

Phoebe started off with a forced, fake smile, but was soon wearing a real one. Harry looked nervous and wary, but his dark eyes soon beamed with warmth, and a wide smile appeared, his famous dimples flashing.

Then he rested his hand on Phoebe's shoulder, just for a moment. Those soulful hands, working their magic again, Maggie fretted.

Finally, Phoebe turned and headed back toward her friends. "At least she's smiling," Maggie murmured.

"Maybe *too* happy?" Lucy asked quietly.

"Not a good sign," Dana agreed.

"Calm down. That could be a victory smirk. Let's hear a full report before we panic," Suzanne said.

Phoebe arrived in their midst moments later. "That wasn't so bad. He just wanted to wish me luck. He loves the way I decorated the stall. He said a lot of nice things, actually." Phoebe straightened a pile of scarves that were already in perfect order. Maggie didn't like the way she was avoiding everyone's gaze.

"You weren't *too* nice to him, I hope?" Suzanne asked.

Phoebe shook her head. "Not at all. But I didn't want to seem like some crazed bunny-boiler. Like I went over the edge, just because we broke up."

"As long as he doesn't get the wrong idea," Lucy said. "Like thinking all is forgiven and he can wheedle his way back into a relationship with you."

Phoebe was smoothing a poncho that hung on one of the mannequins. Her reluctance to answer worried Maggie more.

"It wasn't like that," she said finally. "And not nearly as horrible as I expected. Maybe I am over him."

Dana smiled and nodded with approval. "Good for you. It sounds to me like you're moving on."

Maggie agreed, though she knew in matters of the

heart, it was rarely a straight path. There could be some zigzagging, and backsliding, but Phoebe did seem out of the woods.

Two young women about Phoebe's age had stepped up to the front table, and looked through a display that said, SUPER SALE! SAVE-THE-EARTH SOCKS—100% RECYCLED MATERIALS!

Maggie had taught Phoebe that displaying a bargain out front was perfect bait. Get them in and then they'll soon browse the regular-priced items. It appeared the tactic was working and the little merchant hustled over to make a sale or two.

Lucy had taken a seat and started knitting. "Time to step back and let the magic happen."

Maggie sat beside her. "Phoebe is doing beautifully without anyone's coaching. I'm happy to sit and knit, for stall ambience. And since we're all here, I have a project to share. I thought we should try some socks, in honor of Phoebe's grand opening."

Lucy looked up from her work. "Brilliant. I don't think we've ever knit socks together before."

"Not that I recall," Dana agreed. "Phoebe can give us some pro tips. We're surrounded by inspiration."

"Very true. Though Phoebe's footwear sets a high bar." Maggie happily handed out the patterns she'd found. "These patterns are easy and I brought some organic yarn. It seemed fitting for the marketplace."

Suzanne was the only one who didn't seem excited by the idea, Maggie noticed. She stared at the pattern and frowned. "There's a reason I never tried socks. Maybe I'll do knitted tube socks?"

Maggie laughed. "One stitch at a time. We'll help you navigate the curves."

With Maggie's gentle guidance, they were soon casting off their projects while Phoebe rang up several sales.

* * *

It was sometime later when Maggie noticed an older man and woman approach the stall. They stood close together just outside the entrance and peered inside, taking in the tables and displays. Something about the couple said "longtime married" to Maggie, and their matching white aprons stamped with the words IN A PICKLE! told her they worked together in the market.

"Neighbors dropping by to welcome Phoebe?" Lucy said.

"Could be," Maggie replied. She'd noticed their stall on the way. It sold every possible food one might think of pickling, and many that had never occurred to her. The ubiquitous cucumber, of course, several varieties. Also, tomatoes, cauliflower, cabbage, carrots, onions, and sliced ginger. There were jars of relish, most made of fruits and berries. She'd also noticed an impressive array of horse-radish.

But something about the pair didn't seem very neighborly. The two looked as sour as their inventory.

The pickle husband marched up to Phoebe, his apron strings strained over a round belly. Small, dark eyes gleamed behind wire-rim glasses, his bulbous nose topped by a bushy mustache. His wife crept behind him, a short woman with tightly curled brown hair that peeped out of the edges of a puffy, colonial-style cap.

The knitting group sat on the far side of the stall. Maggie focused on her knitting, her ears set to radar mode.

"You're the sock girl, right? You just moved in this morning?" The man's tone was far from welcoming.

"That's me—Phoebe Myers. Nice to meet you." Phoebe offered her hand in a businesslike greeting, but he ignored the gesture.

"I got nothing against you personally. But you got to pack up your socks and get out. I have a deal with Warren.

If a stall in this section opened up, we were supposed to get it. Period."

Phoebe laughed nervously. "This is a joke, right? Some kind of market initiation thing?"

Pickle Man shook his head, his expression solemn. His wife shook her head, too, as if they were matching bobble-head dolls.

"Do I sound like I'm joking? This stall is mine. The sooner you move this stuff out, the better."

Phoebe was dumbfounded. "That can't be true. Where am I supposed to go?"

He shrugged. "Warren will find you a spot. Our stall will be empty."

Mrs. Pickle stepped up, her tone more conciliatory. "Number five, near the parking lot. It's not so bad."

But in the quietest part of the market, Maggie knew.

Phoebe's dark eyes turned glassy. A burst of anger, or tears about to fall? A mixture, Maggie guessed. "Switch stalls with you? No way. That is so *not* happening."

Maggie and her friends exchanged glances, proud to see Phoebe hold her ground. But the obnoxious visitor was not put off. He stepped closer and leaned over, standing almost nose to nose with Phoebe. About to make another, more pointed threat, Maggie expected.

Suzanne dropped her knitting, jumped up from her seat, and wedged her substantial body between them. "Whoa there, fella. This young woman signed a contract, a legal and binding agreement between two parties, which grants her the exclusive right to this sales space. Not number five. Not number seventy-five. This exact stall. I don't know what you were promised, or by whom, Mr. Pickle. But you'd better slide back into your jar before we call the police."

Mr. Pickle stared at her. His scowl deepened as he turned

back to Phoebe. "You don't know the way things work around here, sweetie. It's not Sesame Street. Believe me."

His wife tugged his sleeve. "You said you were going to talk nice, George."

He spared Mrs. Pickle a glance and tossed up his hands. "I've said my piece. If you're smart, you'll take my advice. Don't get too comfortable."

The pickle people finally stalked away. Phoebe was left wide-eyed and shaken. "Did that just happen? Or am I having some sort of stress-mare?"

Maggie and her friends had already gathered around her in a protective circle. "If that was a hallucination, we all drank the same Kool-Aid," Suzanne said.

Lucy patted Phoebe's shoulder. "Some nerve, trying to push you around. You really stood your ground, honey. Good for you."

"You did us proud," Dana agreed. "You should put a complaint on record about that guy. There must be someone who manages the market."

"Warren Braeburn. He came by this morning to see how I was doing. I saved his number in my phone."

"Track him down and tell him what happened," Maggie advised. "It's obviously a misunderstanding. He'll straighten it out."

"I hope so." A few women had clustered around the hats and ponchos displayed on Phoebe's hip mannequins. Maggie sensed Phoebe was still too rattled to wait on them.

"Shall I take care of your customers?"

"Would you?" Phoebe replied with a grateful smile. "I need a minute to regroup."

As Maggie greeted the shoppers, she noticed Robbie emerge from the crowd with a pile of takeout food boxes.

"Who's ready for lunch?" he greeted them. "Your order

has arrived. A selection of my most popular tacos, drinks, and dessert."

"Robbie, that's so sweet." Phoebe graced him with a huge smile. "I haven't had a bite all day."

"Great, dig in. More where these came from."

The customers both bought hats from Maggie and once they were gone, the scent of warm tacos drew her, though the dish was hardly her favorite. She was wary of most "fun food," which usually meant you ate with your hands and juggled it around to keep the food in question from dripping all over your clothing. Was that the fun part? But her friends were already making their selections and she walked over to see what was left.

"What's in this one? It's certainly . . . green." Suzanne picked up a taco and examined it from various angles. Maggie had rarely seen her give so much thought to eating anything.

"That's my specialty, the Phoebe. Roasted cauliflower with black beans, cheese, and cilantro sauce." Robbie smiled at the honoree. Phoebe smiled back, but looked embarrassed.

"You have a taco named after you? How cool is that?" Suzanne was sincerely impressed. "I've got to try it."

"Is this tofu?" Dana peered into the taco she'd found.

"Toasted tofu, mixed greens, and pepper jack cheese, with siracha," Robbie replied.

"That sounds yummy." Dana's eagerness was enough to distract from the rest of the group's hesitation.

Maggie chose one next without bothering to ask about the mysterious filling, then settled down to eat. First, she coated her summer dress with paper napkins from her chin to her lap.

"This looks very interesting," Lucy said before taking a bite of her lunch.

"What doesn't kill you, makes you stronger," Maggie murmured.

"I like this toasted chickpea filling," Phoebe announced between bites. "I was so hungry, I thought I might faint."

"Not to mention facing down Mr. Pickle. That was enough to make anyone shaky," Lucy said between crunches.

Robbie looked alarmed. "Did someone bother you, Phoebe?"

Phoebe shrugged, then told him the story, making light of the encounter. "It was totally weird. There must be some mix-up. Warren will figure it out."

"I don't like hearing that. I'll speak to that guy myself." Robbie's glasses had slipped down his nose and he quickly pushed them up again. "If you want me to, I mean," he added, dialing back on his manly verve.

"It was no big deal. There's just been a lot going on here today. *Way* a lot . . ."

Was Phoebe going to relate her encounter with Harry? A moment or two passed and she didn't, Maggie noticed.

Robbie offered an encouraging smile. "Your stall looks great and you have plenty of customers. That's what matters, right?"

Phoebe smiled back, looking calmer. Robbie had that effect on her. Maggie liked that about him, too.

Suzanne ate more of her taco than Maggie expected, then politely wadded up the rest in a napkin. "Thanks, Robbie. That was really . . . special."

She sounded so determined to say something polite, Maggie nearly laughed.

"Glad you liked it. Got to run. But before I go . . ." He flipped open another box that had been set aside. "It's churro time."

Suzanne's expression lit up. The cinnamon- and sugar-coated confections made up for the *special* taco, Maggie guessed.

"How can I resist?" Suzanne picked out a churro, and Maggie helped herself to one, too. It was still warm and deliciously fragrant. An indulgence for her, but this was a day to celebrate. She passed the box to Lucy and Dana, but there was still plenty left for Phoebe, who was out front again, talking to a customer.

As Robbie headed back to his truck, they thanked him for the tasty delivery. He insisted on gathering up all the trash and taking it with him.

"How's that for service?" Suzanne whispered as he left. "That kid is a gem. I'll take him, if Phoebe doesn't."

Lucy nearly choked on her churro. "Kevin will love that," she managed, mentioning Suzanne's husband.

Suzanne looked about to reply, then pointed at the crowd. "The police patrol the market? That's weird. Unless it's on their beat?"

Maggie saw two uniformed officers across the aisle, in a stall that was adjacent to Harry's. As one would expect from the banner, Wild Honey sold local, organic honey, handmade soap, bouquets of wildflowers, and related scented products. A pretty young woman about Phoebe's age worked there, and seemed a perfect match for her wares, looking almost ethereal in a long, white sundress, and the flowery wreath that adorned her wavy blond hair.

One of the officers jotted notes on a small pad as they spoke to her.

"Doesn't look routine to me," Maggie said. "It looks like they're interviewing her for some reason."

"Wonder if they'll come here, too," Lucy asked quietly.

Before Maggie could reply, a familiar face stepped out of the crowd, and headed toward Phoebe. "Looks like Phoebe rates a visit from Detective Reyes, not just two uniforms. Something must be up."

Suzanne and Dana had noticed the detective, too.

"We'd better not crowd them. You know how the detective feels about that," Maggie warned her friends, though she was as eager as anyone to know what was going on.

"Let's at least pretend to be knitting?" Dana suggested. "Then slowly slide our chairs close enough to listen in."

"Good plan." Suzanne was already sliding.

If Marisol Reyes noticed the not-so-subtle chair-sliding tactic, she didn't let on. She stood at the front of the booth, waiting for Phoebe to finish a sale. A seasoned detective with the Essex County Police Department, Detective Reyes had been assigned to a few investigations in the area that had involved Maggie and her friends.

Most recently, disturbing events at Piper Nursery that had targeted two sisters who lived there, Holly and Rose Piper. Since Dana was so close to the young women, virtually their only family, the knitting friends had worked hard to figure out who was behind the mayhem and murder, especially after Rose Piper was accused.

Maggie had always found Detective Reyes to be smart, professional, and a bit easier to talk to than most other police officers. But that didn't mean she tolerated amateur involvement in her cases. Maggie knew she hated it.

Detective Reyes usually worked with a partner, but appeared to be alone today. Perhaps her partner was questioning other vendors? That would make sense. But questioning them about what? Maggie wondered.

Detective Reyes looked over a basket of knitted hair bands as Phoebe ran up a sale. She pushed her sunglasses back on her head, her dark eyes and smooth skin free of makeup, except for a slash of pink gloss. She was not very tall, but athletic-looking and dressed today in dark blue cotton slacks and a sleeveless blouse that showed off her lean, buff arms.

"Hello, Phoebe," the detective said finally. "This is your first day at the market, I understand?"

"Yup, my grand opening." Phoebe sounded nervous. Understandably. "What's up, Detective? Why are the police talking to everyone?"

"I think you may have heard that the vendor who used to run this stall died a few days ago?"

"Yeah, I did. Jimmy Hooper. He committed suicide, right?"

"That appeared to be the cause of death, initially. But some new information has come to light. We now believe there was foul play."

Maggie felt a jolt. She glanced at her friends, who had the same reaction.

"Jimmy Hooper was murdered? Is that what you're saying?" Phoebe's shock was obvious and unfiltered. "That's awful."

"Yes, it is. And we need to find the person who took his life." The officer paused, giving Phoebe time to process the news. "I need to ask you a few questions, Phoebe. It won't take long."

"Sure, of course. This was his stall. I just took it over yesterday. I guess you know that?"

Maggie saw Detective Reyes nod. "What was here when you opened the stall? Did Mr. Hooper leave anything?"

Phoebe paused a moment. "Not much. There was a folding table, and two wooden crates. I guess he used that stuff to sell his vegetables? I gave everything to the market manager, Warren. He said he'd bring it back to Jimmy's farm."

"I'll follow up with him on that. I know it's your first day, but have you noticed anything out of the ordinary?" Detective Reyes persisted. "Even if it doesn't seem significant, or related to Mr. Hooper."

Phoebe released a long breath. She glanced at her friends, clustered nearby, who silently urged her to continue.

"There was something. It's probably not connected to Jimmy. But this couple who run another stall sort of threatened me. It was the husband, mainly. His wife mostly tried to calm him down."

Detective Reyes tilted her head back. "What did he say, exactly?"

Phoebe held a fuzzy scarf in her hands and twisted it nervously. "He told me I had to move my things out because he wanted this stall. Well, any stall in this area. He said that Warren, the market manager, had promised him that if one became free it would be his. They run In a Pickle! near the parking lot and he wants a stall in a livelier part of the market."

"I see. Did he say anything else?" the detective asked quickly.

"Something like, 'You'll be sorry. Don't say I didn't warn you. This place isn't Sesame Street.'" Phoebe deepened her voice to imitate him, adding a mocking edge, Maggie noticed. "He tried to scare me."

"What did you say?"

"I said something like, 'No way is that happening.' And when he didn't give up, my friend Suzanne made him back off. You know Suzanne Cavanaugh, right?" Phoebe glanced over at her posse; Suzanne waved and smiled. Detective Reyes didn't wave back, but acknowledged the greeting with a quick nod.

When Suzanne had been suspected of poisoning a coworker, Detective Reyes had not been assigned to the case. But Maggie imagined the entire police force knew of the bold, brassy brunette by now. "What did she say?"

"She told him that I signed a rental agreement and have a totally legit and legal right to be here."

And that he ought to slide back into his condiment jar,

Maggie recalled. Though she was glad Phoebe omitted that part.

"Maybe I should talk to Detective Reyes, too," Suzanne whispered. Dana stilled her with a gentle touch. "I think Phoebe can handle it."

"We'll look into this," Detective Reyes promised. "Anything else?"

Phoebe thought for a moment, then shook her head. "Nope."

"If anything comes to mind or catches your attention, please let me know." The detective handed Phoebe a small white card with a blue police shield printed on the corner. Maggie had seen a few of those. "Thanks for your help. Have a great grand opening."

"It's been pretty wild so far. Not exactly what I expected."

Maggie had to agree.

She and her friends had grown impatient waiting for the interview to end and as soon as the detective left, they scuttled up to Phoebe like one creature with eight legs.

Suzanne spoke first. "Poor Jimmy was murdered. That's big. Do they know how he really died?"

"I didn't ask. She wouldn't have told me anyway," Phoebe replied, which they all knew was true. "She's going to talk to those pickle people. But what can the police do? I'm sure there's no connection to Jimmy's death."

"They are a sour pair, if you don't mind my pun. But would they murder another vendor just to get a better stall?" Lucy asked.

"That pun is awful. But apt," Maggie conceded. "It's highly unlikely anyone would go that far." Though one never knew what might be connected to a crime until all the pieces fell into place.

Phoebe looked stunned, processing the news. "I feel even weirder, knowing he was murdered."

Dana put her arm around Phoebe's shoulder. "Jimmy Hooper's death has nothing to do with this stall, Phoebe." Her tone was calm and even, and very convincing. "You've told the police what you know. Which isn't much. There's nothing more you can do. Focus on your opening day. So far, it's going great."

"If you don't count all the weird and crazy stuff? A panic attack seeing Harry, a shakedown from the pickle vendors, and being questioned by Detective Reyes about a murder investigation. How did I sell a thing with all that going on?"

"You've done a bang-up business for socks in July," Suzanne countered.

She picked up a handful from a display titled DARE TO BE DIFFERENT! The pairs were knitted in the same colors and stitches, but each sock didn't exactly match its mate, which Maggie thought was a clever, imaginative concept.

"I'd like a bunch of these. They're so cute. I need to give a lot of thank-you gifts to my sales force."

Maggie wasn't sure if that was true. Suzanne was so generous; it might have been her way of supporting Phoebe's launch.

"I need some socks, too. The perfect anniversary gift for Matt," Lucy said, sorting through the choices. "He's always complaining my feet feel cold, even in the summer. And some for him. He has the same problem."

"You guys? You don't have buy up all my stuff," Phoebe protested. "You've helped enough, just hanging out with me."

Phoebe's friends ignored her with patient smiles, as the shopping spree continued. Dana moved to a display of shawls and lacy shrugs, stitched in a silk-and-bamboo blend yarn.

She tossed a pale blue stole around her shoulders.

"What do you think? I have a conference coming up in San Francisco. It gets cool there at night."

"That wrap was made for you, Dana. And this little number was made for me." Maggie plucked a sassy purple hat off a mannequin. "I've been eyeing this beauty all day. I'll take the scarf, too." She slung a slim, ruffled-edge scarf around her throat. "I'd never make anything like this for myself. It makes me feel so flirty and . . . French?"

Her comment made her friends laugh, but it was true.

Maggie left the market with Dana, Suzanne, and Lucy a short time later. Everyone felt sure that Phoebe would tally a tidy profit for the day.

A good distraction from the odd interruptions. Most of all the disturbing news that Jimmy Hooper, former resident of stall thirty-two, had not died by his own hand.

He'd been murdered.

Chapter 4

"**D**id Phoebe survive her first weekend at the market?" Lucy took a seat on the rocking chair, and her panting dogs flopped at her feet. Her only request had been ice water for herself. She'd come equipped with water for her dogs and a portable bowl.

Maggie handed her a tall glass and set a steaming mug of coffee for herself on the side table. She had to have real coffee, no matter how hot it was outside. Watered down iced coffee just wasn't the same. Especially on a Monday morning.

"She should be down any minute. I just heard her stirring around upstairs, even though I told her to sleep in. I don't want her working seven days a week and wearing herself down."

"You're right. With two jobs, she needs to be careful of burning herself out," Lucy agreed. "And here she is."

The shop's screen door opened and Phoebe stepped out. Her long hair was still damp from the shower, piled on her head in what she called "a sloppy bun"—which was an actual hairstyle, Maggie had recently learned.

"Geez, it's hot. I'm glad the market is closed. That stall gets stuffy. I need to set up a fan."

"I think there's an extra in the storeroom. Help yourself." A few boxes of new yarn had arrived over the weekend and Maggie carefully slit the first open with a large pair of shears.

"So, how did the weekend go?" Lucy sipped her water, then pressed the glass to her forehead. "I stopped by the market yesterday, but never made it to your end."

"It was okay, I guess. I made some decent sales." Phoebe took a seat next to Lucy and leaned over to pat the dogs. They wriggled in delight and licked her hands.

Maggie and Lucy exchanged a glance. Had Lucy picked up the same flat note in Phoebe's reply? It seemed so. Phoebe was probably tired, but she did seem to have mixed feelings about the market this morning.

"No more visits from irate fellow vendors?" Maggie asked.

"No, thank goodness. Warren said it was a dumb misunderstanding and the picklers won't bother me again. He gave them a new stall and said the spot is even better than mine."

"That's good news," Lucy said. "Though it's hard to picture Pickle Man pleased about anything."

Phoebe sat back in her chair. She had carried out a big mug of hot coffee and took a long sip. "He was right about one thing. The market looks all cheerful and fun. But it's definitely not Sesame Street."

Maggie was concerned to hear that. "How do you mean? Did something else happen?"

"Not exactly. But most of the vendors aren't very friendly. A lot of them have grudges and little feuds going on. It's totally not what I expected."

"Welcome to the wonderful world of commerce." Maggie had been checking the contents of the box against the invoice, but looked up to meet Phoebe's gaze. "The shopkeepers on Main Street aren't nearly as chummy and supportive as we appear, either. You know that."

"Remember Amanda Goran, who owned the Knitting Nest?" Lucy rolled her eyes. "She was so competitive with Maggie; she was actually obsessed." Lucy paused and caught Maggie's glance. "Sorry to remind you, Mag."

Maggie had also been thinking of Amanda, but still didn't like to talk about her.

"It's okay. We all know what happened." The rival knitting shop owners had a long-running feud, and when Amanda turned up dead, Maggie was the prime suspect. She shuddered at the memory. "You'd be smart to keep your head down, Phoebe. Be friendly to everybody, but keep a safe distance."

"I get it," Phoebe replied quietly.

Maggie had a feeling that there was still something on Phoebe's mind. Lucy noticed it too. "Did the police come back and ask more questions? Is that what's bothering you?"

"No, but there's been a lot of talk about Jimmy. A lot of gossip, I should say," she clarified.

"Like what?" Lucy asked.

"How he died. Who may have killed him. Harry heard it was a loan shark. Jimmy had a lot of debt."

"A loan shark?" Lucy clearly wasn't buying. "That explanation never makes sense to me. Why kill someone who owes you money? You can never get it back that way."

"Agreed," Maggie noted. "In the movies, they mostly threaten, or smash up a car. Or inflict painful but nonfatal injuries." Now she'd lost count of the skeins in the box. She shook her head. Why were they even talking about this?

She looked up at Phoebe. "It sounds like the ice is broken with Harry now?"

"I hope he's behaving himself," Lucy added quickly.

"Whatever that means," Maggie murmured. She started from the beginning again, counting out the skeins and setting them in her lap.

"Harry's been very helpful. The nicest person there, so far. I mean, not counting Robbie."

Of course, Robbie wouldn't count for much with Harry anywhere in view. Maggie felt sorry for the guy. Lucy glanced her way. She looked concerned, too.

"The awkward part with Harry was over last week," Phoebe continued. "No harm in talking to him." She unclipped her hair, twisted it, and pinned it up again. A telltale sign that the subject made her nervous. "Harry has been very nice to me. More than nice. I'm getting the feeling that he wants us to get back together. Not that he's been obnoxious about it, or anything."

"That's not good." Lucy looked surprised at her quick, unedited response. "Is it?"

Phoebe shrugged. She wore a yellow sundress with spaghetti straps, her shoulders and slim arms pale as cream, except for two small blue tattoos.

"Hey, gang! Happy Monday! I have an early appointment, but I spotted you out here and couldn't resist."

Maggie had been so focused on Phoebe's reply, she hadn't noticed Suzanne coming up the path.

Suzanne paused at the top of the porch steps as her gaze swept over them. "Looks serious. Figuring out world peace? Climate change? How to lose ten pounds in two days? Believe me, it can't happen in a quantum universe. Even drinking gallons of special soup."

"It's Harry. He's being nice to Phoebe," Maggie said. "Very nice," she qualified.

"Phoebe thinks he wants to get back together," Lucy added.

Suzanne cast Phoebe a disheartened look. "Pheebster? Say it ain't so!"

Phoebe looked embarrassed, then squared her shoulders. "I know. I felt so over it. And I'd promised myself never again. But when I'm with him—I sort of forget? He said he just wants a chance to explain what happened with that other girl, and how he messed everything up. He asked me to hear him out, and make up my mind after that."

"What's left to explain?" Suzanne tossed her hands up. "That big white stripe down his back says it all. He's a skunk. What else do we need to know?"

Phoebe sat back and examined a cuticle on her thumb. Had Suzanne come on too strong? Maggie hoped not.

"We can't tell you what to do," Maggie said in a far gentler tone. "We shouldn't, anyway. If you want to hear him out, or even give him a second chance, that's your choice entirely. We just don't want to see you get hurt again, dear. That's all we're trying to say."

Maggie punctuated her remarks with a strong look in Suzanne's direction.

"I agree," Lucy seconded. "But I agree with Suzanne, too. Though I wouldn't put it quite that way. Anyone can see that Harry is charming and super attractive. But 'when someone shows you who they are, believe them the first time.' That's what Maya Angelou said."

"Big white stripe. End of story," Suzanne persisted.

"I know you're all concerned about me. I appreciate it." Phoebe glanced at Suzanne. "Even if you overdo it a bit. I don't know what I want to do about Harry. He won't be at the market again until Thursday. Maybe I can figure it out by then."

"Good plan. Enough said." Maggie was happy to change the subject. She knew the best way to get Phoebe to ignore their well-intentioned advice was to overload her with it. "We know you'll make the right choice. The one that's best for you."

Suzanne frowned. She looked as if she didn't agree, and was about to remind Phoebe which choice *she* thought was best.

Lucy jumped in just in time. "How did you manage without Phoebe this week, Maggie? Seems you lived to tell the tale."

Maggie had finally squared away the first box and started on the next. A soft and luxurious merino in a smoky lavender shade, a big color for the fall.

"It was touch and go a few times, but I slogged on."

Her reply made Phoebe smile. "Get out. You're just saying that to make me feel good. Or make me feel guilty?"

"None of the above. I missed you terribly. So did the customers. Charles tried to help, but honestly . . ." Her voice trailed off. She didn't like to complain about her soon-to-be husband. She knew she was a very lucky woman. Even if he did have his quirks. *Don't we all,* she often reminded herself.

"I taught him how to work the register and where the button collection is stored. We hardly had any customers and closed early Saturday, then went out on the boat for the rest of the weekend."

Plum Harbor was a sailor's delight. Practically everyone in town owned a boat of some kind—from fifty-foot cruisers to candy-colored kayaks. The harbor was so full of sea craft in the summer it looked like parking for a nautical mall the day before Christmas.

Maggie and her late husband, Bill, had never been boaty types. Bill lived to golf and Maggie loved to garden. They were content to accept invitations to sail on their friends' boats. All that changed when she met Charles, who was a dedicated sailor with a beautiful thirty-five-foot-long sailboat, a classic vessel, fitted with sleek shiny wood and brass. Which Maggie soon learned required a lot of tender loving care. Under full sail at sunset, the sailboat was a sight to behold, and Maggie found gliding along on it an experience both serene and exciting at the same time.

She's was wary of sailing at first. The weather wasn't always cooperative and one was at the mercy of the elements. But Charles was a wonderful instructor, and by the time they'd agree to marry last spring, she felt very comfortable on the boat, hopping from one end of the deck to the other, tying or untying lines, and following the skipper's *requests*. She and Charles had agreed early on that they wouldn't call his directions "orders."

She'd even found a special rhythm to knitting on the bounding sea, which was challenging at times.

"That sounds so romantic." Suzanne sighed.

"It would have been. If Charles hadn't been obsessed with figuring out our wedding plans. I feel as if he trapped me out there on purpose, so I couldn't escape. Though I was tempted to jump overboard." An exaggeration, but only a slight one.

Phoebe's quizzical look was mirrored by Lucy and Suzanne. "Why would you want to? Don't you want to marry Charles?" Phoebe asked.

Maggie paused her counting, taken aback. "What a question. Charles is the best thing that's happened to me in years. How can you even ask?"

As widow, she'd dated a bit, here and there, but never met anyone who even remotely inspired the feelings she'd held for her late husband.

Out of the blue, Charles Mossbacher walked into the shop. He was the lead detective on a complicated case, the investigation of a group of anonymous, knitting graffiti artists who called themselves the Knit Kats. The ominous cabal appeared to be linked to a murder and the mysterious disappearance of a young woman, one of Phoebe's college friends.

The police suspected that the vicious felines were connected to her shop, which was certainly not the case. But by the time the crime was solved, with the help of Maggie and her knitting group, sparks of attraction were flying between Maggie and Charles. And they were both eager to see where their instant, irresistible connection would lead.

Her curiosity about police matters had always been a sticking point between them, and nearly caused them to part. Which Maggie thought ironic, since that's how they'd met. But Charles had proved his love in a very surprising and heroic fashion that had forever won her heart. In order to put aside their conflict once and for all, he decided to retire from the police force. If that wasn't true love, Maggie didn't know what else to call it.

"You know I love him dearly." More than she'd ever thought she could love anyone, after Bill. "That goes without saying."

"So, what's the holdup?" Suzanne got right to the point, as usual. "I have the perfect dress. I swooped it up at half price." She proudly named a famous designer. "Alas, the flimsy material and handkerchief hemline has an expiration date of September one."

"Really? Well, we'll definitely take that into consideration. Your outfit is high on our list of priorities." Maggie wasn't sure her sarcasm registered on Suzanne, though Lucy and Phoebe grinned.

Phoebe turned to Suzanne. "It's practically August. How can they get married by your dress deadline if they haven't planned anything yet?"

"Maybe, maybe not," Maggie said, squinting at the merino invoice. "I'd prefer a small, elegant gathering. Charles wants a longer guest list and it snowballs from there. There's food, music, flowers, and who knows what else to consider. And where will we stick all these people?" She sighed. "I'd be fine with a meal in a good restaurant. Maybe a private room? And not so many guests around the table that we can't carry on a decent conversation."

"Sounds more like a night out with the girls than celebrating till death do you part, with your one and only," Suzanne complained.

"That's another thing. We're writing our own vows," Maggie announced.

Suzanne persisted. "I know it's the second time around for both of you. But go big, or stay home, Mag. You found someone you want to be with for the rest of your life. That's amazing at your age. *Any* age, I mean," she swiftly amended.

Suzanne was more than ten years younger than Maggie, but tried to paper over her faux pas. Maggie wasn't offended. She liked being older. She'd found it had hidden advantages.

She met Suzanne's gaze with a grin. "That's what Charles says, too. We need to celebrate when we can, what we can. You only go around once in life. As far as we know."

Lucy refilled her glass from the pitcher on the table. "Being a bride is big. No way around it. Unless you elope. It's like being picked for the starring role in a high school musical."

Maggie laughed but the insight felt true. "That's it. A bride needs to rise to the occasion and flounce a little. Like a celebrity on the red carpet? Maybe that's what puts me off."

"Maggie, Maggie," Phoebe mused. "Just do *you*. How hard could that be?"

Maggie laughed, hearing her own advice tossed back at her.

Suzanne signaled with one hand, her mouth full of breakfast muffin. She'd been holding a paper napkin under her chin, so as not to mess her dress, one Maggie had not seen before, a smart sheath with a color block pattern, white on top, and turquoise blue on the bottom. The black panels

of fabric on each side were very figure flattering, and for-
giving, and went perfectly with black patent leather sandals. Maggie guessed that outfit signaled an important
meeting on the agenda.

"Out of the mouths of babes. Or should I say, a babe?"
Suzanne finally managed.

Maggie agreed. "That is good advice. I'll take it to heart."

Suzanne's phone buzzed, vibrating on the table. She
snatched it up and tapped back a message. "My ten
o'clock just confirmed. Got to run."

She brushed off her outfit and slung her big bag over her
shoulder. "Wish me luck, guys. I'm showing a drop-dead-
gorgeous mansion on the water to a couple who are pre-
qualified to three mill and totally ripe for the picking. If
this deal goes down, I'm treating everyone to that elegant
evening of fine food and wine, in a private room. For
Maggie's bachelorette party."

"Bachelorette?" The offer was generous but Maggie
couldn't hold back a sputtering laugh. "Last time I heard
that term, women were burning their bras."

"No offense, Mag. But in order to be more bridie you
really need to get more girlie. The two are definitely related."

Phoebe put her hands over her ears. "Am I really hearing this? Stop her, someone, before I puke."

Lucy laughed but looked appalled as well. "You never
fail to amaze. In less time than it takes to drink a glass of
water, you can set feminism back fifty years."

Suzanne dismissed the remark with a wave of her
French manicure. "Don't be so quick to dis. Girl power is
a potent force when applied correctly."

Maggie tried to keep a straight face. "I think this a good
moment to table the question. You can give us more girlie
tips Thursday night, at our meeting."

Once again, the sarcasm floated above Suzanne's freshly blown-out hairstyle.

"Until then, watch and learn . . ." With a cheerful wave, she sashayed off the porch with an extra swing to her curvaceous hips. "Lesson one, use it or lose it," she called back over her shoulder.

Her friends had to laugh, despite themselves. "Enough said," Maggie countered.

Phoebe's phone pinged with an incoming text. She picked it up and smiled. "Harry just sent the cutest video. It looks like one of our knitting group meetings—"

She passed her phone to Lucy, who laughed. "This is fun. Let's send it to Dana and Suzanne."

Lucy passed the phone to Maggie next. Her curiosity was piqued. She had to laugh, too, watching a fast-action Claymation cartoon that showed a group of sheep knitting and chatting. The sequence played over and over, in a quick loop.

Maggie smiled, and handed Phoebe back her phone. "Send it to me, I'll post it on the shop website. On second thought, you'd better do it. That might take me all day," she admitted.

Phoebe was not only her right hand in the shop, she was also her tech support and social media expert.

"Sure, I'll post it right away." She rose from her seat and headed for the shop, dialing her phone on the way. "I just want to thank Harry."

The screen door slammed. Maggie met Lucy's glance but neither spoke. They could hear Phoebe's animated tone in the shop as she spoke to Harry on the phone. Then her lilting laughter.

Lucy leaned closer to Maggie and whispered. "A phone call? Why not a text? I don't feel good about this reconciliation or whatever she's calling it."

Maggie nodded and whispered back. "I don't, either."

"What if he's so vain, he just hates being rejected? And now he's out to prove he can get her hooked again?"

Maggie had also considered that possibility. "We gave her our opinion. What more can we do?"

Lucy shook her head. "Not much. She has to figure it out for herself."

Maggie met Lucy's gaze. There seemed no need to reply.

They all held Phoebe dear, and felt protective of her, like a flock of clucking mother hens. But the time had come for their chick to leave the nest, in more ways than one.

It would be hard, waiting to see what Phoebe decided to do.

Chapter 5

Though the shop was quiet, the week passed quickly. Maggie spent the downtime browsing knitting magazines and websites, searching for projects that would lend themselves to new classes and workshops in the cooler months to come. And she still had stock to order. The shop had seasons, just like the garden outside the door, and she'd learned to appreciate all of them. Even when the cash register wasn't ringing all day.

On Thursday night, Maggie closed for business promptly at six, though she left the door unlatched for her friends. She'd just placed the food she'd prepared for their meeting in the oven to warm and was heading out to the back room with a platter of cold appetizers when she heard Lucy and Dana chatting as they walked in.

She set the platter of hummus, olives, and pita chips on the table and turned to them. "You're early. I haven't even cleared the table yet."

"We came early to help, since Phoebe's at the market today." Lucy set a salad bowl on the sideboard and Dana removed two bottles from her knitting tote, like a magician pulling rabbits from a hat.

"Some wine and sparkling water. I didn't know what you were cooking so I got rosé."

"That sounds just right," Maggie replied. "The menu is a surprise. All the ingredients are from the market. Vegetables, herbs, cheeses."

"Sounds yummy to me." Dana was mostly a vegetarian and Maggie felt sure she'd be pleased with their dinner, though she wasn't sure about the others.

"We'll take it from here. You've done your part, cooking on such a hot day." Lucy's tone was unusually assertive. "Open the wine. Let's have a glass while we set up."

Maggie sat at the table and happily obliged as her friends arranged the sideboard with dishes, napkins, utensils, and everything else needed for their meal.

Suzanne arrived a short time later, bustling in with tote bags and a pie dish covered with foil. "Can I stick this in the oven? I didn't have time to bake it at home."

"Of course. I'm surprised you had time to make anything at all. I thought you were picking up ice cream and berries?"

"I did." She produced a bag full of ice cream containers, a fancy, gourmet label. Suzanne was a firm believer in flavor choices. "The berries cried out to me. Longing to fulfill a greater destiny."

Lucy laughed and handed her a glass of wine. "That's why we call you the Dessert Whisperer."

"Exactly. Though most of the time all I hear is, 'Eat me.'" Suzanne sipped her wine and glanced around the shop. "Where's the Pheebster? I thought the market was closed by now."

"She's waiting for Robbie to finish at the taco truck. He's joining us tonight. He wants to learn how to knit."

"Or just spend more time with Phoebe, doing something she enjoys?" Lucy asked.

Maggie had thought the same. "A little of both, I suspect. I hope you all don't mind. Phoebe asked me after she'd invited him. What could I say?"

Dana had already taken out her knitting but wasn't stitching yet. "I'm glad he's coming. I think it's a good sign and we can get to know him better."

"Since he's cueing up to be Phoebe's next boyfriend?" Lucy asked with a grin.

Before Dana could reply, Suzanne said, "From your mouth to God's ears. Maybe Phoebe will finally listen to us and Harry the Potter's spell will be broken."

"Hard to say." Maggie recalled the phone call she'd overheard between Phoebe and Harry on Monday morning. Phoebe had sounded thoroughly enthralled.

"I wish she could settle these romantic complications. Running a new business is hard enough. And she's not enjoying the market nearly as much as I expected. She says the other vendors aren't friendly."

"Never mind unfriendly. How about downright deadly? Have the police figured out who killed Jimmy Hooper yet?" Suzanne picked out an olive from the platter and popped it in her mouth. "I hate to think his killer was connected to the market in some way. I'd be worrying about Phoebe night and day."

Maggie felt the same, but tried not to think about it. "I've asked Charles if any of his former colleagues have mentioned Jimmy's case. You know how he is. He wouldn't tell me even if he knew."

"Jack heard something," Dana offered. Her husband, Jack, was an attorney with an office in town, but had started his career in the police force, working his way up to detective. He still had a lot of connections in local law enforcement and heard all the inside information on important cases.

"The investigators believe Jimmy knew his killer," Dana told them. "There were no signs of a break-in, or anything stolen from the farm. There were signs of a struggle. Bruises, other than around his neck. It seems his body was moved from somewhere in the house to the barn, where the murderer staged a fake suicide, a hanging from a beam in the barn loft."

"How do they know for sure it was fake?" Lucy voiced the question Maggie had been about to ask. "Couldn't he have had a fight with someone, and then decided to kill himself for some reason?"

"That was not the case. It was easy for the coroner to determine that the bruising on his skin was not consistent with a real suicide and he was dead before his body was hung."

"That's gruesome," Maggie said quietly. "Do they have any idea of who did this, or the motive?"

Dana had finished setting up the sideboard and poured herself a glass of wine. "A few theories, but nothing solid. They did find a wad of cash hidden in an empty paint can on his workbench. About ten thousand dollars."

"Same old story, gang. 'Follow the money.'" Suzanne shrugged with a knowing look.

"Even if he was paying bills, or just got paid by a store or distributor, it's a lot of money to leave lying around," Lucy said.

Maggie had to agree. But sometimes business owners preferred to deal in cash to avoid taxes. Not that she was ever anything less than one hundred percent honest with her records, but she did know it was a common practice.

"Maybe he didn't trust banks," Suzanne said. "There could be more dough stuffed in a mattress."

Maggie knew she was joking. "That reminds me, I saw his daughter, Carrie, this week, coming out of a bank in town. I imagine she has a lot to sort out. Especially since her father died so suddenly."

"You can say that again," Suzanne countered. "I hear Hooper Farm has a layer cake of mortgages to work through. Ten grand would hardly make a dent. The land is worth a tidy sum, but hard to say if much would be left after the debts are settled."

"It's so hard to run a profitable farm these days. I imagine most farmers around here feel the same pinch. They're working for something more than profit, that's for sure." Maggie felt a wistful sadness. "Jimmy also had a lot of medical bills from his wife's illness. Maybe he never caught up, even though it's been years."

"What a sad story." Dana took a seat at the table across from Maggie. "It's a wonder that the poor man *didn't* decide to end it all. He was carrying a heavy burden. All on his own."

Maggie felt the same. "I think he had more social connections when Penelope was alive. She had friends in town, people who helped them deal with her illness. Once she passed on, Jimmy sort of faded into the background. I rarely saw him in the village anymore. I guess I was in touch once or twice. But I didn't know him well. I feel badly now that I never reached out, or did much to help him. Who could guess he was dealing with so much?"

"I remember him, too," Dana said. "He was very friendly. But still not the type to share his feelings easily."

"I don't think you should feel so bad. What could you have done to help him?" Suzanne asked Maggie.

"I can't say. But I will get in touch with his daughter. Maybe there's some way I can help her while she's here."

Maggie couldn't think of much, except to bring over flowers or a homemade cake.

"I don't know what's keeping Phoebe and Robbie," she added. "I'd better check on dinner. Maybe we should start without them."

Maggie stepped into the storeroom and grabbed the pot holders. She didn't want her zucchini and carrot pancakes to dry out, though she had whipped up a yogurt and dill sauce to top them off. There was also a pan of spicy, crispy chickpeas. Along with Dana's green salad, it made a lovely meal, she thought. And one that was kinder to the planet with the absence of meat.

She had just added serving spoons to the platters when she heard the latecomers arrive.

"Just in time for dinner," Maggie greeted them as she set the food on the table.

"Smells great. But I need a minute or two to chill," Phoebe replied. She looked pale, her voice shaky.

Maggie's silent alarm was tripped. "Sure. Have a cold drink. It was hot out there today."

Dana poured a tall glass of sparkling water for Phoebe and one for Robbie, as well.

"It wasn't the weather," Robbie said. "Though Phoebe's side of the market heated up." He met Phoebe's glance, giving her the chance to enlighten her friends. Everyone waited quietly. Even Suzanne.

"I told Harry I didn't want to go out with him. He'd asked me to think about it, and I did." Phoebe paused and gazed around at her friends. "I nearly gave in. But it's really bad timing for me. And I guess I still don't trust him. I told him in a really nice way, I thought. But it didn't go well."

"What do you mean? What did he say to you?" Lucy asked, voicing the concern they all felt.

"At first, he just seemed disappointed. And sad," Phoebe explained. "He almost started crying and asked me to think about it some more. I didn't know he cared so much. I almost caved," she admitted. "But when I held the line, he got really upset and angry. He called me stubborn and mean . . . and all sorts of things. He said I never gave him a chance to explain his side about that other girl. He was mad about that all over again. As if it was my fault,"

Phoebe added, a note of frustration and incredulity in her voice.

"Sounds like quite a scene. Where were you?" Lucy winced.

"In his stall. I ran out and he chased me. But he knocked into a table and a ton of his pottery fell and broke all over the place. It was worth a lot of money and must have taken him forever to make. Which got him even madder. I felt bad, but I didn't know what to do. I just wanted to get away from him."

"Good thing you did." Robbie sounded upset. "I only caught the crash ending. But if Harry had laid a finger on her, I would have broken more than his pottery. I told him to leave her alone from now on. He didn't like that, either."

Robbie, the friendly, floppy scarecrow, looked angry. And convincingly so. Maggie would have never suspected he had it in him. But he obviously cared for Phoebe and was eager to rush to her defense. Even if it meant confronting his friend and roommate.

"Did he try to hurt you, Phoebe?" Dana's voice was alarmed.

Phoebe was silent a moment. Then she said, "Harry's not like that. But he does like to make his point in an argument. He doesn't like it if someone walks away before he's had his say."

"Sounds like more than making a point to me." Lucy sounded angry and upset. "You were smart to get away from him." She glanced at Robbie. "And backup arrived just in time."

"I didn't do much." Robbie looked suddenly shy. "But I would have, if it came to that," he added, stammering a bit.

His gaze came to rest on Phoebe, with a look of adoration. "Don't worry. Phoebe will be fine. I'll keep my eye on her."

"Good to know," Maggie replied.

She was relieved to hear that Phoebe had decided not to date Harry again, but distressed that the young man had acted out in such a frightening way. She so hoped this wasn't going to cause more stress for Phoebe at the market. But how could it not?

"Will Harry be there tomorrow?" Lucy asked.

"His aunt Adele has the stall tomorrow. He doesn't come back until Sunday. I hope he gets over it by then."

"I can meet you there Sunday morning, if you don't want to face him alone," Lucy offered.

"Me too," Suzanne said. "And I'm even scarier and more heavy-duty that Lucy. No offense," she added.

"You're way scarier than me, no question," Lucy replied with a grin. "I mean, in a good way."

Suzanne laughed. "I hope so."

"I think it will be okay," Phoebe said, though Maggie thought she looked wary, imagining their next meeting. Then she suddenly looked angry again. "And that Honey Girl was in his stall, like two minutes later. All over him, like a little blond buzzing bee. I'm so glad I'm not dating him again. I'd have to worry about him flirting with other girls every minute."

"Skunk alert," Suzanne blurted, then covered her mouth with a hand.

"You made your decision," Dana said. "It's too bad he didn't take it well, but now you can move forward."

Phoebe's expression turned thoughtful. She nodded but didn't reply. Robbie looked pleased with Dana's summation. Maggie suspected the words gave him hope. The very fuel of unrealized desires.

Maggie thought it was time to turn the conversation to some other topic. "Let's eat while the food is still warm.

These are vegetable pancakes, made from shredded zucchini and carrots. There's some onions and garlic, too. Of course." Her friends all knew those ingredients were rarely missing from Maggie's menu. "And lots of cheese. And these are crispy chickpeas, a little spicy. You might want to try a small taste first," she warned.

She waited as the group filled their plates and took testing bites. But she was soon rewarded with rave reviews.

Even Suzanne, who she expected to quietly complain about the vegetarian menu, honored her efforts with the highest compliments. "These veg pancakes are scrumptious. I have to get the recipe."

"Happy to pass it on. They're very easy to make."

Phoebe smirked. "Says the woman who can cook anything. I can't even make real pancakes."

"We'll have a little cooking lesson. As soon as you have some free time," Maggie promised.

After the dishes cleared, and even a bit prior, knitting projects emerged and they settled down for some serious stitching.

Phoebe taught Robbie how to knit, starting with casting on stitches, then the simple knit stitch. After a few rows of knits, she showed him how to purl.

He held the needles awkwardly and produced each stitch with effort. But his patience and good humor were admirable and he seemed sincerely interested in learning the craft, not just going through the motions to please Phoebe. Knitting was practically Phoebe's whole world, and it only made sense that someone who wanted to win her heart and be part of that world would want to know more about it.

Had Harry ever tried to knit? Maggie wasn't sure. Maybe it would have helped their relationship if he had. Yarn under the bridge now.

Phoebe was teaching Robbie tonight and they seemed very happy and cozy together. It felt good to see that. Especially in light of Phoebe's disturbing day.

Lucy and Suzanne were still working on socks. Dana had completed a pair and was starting a second. Maggie decided to ask their opinion on project ideas she was considering for fall and winter workshops. She'd found a number of possibilities in the latest knitting magazines and opened a copy of *Vogue Knitting*, turning to the page she'd marked with a yellow sticky.

"What do you think of this ruffle-edged cardigan? I thought it would be perfect for holiday parties."

Suzanne crooned. "Love that. It's so cute."

"A little *girlie* for me," Lucy said in a pointed tone.

"As we've already heard," Suzanne countered.

"What's this, some private joke I missed?" Dana looked over the edge of her reading glasses, her expression curious, and Maggie recalled she had not been at the shop Monday morning.

"Suzanne promised to share pro tips on using our 'secret girlie power' to win friends and influence people," Maggie explained in a sly tone. "We all feel it's a giant step backward for feminism."

"And I suppose you agree?" Suzanne challenged Dana.

Dana thought for a moment. "If by 'girlie' you mean the divine feminine, the matriarchal Earth Mother force, I don't disagree entirely. Goddesses were central to practically every culture and faith tradition before the patriarchy pushed them aside and made women doubt and suppress their powerful natures. Men are still afraid of powerful women. Most men."

"I think Suzanne's talking more Barbie doll than Goddess Gaia," Lucy countered.

"Never heard of her. That's not even fair." Suzanne shrugged. Her socks were turning into tubes, but Maggie didn't think this was a good moment to swoop in for adjustments.

"Gaia was the Greek goddess of the Earth, who symbolized all creation," Maggie explained quietly.

"Uh, guys? Can we skip the women's studies lecture tonight?" Phoebe sounded embarrassed. "We have a guest. Remember?"

Robbie laughed and pushed his chair back. "Don't mind me. I have to go."

"So soon?" Suzanne sounded genuinely sorry. "We're just getting warmed up and we didn't even have dessert. My own homemade blueberry tart with ice cream."

"Sounds delicious, but I have a night job."

"I thought Phoebe had a rough schedule. Yours is even worse," Lucy said.

"It's not so bad. I stock the supermarket, from about ten till one. There's a fun bunch of people there. We goof around and snack all we want from the broken packages of cookies and chips. And I get to drive a forklift."

"How cool is that?" Suzanne's eyes grew wide. "How do I apply?" She sounded so sincere Maggie wondered if she was joking.

Robbie said goodbye and thanked everyone for letting him join the meeting. "Come back anytime," Suzanne oozed. "We'll keep a lid on that goddess talk, promise."

Phoebe walked Robbie out to his truck and once they heard the shop door close, Maggie and her friends ducked their heads together in a huddle.

"I can't believe he has a night job. After slaving all day on a hot taco truck." Suzanne whispered. "That shows character. I'm impressed."

"I am, too," Dana said. "They seem totally in tune. It was cute to watch her teach him how to knit."

"Very," Lucy seconded. "And the perfect distraction from her encounter with Harry."

Maggie could not have agreed more. "Let's hope sweet, responsible Robbie continues to distract her. I think Phoebe has finally turned a page with Harry."

"Let's hope Harry has, too," Dana mused, "and he won't bother her again."

"If he does, her knight in shining armor will protect her." Suzanne sounded content with the happy ending she imagined.

Maggie smiled at the notion. To her, Robbie seemed more like the good-natured family dog who barked his head off if a stranger knocked on the door, but rarely showed much follow-through.

Hopefully, his heroics would not be put to the test.

Chapter 6

"Phoebe, can you stop crying? Just for a moment, please? I can't understand a word you're saying, dear." Maggie was beside herself, trying to simultaneously comfort and comprehend her young friend, who sat sobbing uncontrollably in the middle of the shop's back staircase.

It was eight thirty, almost time to open the shop, but Phoebe was still in her nightwear, pink cotton boxers and a black tank top with a yin-yang sign. She held her cell phone in one hand and had her laptop balanced on her knees.

Maggie tried to hold her wandering gaze. "Are you hurt? Are you sick? . . . Did Van Gogh run away again?"

Phoebe shook her head, her expression bleak. "Just look at this! It's a dumpster fire!" She thrust out her phone. "I've been trashed all over the internet! It's a total nightmare! An absolute, freaking disaster!"

Maggie took the phone in hand and slipped on her reading glasses, not exactly sure what she was looking at. She recognized Phoebe's Facebook page, and a scroll of customer comments and reviews on the sidebar.

Maggie had read such comments before, many times—always the most glowing, five-star reviews. This morning the entire page was filled with complaints and criticism, ranging from cranky to downright degrading, insulting and libelous.

Cheap junk. Don't waste your money.

She claims this stuff is handmade? If robots have hands these days.

Wore sox once. My feet turned purple, like Easter eggs and socks unraveled in one wearing.

Sox by Phoebe sent me to the ER. My body broke out in hives. Stay away from this stuff, unless you have good health insurance.

Is this site a sham? Sox by Phoebe took my money and I never got any socks. When I tried to follow up, my emails were never answered. I have alerted the Better Business Bureau. Save your money. Stay away from Sox by Phoebe.

The pictures look so cute but this is a terrible product! My five-year-old could do better. This site never replied to my complaints or my request for a refund.

Run the other way from Sox by Phoebe. Barefoot or not.

And on and on it went . . . Maggie felt sick to her stomach, but forced a brave face.

"Oh, my goodness. This is simply . . . abominable!" She handed the phone back. She didn't need to read any more. "How in the world could that have happened?"

"There's more on my website and my Amazon and Etsy

pages, too." Phoebe showed her the laptop and Maggie peered down briefly. "I'm ruined. My business career is over. I'll never come back from this. Never *ever*."

She seemed on the verge of melting down again. Maggie touched her shoulder. "That's just not true. I know it seems awful right now. But we'll figure it out. There must be something we can do. Let's sit down and try to approach it in a calmer frame of mind."

"I'd better take a shower and get dressed first."

"Good idea. A long, hot shower always helps me tackle a problem. You do that and come right down. We'll strategize." Maggie felt so bad for Phoebe, she didn't know what to say or do. "Lucy is probably nearby," she added, pulling out her phone. "She's good with computers. I bet she knows how to fix this. Or knows someone who can?"

Phoebe nodded and sighed, then slipped inside her apartment and shut the door.

Maggie's body sagged with the shock she'd worked hard to hide. So, this is what people called a cyberattack. Now she understood the full meaning of the word. Who in the world had assaulted Phoebe in this cowardly, shameless way? What diabolical mind had cooked up this heinous prank?

"It's mind-boggling, isn't it?" Maggie asked Lucy a few minutes later. They spoke in low voices. Phoebe was still upstairs and Maggie heard the shower running.

Lucy had been walking up from the harbor when Maggie called and practically ran the rest of the way up Main Street to the shop. Using Maggie's laptop, she quickly reviewed Phoebe's website, Facebook, and sales pages on various sites. Maggie watched her expression turn grim.

"This is just . . . unspeakably awful. It's cyberbullying to the max. More than that. I can't believe someone would attack poor Phoebe this way. You'd have to stay up all night to create this kind of havoc. More than one night. You'd have to plan it, with fake usernames and passwords, and burner phones that aren't traceable. You'd really need to put time and thought into this mess. It's just so . . . unbelievably creepy. I've got the chills thinking about it."

"Me too," Maggie replied. "And I never get the chills. The idea that someone struck out at her this way is disturbing. The internet is bad enough. What if they try to hurt her for real?"

"I thought of that, too. I think she needs to report this to the police. Though I'm not sure if there's anything they can do." Lucy sat back and sighed. "The first thing is to take screenshots of the damage, then take down all this trash talk. Matt has a friend who's a super tech whiz. He helps me all the time when I have computer glitches. I'm sure he'll help us clean up this mess."

Maggie felt a wave of relief. A small wave, but at least there was some hope and some good news to tell Phoebe when she came downstairs. "That's so good of you, Lucy. But I knew you'd be able to help. Don't you need to work today?"

Lucy shrugged, her gaze fixed on the computer screen. "This is more important."

Maggie heard Phoebe's apartment door open and her quick, light step on the staircase.

"Lucy—did you see what happened to me? I've been trolled. Trashed. Slandered and smeared . . ."

"It's ugly, honey. No question," Lucy cut in. She shut the laptop and came to her feet. "But we'll fix it. Matt has a friend who's an IT genius. He'll know what to do."

Lucy put her arm around Phoebe's shoulder and gave her a hug. Maggie had slipped into the storeroom, but now returned with a mug of coffee. She handed it to Phoebe.

"Who do you think did this?" she asked quietly. "Who would want to spend that much time causing trouble for you?"

"The pickle people? Trying to push you out so they can finally get that stall?" Lucy guessed. "The husband especially looked like a grudge holder. He didn't strike me as the computer-savvy type, but you never know."

"Warren moved their stall last week, right next to the village green. It's a prime location and they even came by to brag about it."

The pickle people were Maggie's first choice, too, but it seemed they had no reason now to retaliate.

"What about Harry?" Maggie hated to bring him up, but she had to. "Maybe he was so upset when you refused to see him, he did this to get back at you. He knows how long you've planned to open your own business and how much this would hurt you."

Phoebe frowned and ducked her head. Maggie couldn't tell if she was surprised at the idea, or had already considered it.

"He was upset. More than I'd ever seen him. He's not that great on computers, but I guess he could have done this to get back at me. Or had some help?" She sighed and bit her lower lip. "I don't know what to think."

Maggie didn't know what to think, either. Or how to find the words that would comfort her.

Phoebe's phone rang. She checked the caller and quickly picked it up. "Hey, Warren. What's up?"

It was the market manager, Warren Braeburn. Had he seen the trash talk on Phoebe's social media already? Warren didn't seem like the social media type. He was probably too busy running the markets and his farm to post and tweet, and all that.

But it seemed there was some other news, and just as

bad, Maggie realized, when Phoebe's expression melted into dismay and tears again.

"Sure . . . I understand." Phoebe struggled to keep her voice steady. "I'll be there right away."

Phoebe ended the call and took a deep, shaky breath.

Maggie went on high alert and knew Lucy felt the same. "What is it, Phoebe? What's happened now?"

"Warren said my stall is filled with trash. Fishy-smelling garbage that's stinking up the whole aisle." The words sputtered out as she fought back tears. "All the customers are complaining and the other vendors on my aisle want to kill me. I have to go down there right away and clean it up."

Lucy looked baffled. "Garbage? How could that be? Aren't the stalls secure at night?"

"Someone slashed the canvas and dumped it. Thank goodness I don't leave anything in there besides tables and chairs." She sniffed and wiped her eyes with the back of her hand. "Why is this happening? What did I ever do to deserve this?"

Maggie and Lucy stood on either side of Phoebe and patted her shoulders. "Don't cry, Phoebe. I won't say it doesn't sound bad. But it's not irreparable. Messes can be cleaned. Many hands make light work, and all that?" Maggie remined her. "You'll be up and running by this afternoon."

Phoebe sighed. "I have to clean up the trash. But after that, what's the point? Obviously, someone wants me out. Maybe I should take the hint. This vendor gig has turned into a total disaster."

Lucy had been rubbing Phoebe's back with a comforting touch, but suddenly looked serious, her tone stern. "Hey, none of that giving-up talk. Whoever trashed the stall probably trashed you all over the internet, too. They're out to intimidate you, to wear down your confidence. You can't let them win, kiddo. The best revenge is to dust your-self off and march on. In a pair of Sox by Phoebe, of course."

When Phoebe didn't reply, Lucy added in a more playful tone, "What kind of feminist lets a little garbage—real and virtual—push her out of business?"

Maggie felt the impulse to chime in. "Women have been taking garbage on the chin for centuries. Where would we be now if our ancestors had let that get in their way? We wouldn't vote, we wouldn't drive, we wouldn't hold good jobs and start our own businesses . . ."

Phoebe finally raised her head and whisked her fingers under her eyes to wipe away her tears. "I hear you. Sorry for being such a pushover." She sighed and stood up straighter. "You're right. I'm not throwing in my socks yet."

Maggie was pleased to hear Phoebe's change of heart. She was already putting out an SOS to Dana and Suzanne.

"I have some cleaning supplies in the storeroom. Gloves and trash bags, and such. We can pick up more later. Let's survey the damage first." Maggie grabbed her essentials, keys, wallet, and phone. "I almost forgot . . . what will you do with the dogs, Lucy? Don't you need to bring them home?"

"I'll drop them off with Matt. The practice has doggie daycare there now. Tink and Wally are always welcome."

Lucy headed off on foot with her pals, and Maggie locked up the shop and tossed the cleaning supplies in the back of her Subaru. Phoebe had already jumped in the passenger side.

As they headed to the market, Phoebe said, "I'm going to text Robbie. Maybe he'll help, too."

"Good idea. The more the merrier." Maggie could have almost guaranteed Robbie would join the effort, happy to even dive into a pile of trash for Phoebe.

Maggie tried to remain cool and no drama about the

morning's surprising events, but it was all very strange and unsettling. Was Harry's wounded ego behind these vicious pranks? More of an attack than a mere prank, Maggie had to say.

Or was there someone unfamiliar lurking in the background, who wanted to push Phoebe out of the market? Maggie had no idea why that would be, but the more she thought about it, the more complicated the question seemed.

Maggie and Phoebe were the first to arrive at the scene of the crime. The stall was closed, but Maggie could see where the canvas had been torn and now hung loose. While that could be repaired with some duct tape, she thought, the rest would be a little harder to set right.

The smell of spoiled fish was powerful and sickening, even from a distance. It hung over the space like a toxic cloud. The still, humid air made the situation even worse. Low dark clouds promised rain, which Maggie hoped would help wash the mess away. But not before they had a chance to clean things up.

Phoebe pressed her hand over her mouth as she opened the stall all the way. The space was almost filled with broken bags of garbage, spilling their guts all over the wooden floor. "This is bad. I hope I won't be sick. I'm glad I skipped breakfast."

Maggie hoped she wouldn't be sick, either. And she had not skipped breakfast, unfortunately.

"Gloves. Mask. Bag." Maggie handed the equipment to Phoebe and took the same for herself. Holding her breath, as if about to jump into the deep end of a pool, she bravely waded into the mess as Phoebe followed.

"We should have brought a shovel," Maggie said finally. "It would have gone faster."

"I just thought of that, too. I'll text Suzanne and Dana. Maybe they can find one."

They picked around the edges, working their way to the middle. Maggie felt the nearby vendors watching them. They didn't have much else to do. The smell had driven customers into other areas of the market. Idle as they were, no one stepped forward to help, she noticed.

Was she imagining a hostile vibe? Of course they'd be angry about losing business due to the toxic cloud, and probably blamed Phoebe, thinking she must be at fault in some way.

But the hostile vibe seemed something more. She shook her head, feeling silly for letting her imagination run amok.

Maggie had brought a box of plastic gloves that she kept in the shop for fiber dying projects, and she'd also brought some dish towels, to cover their noses and mouths. Rubber boots had felt like an overreaction back at the shop, when she'd considered taking them, but they definitely would have come in handy. As she filled one trash bag, tied it, and started on the next, she tried not to dwell on the future of her new sandals.

"Hey—too bad about what happened to your stall. What a bummer." Maggie looked up. It was Honey Girl, holding up the hem of a long, floral prairie dress, her thick tresses woven in braids that wrapped around her head.

Phoebe stopped working and stared at her. When she finally replied, she sounded annoyed. "Yeah, totally. Did you see anybody near my stall this morning?"

"Me? Nope. It was already smelly." Her blue eyes were wide. "So, you don't know who did it? Was it just, like, a random thing, you think?"

She sounded worried it could happen to her, Maggie thought. Or was that just an act, to throw off suspicion?

"I don't know who or why," Phoebe replied in a sharp tone. "If I find out, there's going to be trouble."

Honey Girl nodded solemnly. "I hear you. But it never helps to feed the bad wolf inside of us. I brought you some sprays and scent sticks—lavender and lemon verbena. And this is a diffuser. It's all pure essential oils."

Phoebe took the gifts, fumbling a bit to hold them with her gloved hands. Maggie could see she didn't know what to say. The scent solutions seemed like offering a water pistol to extinguish a forest fire, but Honey Girl certainly meant well. She was the only neighbor who had tried to help.

"Thanks. I'll use this stuff later. Hey, I'm Phoebe. I don't even know your name."

"Yeah, I know. From your socks. I'm Samantha Newton. See you later. Looks like I finally have a customer. She must need a neti pot," Samantha mused as she walked away.

Phoebe set the gifts in the only clean spot, outside the tent. "Maybe Honey Girl isn't so bad after all?" Maggie murmured.

Phoebe pulled up her dish towel mask and Maggie realized they must look like old-time bank robbers. "Or maybe she just stopped in to gloat."

Before Maggie could speculate, Lucy appeared, a large tote bag hanging from each arm. "Mother-of-pearl, it smells worse than low tide during crabbing season. This stuff must have come from the Yankee Chowder stall. From the dumpster where they throw their trash, I mean."

"That seems likely. It's the only stall that sells anything fishy. And I did spot a few oyster cracker cellophanes, now that you mention it." Maggie glanced at Phoebe. "Any reason the chowder vendors would be mad at you?"

"Zero," Phoebe replied quickly. "I've never even met them. I think it's more like someone just looked for the smelliest garbage, and they were the nose-down winners."

"Maybe we should ask them what they use to clean up at night," Maggie suggested. "Once we get the trash bagged up, we move to phase two—odor removal."

"Got it covered, girls." Lucy had already donned her gloves and mask, and showed them large, white plastic bottles. "Super cleaner, from the animal hospital. It breaks down the absolute worst dog and cat messes and gets rid of all the odors."

"Good thinking. We'll certainly put it to the test," Maggie said.

Dana arrived and jumped right in, catching up on the situation as they bagged up the last bits of trash. The day was growing warmer and the weather even stickier. The smell was still noxious and the task was wearing on their resolve.

Suzanne was the last to arrive, but laden with more supplies. She swept into the stall, carrying buckets, mops, and bags full of cleaning potions. "Hey gang, sorry I'm late. You know how I love to shop."

She quickly dropped her contributions and waved a hand in front of her face. "I know who did this. The CIA is developing stink bombs and dumped one here as a test."

"That would definitely explain it," Dana said drily. "I think I saw something about that last night, on the conspiracy channel?"

"I'm serious. Well, almost." Suzanne pulled a plastic poncho from her purse, then yanked it down over her clothing.

"Good idea, but you'll melt under there in this heat," Maggie warned.

"That's partly the reason I'm wearing it. It already feels like a portable sauna. Maybe I'll lose a few pounds." She opened another bag and passed it around. "Which reminds me, I brought cold waters and snacks."

The bottles of cold water were welcome. Maggie twisted one open and gulped it down.

They had just set back to work when Robbie arrived. He waved cheerfully, rolling along a metal hand truck, with a garden hose draped over one shoulder. "Wow, you guys work fast. Want to clean out my truck tonight?"

Maggie paused to wipe her brow with the back of her hand. "I think I'll pass. The rest of you go ahead, if you like."

Her friends rolled their eyes. Robbie was the only one who laughed. He grabbed a bulging trash bag in each hand and secured them to the hand truck with bungee cords.

"I'll take all the bags to the dumpster, then hook up the hose so you can spray the floor down. There's a connection somewhere around here. Be right back."

"Robbie to the rescue. Again," Suzanne murmured. She and Maggie exchanged a look. Luckily, Phoebe had not heard them.

When the stall was finally cleared, Maggie stepped back to survey their work. Phoebe's lovely murals of falling snow, painted on big sheets of drawing paper, would all have to come down. Would she bother to duplicate them? Hard to say.

The floor definitely needed scrubbing. A simple rinse, even with a hose, would not do. It appeared to be old wooden planks, set into some sort of frame that held them in place. They could use Lucy's odor blaster, but doubtlessly, some of the stench had leaked into the cracks between the boards. That would be harder to remove and far more insidious.

While she mused about the rest of the job, Phoebe tugged her arm. "Look, Harry's aunt Adele is here. I'm going over to talk to her."

Maggie wondered about that. "Do you think that's wise? No sense stirring the hive."

Suzanne waved her arms under the poncho. She looked like a big yellow bird about to take flight. "I'm all for it. His aunt will probably cover for him, even if she knows something. But Phoebe might get some idea of whether or not Harry is behind this garbage attack. Want some backup, sweetie?" she offered.

"Maybe I should go," Maggie said. "Adele stops in at the shop from time to time. I'd be a friendly face?"

Maggie hated to cut in on Suzanne's offer and imply that she was *not* a friendly face. But things could quickly escalate with the fiery brunette riding shotgun. They all knew Suzanne's bold tongue often ran far ahead of her brain.

"Thanks, Suzanne. But I think Maggie should come." Phoebe pulled off her plastic gloves and rubbed her hands with sanitizer, then passed Maggie the bottle. "Let's catch her while she's setting up."

Maggie followed Phoebe, rubbing her hands with anti-bacterial potion as they trotted across the aisle. It was going to take more than hand sanitizer to restore a normal level of hygiene. Maybe a bath in Chanel No. 5?

They found Adele McSweeney waving a pink feather duster over her miscellany of semi-antique treasures, as if casting a magical spell. Chipped china dishes, carnival glass ashtrays and perfume bottles, and desk clocks in various states of disrepair had been displayed with care on a folding table covered by an old lace tablecloth.

It was hard to guess Adele's age. Her hair was white, gathered in a wispy bun at the back of her head, random bobby pins not quite succeeding in holding the construction together. A small hat was perched on top; the black velvet looked rusty in spots, the veiling tattered. Her long cotton dress, a floral print on a gray background, was partly covered by a checkered apron, the type favored by nineteen fifties housewives. A large, gaudy broach was pinned near the shoulder of her dress, a flower with petals made of fake gems.

She always wore clothes from some distant era, a thrift

shop chic that millennials like Phoebe admired. But Maggie suspected it was not a fashion statement. The garments had simply been hanging in Adele's closet all this while.

Adele called over her shoulder as Phoebe and Maggie approached. "I'll just be a minute. You can browse a bit if you like."

"Her eyesight isn't too good. Cataracts," Phoebe whispered, then in a louder voice added, "It's Phoebe, Mrs. McSweeney."

Adele turned and looked at them. "Oh, hello, dear. How are you doing with your stall? I noticed you aren't open yet today."

"I had a mess to clean. Someone broke in last night and filled my stall with garbage."

Phoebe waited, and Maggie did, too, to see what Adele would say. "For goodness' sake. I've been at this market ten years. I've never heard of such a thing." She shook her head with dismay. "You poor thing. I did smell something distasteful wafting this way. Who would do a thing like that to you, dear? Do you have any idea?"

"I was wondering if you knew," Phoebe said.

Adele seemed surprised by the question. "I have no idea. None at all. I wasn't here yesterday. It was Harry's day. Didn't you see him here? You ought to ask him if he knows anything about it. Maybe he can help."

If Adele had the slightest suspicion about her grandnephew, she was putting on a very good show. She'd moved from the knickknack table to her jewelry trays, and began sorting out the rings, bracelets, and earring sets.

"I did see him, Mrs. McSweeney. We had an argument. Now I think he dumped the trash to get back at me." Phoebe's voice quivered just a little, but Maggie was proud to see her stand up for herself.

The old woman looked up and stared at Phoebe, her complexion waxy under pancake powder and rouge.

"My Harry?" She sounded partly shocked, and partly as if she thought Phoebe was joking with her. "He'd never do a thing like that. He's not that sort of boy. Yes, he has a temper from time to time," she admitted. "But he can't even squash a bug. He's a kind, sweet, considerate soul. He'd never do that to you. No matter how upset he was."

Her tone was suddenly emotional, rich with feeling. Adele truly loved her grandnephew. Phoebe had said they were close. Harry didn't have much family—a reason that he and Phoebe were drawn to each other—and Adele was like a grandmother to him. A doting grandmother, who would like to deny or ignore certain character flaws in Harry the Potter?

"He wasn't kind and considerate to me yesterday," Phoebe countered. "Not the least bit. I've never seen him so angry. He was like another person."

Adele shook her head, her little hat sliding to one side. She seemed distressed by the conversation. "He gets upset but quickly gets past it. He'd never make a mess like that and cause you so much trouble, dear. No matter how mad he was. Believe me . . . Better yet, you ask him yourself. I'm sure he'll tell you the same thing."

"I will," Phoebe replied, though her tone suddenly lacked the clear note of conviction Maggie had heard earlier.

"Good luck. I hope you don't lose too much time getting your stall back in order."

"Thanks." Phoebe's tone was sharp. She turned and Maggie followed.

"Goodbye, Adele," Maggie said. "Phoebe is upset today. I'm sure you understand."

"I do." Adele adjusted her hat, though it still sat at a funny angle. "But she's barking up the wrong tree if she thinks my Harry had anything to do with that mess. He's very particular and has so many allergies. He could never tolerate handling garbage, even if he'd wanted to. Phoebe should know that, too."

Maggie said goodbye again and headed for Phoebe's stall. She'd have to ask Phoebe about Adele's alibi for her nephew. Perhaps Harry had worn protection from the smell, or had help. If he wasn't the one behind this mischief, then who?

By the time Phoebe and Maggie returned to the stall, the wooden floor had been scrubbed with cleaner. Robbie had hooked up the hose and Suzanne had sprayed down the boards.

"Good, you're back. I know we're all traumatized, but it's time to use those old schnozzolas and give this place a good sniff." Suzanne tapped her finger to the side of her lovely, straight nose.

"We should bring the dogs here," Phoebe said. "They would tell us if there was still a fishy smell."

"We'll just have to pretend we're canines for a few minutes." Suzanne glanced at Lucy. "That won't be too hard for some of us."

Lucy smiled. "What a lovely compliment. Most dogs are nicer than most people. That's a fact."

"All right, let's just do this," Maggie said, focusing their attention again. "The sooner we're done, the sooner Phoebe can get back to business."

"If Wi-Fi has gone down all over town," Phoebe muttered. "Which is highly unlikely."

"We'll take care of the virtual mess later, sweetie," Lucy promised. "My IT buddy said he can help us this afternoon."

Maggie was encouraged by that news and so was Phoebe. She led the way back into her stall, bending low and sniffing the air. Someone had tested Honey Girl's lavender mist. Maggie smelled that at first. But underneath, the fishy odor persisted. Everyone seemed to notice at the same time.

Suzanne lifted her head and covered her nose with her hand. "Ugh . . . it's still there. I'll never eat chowder again."

"I smell it, too," Dana agreed. "But I didn't want to say."

Phoebe looked flummoxed. "What can I do now? Tear the whole thing down?"

"At summer camp we had tents with wooden floors just like this. A mouse died under the boards and it really stunk," Lucy explained. "Maybe if we pick up the planks and spread some of the super cleaner underneath, the rest of the smell will go away?"

They agreed it was worth a try. The stall floor was only about ten planks wide. Phoebe found her heavy shears and used them to pry up the sides of the boards. They found a layer of gravel underneath, which was a good thing, Maggie thought. It would drain quickly once they hosed it down. They worked together to set the boards behind the stall.

"We can hose the boards down again, too," Maggie suggested. "It couldn't hurt."

Phoebe and Lucy were lifting the last two planks, when Phoebe suddenly reached down and pulled something up. "Look . . ."

"Not a dead rodent, I hope?" Suzanne squeezed her eyes closed, afraid to see Phoebe's discovery.

"A hat." She held the visor and pushed the rest open with her hand. "It says, 'Hooper Organic Farm.'" She looked up at her friends. "That's sad. It must have belonged to Jimmy."

Maggie stepped over and took the cap from her hand. "I guess so. Or someone working for him." The unexpected reminder of the lost farmer felt jarring, even spooky.

"I'm going to visit his daughter, Carrie, soon. I'll bring

it to her." Maggie put the hat in an empty plastic bag, then shot a bit of spray inside. She'd need to clean the hat off before she delivered it. It hadn't fared well, stuck under the floor for who knows how long.

With the planks cleared, they followed through on Lucy's suggestion and poured the rest of the super cleaner on the gravel under the floor and the undersides of the boards, too.

A few minutes later, they all agreed, the putrid smell had finally been banished.

"That was a job and half," Lucy said, sounding breathless.

"I was thinking, we could probably clean up crime scenes now," Suzanne suggested. "I mean, if we wanted a little extra cash for the holidays?"

"Suzanne, only you would say that," Lucy laughed.

"Always enterprising, I'll grant you that." Maggie was happy to pull off the fifth pair of plastic gloves she'd donned that day. Was this cleaning episode finally over?

Earlier today when they'd started working, she never thought she'd eat again. But now she was hungry for lunch. She wondered if Robbie would bring them more tacos. He had not been a huge help, but he had a job to do and was certainly facing the midday lunch rush now.

Maybe it was better if they took Phoebe somewhere else for a bite. She needed a break from the market, Maggie decided. She was just about to suggest it, when Phoebe grabbed her arm. "Look, there's Harry. I can't believe he came here today."

They all turned and looked across the aisle at Adele's stall. Harry was speaking to his great-aunt, his back turned toward them.

"The culprit always returns to the scene of the crime," Suzanne whispered. "You should ask him if he trashed your stall . . . and trashed you online, too."

"He'll just deny it." Maggie didn't want Phoebe to get into another row with her combustible ex-boyfriend. "You don't want a replay of yesterday's scene. Or worse."

Phoebe met her glance, then looked over at the rest of her friends. "I just want to see the expression on his face. I'll know if he's lying or not."

Maggie was about to debate, then swallowed back her words. "Looks like we'll all have a chance to see that. Circle the wagons, ladies. Harry McSweeney is coming this way."

Chapter 7

"My aunt said you're looking for me?" Harry walked straight up to Phoebe, his expression cold and blank. "You want to ask me something?"

He towered over Phoebe's slight form. A stark white shirt tucked into black jeans made his shoulders look even broader than usual. Especially when he crossed his arms over his chest.

Phoebe was not the least bit intimidated. She lifted her chin to confront him. "Did you dump a ton of garbage in my stall? And post nasty comments about my socks all over the internet?"

Harry's eyes narrowed. He didn't look angry, exactly. He did look confused. Maggie was surprised by that.

"What? No way. That's plain crazy, Phoebe. Even for you."

"Don't lie to me, Harry. You're the only person who has any reason to be mad at me and do something like that."

"I lost it last night. I'm sorry. I came here today to apologize to you." Harry ran a hand through his thick, dark hair. "I really, *really* hoped that you'd go out with me again. I was totally bummed when you said you just wanted to be friends. But I'm sorry for the way I reacted.

That wasn't right." His tone had softened and he tilted his head to catch Phoebe's glance and hold it. "I still have a lot of feelings for you, Pheebs. Even if you don't feel the same anymore. I know how much it means to you to open this stall. You've been talking about it for months. I could never spoil that for you. Never."

Was Harry telling the truth, or casting his spell again? The former, Maggie feared. Phoebe was practically melting on the spot.

His dark hair, deep brown eyes, and chiseled features were a potent combination, no question. A brooding, passionate Heathcliff type. Maggie didn't underrate the attraction. She also knew a relationship with someone like that was like juggling a stick of dynamite. A fact Phoebe should know by now, too.

"You believe me, don't you?" he persisted.

Phoebe looked down and shook her head. "I don't know, Harry. I'm not sure I should."

Harry took a deep breath. "I know it's hard for you to trust me. That's all on me. I'll tell you where I was last night. On campus, in the ceramics studio. I pay to use the space on the off-hours. I was there from about eight until three this morning. Glazing and firing. I need to replace all those pieces that broke the other day." When she didn't reply, he added, "You know how lame I am at that social media stuff? And how crummy the Wi-Fi is in that building? Even if I knew how to troll someone's pages, I wouldn't have been able to do it out there."

Phoebe let out a frustrated sigh. Maggie couldn't tell if she believed him or not. "Was anyone at the studio with you?"

"Not the whole night," he admitted. "But that's the truth. I guess it's your choice to believe me or not."

Phoebe didn't answer. She stared up at him a moment,

then looked away and let out a long breath. It seemed they'd hit an impasse. Maggie wondered if it was a good time to interrupt, before someone lost their temper?

Robbie swung around the corner carrying another garden hose. "I can give you a hand now. Did that hose reach far enough? I just found another one."

His cheerful expression faded at the sight of Phoebe and Harry standing toe to toe. He quickly strode up to them.

"Didn't you cause enough trouble yesterday, Harry?" Robbie stepped between Phoebe and Harry, sounding angry and spoiling for a fight.

"Chill, Robbie. We're just talking." Harry backed up, raising his hands in a sign of surrender. He had almost six inches and about twenty pounds of muscle on Phoebe's champion, but he clearly didn't want to fight him.

Robbie laughed. "Good one. If the pottery doesn't work out, you'd make a good garbage man. You definitely know how to sling trash bags around."

"I didn't vandalize Phoebe's stall. I never would," Harry insisted.

"You're buying that, Phoebe? I don't." Robbie's tone was steady and controlled. But he took a step closer to Harry, causing Harry to take another step back.

"It doesn't matter what you think," Harry countered. "Phoebe believes me."

"I don't know what to think," Phoebe cut in. "But you two arguing is pointless. It doesn't solve a thing."

"He started it." Harry stepped closer to Robbie and stared down at him. "I don't know what your problem is. You scare me lately, man. Truly."

Robbie looked surprised. Then about to laugh. "I scare you? Give me a break. I want you to move out, Harry. I've been meaning to tell you for a long time. This is the last straw. I don't want to find you or your stuff in the apartment when I get back."

Harry's expression darkened and his fists curled at his sides. Was he going to defile those soulful hands by throwing a punch?

"No problem. I was going to move anyway." He pushed his face close to Robbie's. "I know what you're up to, Taco Boy. This isn't over yet."

Robbie squared his shoulders and swallowed hard. Was he the least bit afraid of Harry? It seemed so, though he managed to hold his ground.

The two young men glared at each other a moment, then Harry stalked back to his aunt's stall. Maggie heard a unified sigh of relief rise from her friends.

"Glad that's over. I was about turn that hose on them," Lucy admitted. "Works great on snarling dogs."

"Young males of the species, butting heads like bighorn sheep," Dana said. "Dueling testosterone in action."

"Sparring over the choice young female in the pack, you mean," Suzanne noted.

Phoebe had returned and heard the tail end of the postgame commentary, unfortunately. "Thanks a lot. This isn't the nature channel. It's my life," she reminded everyone.

Robbie had followed her, a few meek steps behind. She suddenly turned to him. "Maybe I should thank you for stepping in. But sounds to me like you and Harry have your own baggage to unpack."

He offered his soft, apologetic smile. "I'm sorry you had to hear that. The way he treated you, Phoebe—that meltdown last night and that stupid prank with the garbage—it just put me over the top."

Apparently, Robbie had no doubt that Harry was responsible for the cyberbullying and the mess in her stall, but Maggie wasn't sure if his opinion had much sway with Phoebe.

Suzanne slipped off her plastic poncho and whisked her damp brow with a tissue. "That's the way it goes sometimes with college friends. It's sad, but most of the time, you outgrow those ties."

"It's more than that." Robbie paused and sighed, reluctant to elaborate. He glanced at Phoebe. "I didn't just throw him out because of you. He's been so moody lately. I never know what to expect. He's like two different people. I know I sound like a wimp, but living with him scares me now."

He seemed embarrassed to admit the last part, perhaps for looking far less macho in front of the choice young female?

"Maybe he's been upset over the breakup," Lucy offered.

"Could be," Robbie agreed halfheartedly. "I kept asking him what was wrong. And if he wanted to talk, but he always brushed me off. I don't know what's going on with him. But I don't think it's good."

Maggie could see that Phoebe was disturbed by Robbie's disclosures. "If he's in some sort of trouble, we should help him. I don't want to date him anymore, but I don't hate him. We were all such good friends in school."

Robbie answered with a soft smile. "That's just like you, Phoebe. The guy trashes your entire life, and you still want to rescue him. Like another stray cat."

His observation hit a nerve and Phoebe flushed. "He swears that he was in the ceramics studio all night. You know how spotty Wi-Fi is on that end of campus. You have to step outside to get any kind of signal. I don't know how he could have put up all those posts if he was really there."

Robbie looked about to argue, then shrugged. "If you want to believe him, I won't argue with you. I do think you should steer clear of him right now. He's up to something. I just don't know what it is."

He glanced over at Maggie and the rest of Phoebe's

friends, his expression urging them to agree. Maggie didn't want to interfere, but some of Robbie's disclosures and complaints about Harry were unsettling.

"It's probably best to keep your distance from Harry until you look into his alibi," she said finally. "Do you know anyone who might have seen him on the campus last night?"

"I'll ask around and see if his story checks out. I owe him that much."

Maggie wondered if Phoebe owed Harry anything. But that was Phoebe, fair-minded to a fault. Once she let someone into her heart, it was hard for her to evict them. Much harder for her, apparently, than it was for Robbie.

Lucy proposed that they put the stall back together and test for the smell again. As everyone jumped into action, Maggie was relieved that another episode with Harry was behind them.

They soon agreed that the wretched stink was finally and totally banished. Dispensing a few of Honey Girl's scented gifts made the area smell even better. But Phoebe felt too weary to set up her displays and she still had the cyber mess on her social media accounts to address.

Suzanne and Dana went back to work while Maggie, Lucy, and Phoebe returned to the shop. Maggie handled customers while Phoebe and Lucy got to work in Phoebe's apartment, clearing the fake reviews from various websites. With some coaching from Lucy's techy friend, they managed to take down all the complaints. By the time Lucy left, Phoebe was ready to start fresh, in more ways than one.

By the time Maggie arrived at the shop Saturday morning, Phoebe had already left for the market. She didn't receive any messages from Phoebe all day, but reminded herself that no good news was good news.

On Sunday morning, just before she and Charles and Daisy set out for a sail, she sent Phoebe a quick text.

Hope all is going well and smells good at your stall.

Still want to visit Carrie Hooper with me? She said we can come by around six o'clock. I can pick you up at the shop around 5:30.

Phoebe replied almost instantly. A tiny image of a hand making the "okay" sign. Then she wrote:

I'll bring her some flowers and write a note about her Dad.

Maggie was glad to see her reply. She was grateful to have company for the visit. She hadn't known Jimmy very well, but it seemed the right thing to do. And she did want to return that cap they'd found under the floorboards, such as it was.

Maggie suddenly wondered what had happened to the hat. She'd stuck it in one of the bags of cleaning supplies she'd brought back from the market on Friday. She'd dropped the bags in the storeroom, in a cupboard with a mop and bucket.

She'd have to get to the shop a little early, in time to find the cap and spruce it up. It might prove to be a meaningful memento. Or Carrie might just toss it in a bag of clothes for charity. Maggie knew that wasn't her call to make. Returning it seemed to be the right thing to do.

The Hooper Farm was about half an hour from the village, and the sun was still shining as they set off from the shop early Sunday evening.

"She probably has a lot of flowers on a farm, but I thought this bouquet was so pretty. I didn't know what else to bring her." Phoebe held a large bouquet of flowers in her lap that she'd bought at the market. She'd showered and changed into a summer dress in record time. Her hair was still shiny and wet, pulled back in a tight ponytail.

Her dress, navy blue cotton with cap sleeves and red

buttons on the bodice, was one of her most sedate outfits. And very becoming, Maggie thought.

"The flowers are beautiful. I'm sure she'll appreciate them. Who knows if Jimmy ever kept a cutting garden and what state it's in now. I made peach crumble for her this morning from some fruit I picked up at the market. The stand was already selling apples. Can you believe it? Seems early for that but I guess the summer is flying by." Maggie glanced in the backseat. "Oh, and I brought the hat you found. I'd almost forgotten it."

"Oh, right. The baseball cap. You cleaned it, I hope?"

"Indeed, I did. It wasn't too bad. It might be meaningful to her. Or maybe Jimmy had a dozen, who knows? I got out most of the dirt. There was a little X on the back. Looked like indelible marker. The oddest thing though was when I wiped the inside down, I found a note on a bit of paper. All folded up and tucked into the inside band."

Phoebe had been watching the green fields and marsh grass fly by her window but now turned to Maggie. "What sort of note? What did it say?"

Maggie shrugged. "It's a list, of vegetables and fruit, in different amounts. Fifty pounds of that, twenty pounds of this. It looked like a sales tally or record of some kind. I saved it in an envelope. It's in my purse. You can look at it if you like."

Phoebe reached back and picked up Maggie's purse, a hand-knit and felted shoulder bag she'd made last summer. Phoebe quickly found the slip of paper, which was yellowed and stained, and carefully unfolded it.

"There's nothing special about it," Maggie said. "It's just that he passed away under such strange circumstances. Everything connected to him feels like it *might* be significant."

Phoebe was still reading the list. "Tell me about it. I still feel like that stall is haunted. Or at least jinxed."

Maggie gave her a look. "Honey Girl probably has some scented oil or candles that can chase away unhappy spirits. You ought to ask her."

Maggie was teasing, but Phoebe replied in a serious tone. "I think I will. I've heard that burning sage clears bad vibes. Maybe she can give me something like that." Phoebe folded the note and slipped it back in the envelope. "The list looks pretty normal to me. The only weird thing is the last line," she remarked. "He wrote big amounts for the vegetables and foods, cucumber pickles, peaches, and clams. But at the bottom it says two Button apples. I never heard of that type."

"Me either." Maggie had noticed that, too. "But I didn't get a chance to look it up. There are so many different kinds of apples. Button could be one we've never heard of." Maggie glanced at her, then looked back at the road. "Carrie might know. We can ask her."

There were many question Maggie wanted to ask Carrie Hooper. But this was a sympathy call and she felt that sincerely. She didn't want to leave poor Carrie with the impression she'd to come visit out of some macabre curiosity about her father's murder.

Maggie turned at the sign for Hooper Organic Farm and her little SUV suddenly bounced along a dirt and gravel road that led to a small white farmhouse. The dark green shutters were in need of paint and hanging at odd angles, like loose teeth. The roof was patched in places, and mossy in other spots.

They passed a pen that enclosed a few yellow and dark red chickens, who strutted about and pecked the dirt. A wooden corral held a few sheep and a cow, and behind that a large barn, painted dark green, loomed up, casting a long, dark shadow over the animals.

Behind the barn, wide fields, plowed in neat rows, boasted a lush green bounty that looked ready to harvest, and it made her sad to think that he'd passed away just before the harvest season, the hard-won rewards for his labor left on the land.

They stepped up to a porch filled with cast-off household items, an old washing machine, and a three-legged wooden chair. Jimmy had obviously found it hard to keep up with repairs while running the farm on his own all these years. Understandably, but it certainly made it harder for his daughter right now.

Carrie appeared at the door before they'd even had a chance to knock. She greeted them cheerfully, grateful for their gifts, and led them through a cramped center hall, decorated much like the porch, and then into a sitting room.

"Please excuse the mess." She cleared boxes from a low couch so they could sit. "My father wasn't much of a housekeeper, and a real pack rat. I'm trying to sort things out but it's slow going."

Maggie had expected as much. She didn't envy Carrie the job. The room looked upended, filled with open cartons, black plastic trash bags, piles of *National Geographic*, *Modern Farmer*, and equipment catalogues. There were also boxes of documents Maggie couldn't help but notice as she walked by. Most of it looked confidential—bank statements, bills, and even handwritten letters. She gave the lot a glance, then averted her gaze. The last thing she wanted was for Carrie to think she'd come here to snoop.

A battered rolltop desk stood in one corner, with more papers and envelopes bulging from every cubbyhole and drawer.

Maggie took a seat on a worn tweed sofa, and Phoebe

sat beside her. Two armchairs, covered with hand-stitched afghans, probably made by Carrie's mother, completed the ensemble.

The oval coffee table was covered with photographs and albums that held newspaper clippings and various memorabilia. Carrie had cleared a space, and set out a plate of cookies and a jug of ice tea. As they found seats, she poured everyone a glass.

"We won't take up much of your time, Carrie. I just want to say how sorry I was to hear about your father." Maggie searched the table for a coaster, but finding none, she balanced the glass in her lap. "I knew your parents a little. I often met up with your mother in knitting shops around town. Before I opened the Black Sheep, I mean. Your dad always had a smile and a cheerful word when he came to pick her up. I have to admit, I didn't see him much after she passed away."

"That's a nice memory. My mom loved to knit. As long as she was able. It was a wonderful distraction for her." Carrie smiled softly, remembering. "You weren't the only one who lost touch with my dad. He isolated himself out here after my mom was gone. Except in the summer, when he worked at the market."

"That's how I knew him. Sort of," Phoebe explained. "I used to shop at his stall. When he passed away, I got his spot."

"Really? I hope it's working out for you. He helped start that market, years ago. It was only open to farmers back then. It's certainly expanded. Though my father's social circle probably got smaller," she added with a wry smile.

She stepped over to the window and raised a bamboo shade, a style Maggie had not seen for decades. Scraggly, parched plants in macramé hangers looked desperate for attention. Maggie looked away, holding herself back from rushing in with houseplant CPR.

"Your father was a very independent man. Certainly in his opinions and the way he lived his life," Maggie said.

Carrie seemed pleased by that version. "Both of my parents were iconoclasts, happy in their own company." She smiled and gazed at the framed photos on the fireplace mantel. "I guess you could have called them hippies."

Maggie agreed with a small smile. "A compliment in my book."

"I was teased about it at school. I hated having parents who were so different. So out of sync with my friends. I just wanted a normal family, that wasn't 'antiestablishment.' Or, anti-anything," she said with a laugh. "But when I got older, I was proud of them. I realized they were interesting and original. They had ideals and stayed true to them."

"I give your folks a lot of credit for that. Your father was well ahead of his time, one of the first to go all in with organic growing."

"Most people didn't understand what he was doing, or why," Carrie said. "But times change. Organic produce is trendy now, and he had a lot of competition around here."

"Is that their wedding photo?" Phoebe gazed up at the row of framed pictures on the mantel.

Carrie took the framed photo down so they could see it. "They were married in a field behind the house and had a party in the barn."

A much younger Jimmy Hooper, with reddish brown hair tied back in a ponytail, stood with a lovely, long-haired bride. He wore a denim work shirt and blue jeans and she wore a long yellow prairie dress. Both wore garlands of flowers in their hair and around their necks. They stood facing each other, hand in hand, in a field of tall, amber grass. The sky behind them was clear blue, the sun casting a mellow light. What a perfect moment in their lives, Maggie reflected. When you're so young and in love, with your whole life ahead of you, how can you ever imagine what the future will bring? That was a blessing, when you thought about it.

"That's a beautiful picture." Maggie looked up at her. "I see you have a lot of photos to keep their memory alive."

"Some of happy days, and some not so happy. We did our best for my mom. But a long, drawn-out illness takes its toll on a family."

Maggie nodded and sipped her ice tea. Carrie was petite, but fit-looking, and Maggie guessed to be in her mid-forties. Her short, stylish haircut and small pearl earrings were at odds with her housecleaning outfit—a baggy sweatshirt, jeans, and sneakers. Maggie could easily see her dressed in a tailored suit, conducting a business meeting.

"Where do you live now, Carrie?" Phoebe asked.

"Just outside of Hartford. I'm the VP of marketing at an insurance firm. I rebelled, too. But in a different way." She smiled at the irony. "My folks hated it when I announced I was going for an MBA. They felt I'd rejected their values. But they tried to understand," she joked. "I think they were even proud of me later, in their way."

"I'm sure they were," Maggie said. "Are these your children?" Maggie picked up a photo of Jimmy and Penny and two little boys, engaged in a big huddle of hugging in a pile of hay with pumpkins all around. Maggie recognized the farmhouse in the background. It looked like a perfect autumn day.

"Those are my sons, James and Scott. They're all grown up now," she said proudly. "My dad put them to work here every summer. He was a good influence. Their father, my ex-husband, dropped out of the picture when they were very young. My dad even talked about one of the boys taking over the farm someday. My brother, Brad, never had any interest in battling the weather or rusty old machinery. Neither do my boys. A good thing, too. We'll need to sell the property to cover my dad's debts."

Suzanne had been right about that, Maggie recalled.

"That's too bad. Not only for your family, but for this area to lose another farm. A new buyer will probably build condos or mini mansions."

"I hope not. I haven't looked into it yet. There are so many other issues to untangle first. My father's finances are a mess. I asked the police if they think that had anything to do with his murder."

Phoebe's speculation about loan sharks came to mind. And the paint can full of cash that the police found in the barn. Maggie nearly asked about that, but caught herself just in time.

She had not intended to quiz Carrie about the investigation. She thought that would be tactless on this sort of visit. But now that Carrie had raised the subject, she did have a question or two.

Chapter 8

"Do the police have any idea who killed your father? Or why? I haven't seen anything in the news about the case for days."

"They told me that they're working on several possibilities, but won't go into specifics. They asked a million questions when I first got here. But I haven't heard much lately. Except for bits of gossip here and there." She shook her head. "Most of it farfetched."

"There will always be gossip," Maggie said, though she wondered what rumors Carrie had heard, farfetched or not.

"When I was a kid, my teachers would always invite my father to talk to my classmates. He was proud to grow good food for people to eat. A simple mission in life, but it was very satisfying to him." She smiled, remembering, then looked up at Maggie and Phoebe. "It's hard for me to imagine why anyone would hurt him. They must have known he was alone and defenseless. Whoever did this awful thing must have planned it. It's a very frightening thought."

She picked up a photo from the table, her expression softening. It was an image of her father, in the seat of a dusty yellow tractor, smiling and squinting in the sunlight, his clothes dirty and sweat-stained. He waved his cap at the photographer. Maggie wondered if Carrie had taken that photo but didn't want to interrupt her reverie.

"I know he was his own man, but I never imagined that my father had a single enemy. Dry spells, or an early frost, insects and mold that attacked his crop—those were the only foes he talked about."

She put the photo down again and Maggie glanced at it. A wave of sympathy for Carrie's loss washed over her. And made her remember the cap Phoebe had found.

"That's a lovely photo. It just reminded me, we had to clean the market stall and when we raised the floorboards, Phoebe found this cap." Maggie took the plastic bag out of her purse and handed it to Carrie. "It says Hooper Organic Farm. I thought it may have belonged to Jimmy."

Carrie took the cap out of the bag and turned it in her hands. "All the helpers here wore these caps, too. But there's a little X in the back, see?" Carrie showed Maggie the back of the hat. "That was his mark. My dad hated when his hat got mixed up with the others."

"I did notice that." Maggie hadn't been completely sure until now the cap had belonged exclusively to Jimmy, but Carrie's disclosure made the list even more interesting.

"I found something else, when I was cleaning it." She took the envelope out of her purse that contained the folded note. "This slip of paper was tucked under the inside band. I thought you'd want to see it."

Carrie's expression lit with interest. She unfolded the note and read the short list. She looked puzzled, then amused. "That's definitely his handwriting. He had a very recognizable scrawl."

"I thought it might be a sales tally or an order from a store?" Maggie suggested.

"Dad was a compulsive list maker. There are bits of

paper all over the place." She stared around the room and shrugged. "He sometimes made a note like this for his farm-hands, to tell them what to bring to the market to sell."

"That makes sense." Maggie felt silly now, trying to read some mysterious meaning into the find.

"But these amounts seem off-kilter. Some are way too large for a store order or the market," Carrie noticed. "Or not large enough. Maybe it was a special order of some kind?" she wondered aloud. "And what about that line at the bottom, about the two apples?"

"We noticed that, too." Phoebe leaned forward and peeked at the list again. "Do you know what Button ap-ples are? We never heard of that kind."

"Me either." Carrie shrugged and looked up at them over the edge of her reading glasses. "We didn't grow ap-ples here."

Maggie hadn't been sure and was glad to have the ques-tion answered and without asking, either. "It's probably not important. But you might show Detective Reyes. See what she thinks?"

"I will." Carrie took her glasses off and set them on the table. "You found the hat under the floor of the stall?" she asked Phoebe. "I wonder how it got there."

"The stalls come apart easily and are moved around a lot. Maybe your dad had to move his, or was cleaning up one day, and he didn't notice when his hat fell off?"

"I think he wore that hat to bed, but I guess that could have happened." Carrie stared down at the hat again. "I will pass the list to Detective Reyes, but I hope she lets me keep the hat. It feels like a little part of him."

Maggie could easily understand why. It seemed like a good time to go, too. "Then I'm very glad we were able to return it to you. Thanks for having us. Is there any way I can help you while you're here, Carrie?"

Carrie seemed touched by the offer. "There is something, now that you mention it. I found a lot of my mother's knitting supplies in the attic. Yarn, needles, all kinds of little gadgets. She used to call it her 'stash'?"

"Yes, that's what we call it." Maggie smiled. "A true knitter always has a stash, squirreled away somewhere."

"There's enough there for several squirrels," Carrie quipped. "Do you know where I can donate it?"

"That's easy. Nursing homes and rehab centers can always use knitting supplies. I could sort it out and deliver it for you."

"That would be great. I'll give you a call when it's boxed up."

The sun was low as they set off for town. Maggie loved the amber light of a summer evening, streaking the horizon with lavender and apricot hues. She often wished she could capture the essence of a sunset in a sweater or scarf, but the color combinations were more suited for watercolor paintings than yarn combinations.

"Carrie seemed eager to talk," Maggie said. "I didn't expect to stay that long. I think she was happy to have some company."

"I got the feeling she was lonely, too. Going through all those papers and family photos. All those memories. That must be rough."

"Not to mention, figuring out her father's finances," Maggie added. "I was going to ask if she, or the police, think Jimmy's death is connected to the market. But she doesn't seem to have much idea of why he died, or who killed him. I didn't see the point in pressing her about it."

"I wonder about that, too. She did say he helped start the market. I thought that was interesting."

"I thought so. Even though he was a loner, it seems that

Jimmy had ties to a lot of the farmers at the market. Ties that go back a long way. Maybe that has something to do with his murder."

"Possibly." Phoebe turned to face her. "But it doesn't make a person feel great about working there. On top of everything else."

Maggie nodded, her gaze fixed on the road. By "everything else" she knew Phoebe probably meant Harry. Maggie had been so focused on their visit with Carrie, she'd forgotten to ask Phoebe about that situation.

"How did it go? Did Harry bother you the last few days?"

"His aunt was in the stall all weekend. It was his time, but he never showed."

Maggie felt relieved. "Maybe he's taking a break, to cool off. Maybe he won't come back at all," she speculated.

She thought that Phoebe would be pleased to consider that possibility, but instead, she looked alarmed. "I'd hate to think he'd give up selling his work there just because of me. Harry was very upset when I broke up with him the first time, and probably feels even worse now."

Maggie sighed. She was only concerned about Phoebe. And her feelings. And her personal safety. But it seemed this conversation had stirred up another pot, all about Harry again.

"Maybe he's settling into a new apartment. He moved out of the place that he and Robbie shared, right?"

"His aunt Adele said he moved in with her and can stay as long as he likes. Which is bad news since her place would be the last choice for anyone. Unless your dream is living in a cat sanctuary."

"Sounds charming," Maggie quipped, though she knew Phoebe was in no mood for jokes. She was taking Harry's situation very seriously, and very much to heart.

"And she's a bona fide hoarder. Harry has really bad allergies and asthma. He can't even stick a toe in her house. He's staying in a little cottage on the property, but I bet that's a mess, too."

"I'm sure it's only temporary." Maggie stole a quick glance at her passenger. She seemed upset, staring blankly out her window at the passing scenery.

"I was worried about seeing him, but now I'm wondering if he's all right." Phoebe turned back to Maggie. "Maybe he didn't trash the stall, or post the bad reviews. Maybe it was someone else who is out to get me. When I accused him, he looked at me like I was crazy. Like it was the first he'd heard any of it."

"His reaction might show he's a good actor. Of course he'd deny it. I know there's no real proof. But Harry still seems the most likely."

Phoebe didn't answer. She turned away and looked out the window again. Maggie wondered if she'd gone too far.

"I know what you're saying. I sort of agree," Phoebe said finally. "But what if something is really troubling him, like Robbie said? And my rejection—second rejection—and then, my accusations, put him over the top?" She shook her head. "I think I should talk to him. Tell him I'm not so sure he was behind the mess on Friday. I never really heard him out when we broke up. I think we should clear the air about that, too. For once and for all. Like he wanted to do."

"Phoebe . . ." Maggie sighed. "After the way he lost his temper last week? I wish you'd let this go. Sometimes, that's the best thing." Maggie tried to catch her glance, but Phoebe looked away. "Well, if there are any more face to face conversations, I hope you won't be alone with him. That's what I'm most concerned about."

"I understand. I'll wait until Wednesday and see if he comes back to the market."

Maggie was relieved to hear that. "That gives you some time to think about it, too."

Maggie promised herself she wouldn't bring it up again, either. She didn't want her concern and advice to backfire. She did hope Phoebe would realize that more "talking things out" might not yield the closure she sought, but could end up opening another emotional Pandora's box.

On Wednesday morning, Maggie was disturbed to hear that Phoebe was still determined to talk to Harry. Lucy had just arrived, and Maggie was glad for the backup.

"Phoebe . . . you're being very generous, after what he's done," Lucy said.

"That's just the thing. I really *did* think it was Harry at first. But I don't have any proof. The market is so pretty and all the vendors are so nice to their customers. But Pickle Man was right. It's totally not Sesame Street. Maybe somebody down there thinks I'm stealing their sales and they're trying to push me out. It didn't have to be him."

"Okay," Lucy conceded. "But if it's not, which vendor is it? I don't see how your socks and things cut into anybody's sales. And it seems too much of a coincidence with Harry's angry outburst the day before."

Maggie agreed, but held her tongue. Phoebe had already heard enough of her opinion.

"That's just the thing. Every time Harry and I argue, I run out. The first time we broke up and last week, too. I think I can figure out for sure if he did it, if I just hear him out. About what happened between us when I broke up with him, and about this latest mess, too." Phoebe had filled her knapsack with her necessary items for the day: water bottle, healthy snacks, her knitting, and her laptop. "For once and for all," she concluded, slipping the straps on her slim shoulders.

Maggie sighed. "I hoped you weren't going to say that."

Phoebe met her glance but didn't answer.

"You have a soft spot for him. We can see that," Lucy persisted. "But a guy like that will just weasel his way back into your life." Into her heart and her bed, Maggie knew Lucy meant. "We're just worried about you."

"I totally get it. My weasel radar is tuned to super alert. I just want to clear the air between us and make sure that he's okay. Harry meant a lot to me, at one time. I don't hate him."

Maggie met Lucy's gaze. They both knew generous hearted Phoebe would not be persuaded to give up this plan.

"Good luck. Let us know how it goes . . . if you get a chance," Maggie said.

Phoebe grinned at Maggie's lame attempt to sound casual about her interest. "I'll send a full report. No worries."

Maggie and Lucy stepped out to the porch to watch Phoebe head down Main Street. She set off with a bounce in her step, clad in black spandex biking shorts and a bluish-purple tank top that matched her tattoos. Her slight form leaned forward to balance the overloaded backpack and tote bags that swung from each hand, but she hardly seemed to notice.

"I don't have a good feeling about this," Lucy said. "I know we shouldn't butt in, but what if he blows up at her again? Even if they talk out in the open, who's to say he won't hurt her this time if he loses his temper?"

Maggie was worrying about the same question. "I totally agree. But what can we do?"

Moments later, Maggie had locked up the shop and taped a hastily dashed BACK IN FIVE MINUTES sign to the door. She and Lucy set off for the market at a swift pace, estimating that Phoebe's big pack and bags would slow her down enough to accommodate for her head start.

Trying to keep up with Lucy, Maggie was reminded she needed to get back to the gym, or at least walk Daisy more.

"Can you dial down the speed a notch or two? I can't keep up with those long legs," Maggie said finally.

"You're doing fine. Speed walking is great cardio. We are racing to the rescue."

"I'll keep that in mind," Maggie managed between breaths.

At the market, most of the stalls were just opening. As they drew closer to Phoebe's space, they paused in front of a display of perennials—black-eyed Susans, orange tiger lilies, and large pots of hydrangea with heavy blue blossoms.

Maggie slipped behind a table of tall, pink phlox for cover. "I'm not sure we should let Phoebe know we're here. What if she gets mad at us for hovering?"

Lucy stepped beside her, pretending to look over a pot of yarrow. Maggie never included that plant in her gardens. She thought it was very weedy-looking.

"Let's stay out of sight and see how it goes."

"It's early," Maggie noted. "Harry may not be here yet."

"Uh, yeah he is." Lucy tipped her head and Maggie followed her gaze.

Harry stood just outside of his stall and Phoebe walked over to meet him. Luckily, Phoebe's back was turned their way. Maggie hoped they'd still get some idea of what she was saying.

Harry stood with his hands crossed over his chest, his expression impatient, as if he could barely wait for Phoebe to finish talking. Maggie could hear her voice but couldn't make out her words, though Phoebe gestured in her animated way.

Finally, his expression softened and he smiled, his white teeth and dimples working their magic. He began talking—telling his side of something, Maggie guessed. Unable to see Phoebe's expression it was impossible to tell if she was buying his story.

Maggie glanced at Lucy. "As long as he doesn't have another meltdown. Whatever else happens is her business. Let's just wait a minute or two, and then we'll go back to the shop."

"Good plan," Lucy said. "But my weasel radar is going off big-time. Just sayin'."

"Mine is, too," Maggie replied. She'd noticed two uniformed police officers walking down their way and was surprised to see them head for Harry's stall. More questions about Jimmy Hooper's murder? But why ask Harry?

Lucy had noticed the law officers, too. "Now we really have to move within earshot. Even if it means blowing our cover."

Maggie followed her into the flow of shoppers who were starting to fill the aisle. Phoebe was so focused on Harry and the police officers she didn't notice her friends approach.

Maggie couldn't hear what the officers said, but Harry suddenly looked pale and shaken. Phoebe grabbed his arm, partly a comforting gesture and partly to keep him steady.

"Harry, that's awful! I'm so, so sorry," Maggie heard her say.

Harry stared at the officers blankly, as if he couldn't speak. Then he said, "Aunt Adele? Are you sure? She can't be dead. I don't believe you."

Maggie felt her stomach drop, as if she was in an elevator that had skipped a floor or two. She felt Lucy squeeze her arm. "I don't believe it, either," Lucy whispered.

"Sorry, son," one of the officers replied. "A neighbor found her. We need a family member to make the official identification. Can you come with us, please?"

"Yes, of course." Harry brushed his eyes with the back of his hand as tears began to fall.

"I'll close up here. Don't worry." Phoebe touched his arm again. "I'll take care of everything. Text me later if you need any help. Or if you just want to talk?"

He nodded, but didn't speak. Then walked away between the two police officers.

Lucy stepped behind a hydrangea bush. "First Jimmy, now Adele? Working at this market is dangerous to a person's health."

"It might raise the rates on one's life insurance policy," Maggie agreed. "But we don't know how she died. It could have been natural causes. Unlike poor Jimmy."

Maggie was still watching Phoebe. She'd slipped inside Harry's stall, beyond their view. "Should we slink away, undetected, or magically appear? She might be upset and want company."

"Magically appear. Let's hope she's so distracted by the news she doesn't realize we were stalking."

"Hovering, like guardian angels," Maggie corrected. "Either way, I hope you're right."

They strolled over to Phoebe's stall. She looked surprised to see them, then quickly ran their way.

"Lucy . . . Maggie . . . You won't believe it. The police just told Harry that his aunt died. He has to identify her body."

"What a shock. Poor guy," Lucy replied.

"That is terrible news," Maggie said sincerely.

"He was, like, stunned. He could barely talk." Phoebe shook her head, looking as if she might start crying, too. "I feel so bad for him."

Maggie knew that was coming, but tried not to dwell on the ramifications of Harry's new sympathetic situation.

"It's very hard to hear such bad news, especially when it's so sudden. Did she have any health problems?" Maggie asked.

"Not that I know of." Phoebe opened the lock on her stall and Lucy helped her roll back the canvas curtain that covered the front opening. "I think Adele has a son. He lives in California. Harry sometimes mentions him. I guess the police are tracking him down, too."

"I'm sure they are. And her son will take over arranging things. It will be easier for Harry." Maggie put her arm around Phoebe's shoulder. "This is a shock for you, too. Would you like to come back to the shop with us? To clear your head? You can open the stall in the afternoon."

Phoebe looked tempted, then determined. "It feels better to keep busy. I may close early if Harry needs some help. He's going to stay in touch."

She couldn't shake free of him, could she? Maggie glanced at Lucy and could tell she was thinking the same thing.

"So, how was the play, Mrs. Lincoln?" Lucy asked. When Phoebe answered with a blank look, Lucy added, "Aside from this awful news, did you and Harry get a chance to talk things out?"

"Oh, right . . . yes, we did. It was tough at first. He was sort of distant and, like, what now? But once I apologized for accusing him, he seemed relieved and kept telling me he didn't do it and he was glad that I finally believed him. We talked a little about why we broke up, too. He says he can explain everything about that other girl."

Maggie wasn't sure how she felt about that. Was this good news, or bad? Phoebe seemed to think the former.

Lucy seemed to think the latter. Maggie could tell from

her expression. "Too bad that part was interrupted. I'd be curious to hear him explain why he cheated on you."

"He claims it's a huge misunderstanding." Phoebe shrugged. "Maybe it was."

Maggie wanted to mention a bridge that was for sale, but bit her tongue. "I guess you have to hear him out at some point, and see what you think." She checked her watch. "I'd better head back to the shop. Coming, Lucy?"

"I'll hang out here awhile. Want some company?" Lucy asked Phoebe.

"That would be great." Phoebe seemed happy to hear that Lucy was staying.

Maggie waved as she left. "I'll see you later."

She wondered if Dana and Suzanne had heard yet about Adele McSweeney. News of her death would spread like wildfire around the market and through the village, too, though little was known. Had Adele died of natural causes? Or something else?

She was impatient to find out, but knew she had to wait.

Chapter 9

Maggie was not surprised to find Lucy at the shop the next morning, waiting on the porch with Tink and Wally.

"You're an early bird," Maggie greeted her. "With your early bird dogs."

"I didn't want to miss Dana," she admitted. "She's dropping by the shop this morning to give us an update on Adele. Jack's heard a few things from his connections."

Last night, Dana had passed along the information that a neighbor had found Adele at the bottom of the cellar steps. It appeared that Adele had suffered a fall. But the medical examiner's findings weren't on the grapevine at that time, and an autopsy would also be performed. Since Adele had died alone, the police were required to conduct a full investigation, even if her death seemed accidental. Dana thought that by this morning, she would know—via Jack's connections on the police force—even more.

"I'm waiting for her, too," Maggie admitted.

Tink rested her head in Lucy's lap, her signal that she wanted some attention. Lucy responded with absent-minded strokes on the dog's silky fur.

"What does Phoebe say? Has she been in touch with Harry?"

Maggie took a seat in the rocker. It was so hot today she'd actually picked up a cup of ice coffee at the diner, but didn't like the taste much. She took out her knitting to settle her nerves and began to stitch.

"Phoebe came over for dinner last night. I thought she could use some company. Harry was texting every five minutes. He was very upset. His cousin, Martin, Adele's son, hadn't arrived yet." Maggie paused, expecting Phoebe to appear at the shop door any moment. She didn't hear footsteps inside, and continued in a near whisper. "Phoebe said Harry was questioned a long time, first by uniformed officers, and then by detectives. The property has been secured as a crime scene, and they're still searching the house and the cottage where Harry is staying. I guess he ended up on someone's couch last night."

"Not good old Robbie's. Harry burned that bridge," Lucy reminded her.

"Blew it up with dynamite, more like. Despite what I've said before about Harry, I feel bad for the boy. Phoebe said Adele was his only close family. But I still don't like the idea of him crying on Phoebe's shoulder. She's completely forgotten why she broke off their relationship. And that he may have done her real harm last week, online and at the market."

"That's Harry the Potter, boy wizard, casting a memory loss spell on our Phoebe." Lucy sounded unhappy, too. "What can we do? Besides gently encourage her to return to her senses. Harry can't play the sad guy card forever."

"Maybe not. But probably longer than we'd like."

Maggie's worries were interrupted by the sight of Dana and Suzanne coming toward the shop, approaching from opposite ends of Main Street. They met at the gate and walked up the path side by side. Suzanne had parked her grand SUV up the street, and Dana was on foot, walking up from the village in her yoga outfit. The rolled rubber mat was tucked under her arm and a large cup that doubtlessly held her morning smoothie was in hand.

Suzanne carried a frothy coffee drink. She sat down and slipped a golden pastry from a little white bakery bag. "Just lost a juicy deal on that waterfront mansion. I really need a treat."

"You'll reel in the next one. You're a champ," Lucy said. "What doesn't kill us, makes us stronger. Right?"

"Maybe so. But these little defeats sure make my clothes tighter," Suzanne replied around a mouthful of chocolate croissant. "So, what's the nine-one-one? I can't hang out long."

"Should we wait for Phoebe?" Maggie said.

"It's probably best if she's not here. The details might upset her." Dana set her cup down. She sounded serious. Maggie didn't dare interrupt and neither did any of her friends.

"Jack didn't hear much more than I told you all last night. But the police are certain Adele's death was not an accident. She died from a head injury, which wasn't consistent with her fall. She may have been struck before she was pushed down the stairs. Or her killer may have finished her off in the basement afterward."

"Ugh, that's sick." Suzanne lifted a hand to her throat. It appeared that her indulgent breakfast was not going down well.

"There were no signs of a break-in, or a robbery. Though the house is such a mess, it was hard to tell. Hoarder's paradise, one cop described it."

"And a feline paradise as well, I've heard," Maggie said.

Dana rolled her eyes. "They had to wear hazmat suits to protect them from the cat hair . . . and the rest of it."

"What will happen to the cats?" Of course Lucy would be the first to speak up for the animals, since Phoebe wasn't there.

"That depends on her son, I think. If he doesn't want to take care of all the cats—and I can't see how he'd do it, living so far away—they'll probably be brought to a shelter." Maggie was glad Phoebe hadn't heard that part, either.

Suzanne had put the pastry aside, and sipped some foam off her coffee. "When did she die? Do the police know?"

"Late Tuesday night, sometime between ten and midnight, they think. A neighbor found the body just by chance. Adele's cats slip out of the house from time to time, and the neighbor came by to return one of them. When no one answered the door, she went around the back and found that door unlocked. She went inside to look for Adele, and, well . . . found the body down in the cellar."

"That sure isn't what I want to find when I visit a neighbor," Suzanne said.

"Who knows what she *really* found? There was something else," Dana said. "Some detail that the police are keeping under wraps. It's not in any of the news reports and Jack doesn't even know what it is, exactly. Only that the search team found something odd at the crime scene, on the body maybe? Something only the killer knows about."

"That's weird. Like the murderer left a message? Or has some weird, twisted trademark?" Lucy asked.

"Seems so. Though no one's saying what the message is," Dana replied.

Suzanne patted her lips with a paper napkin. "Thanks for the gruesome details. And for keeping me from devouring this fat bomb." She'd hardly taken a bite of the croissant and slipped the rest back in the bag.

"Happy to help." Dana's tone was polite and matter-of-fact, her focus quickly returning to Adele. "This is why I really didn't want Phoebe here. Jack said that so far, the police have no witnesses, or hard evidence. But they do have their eye on Harry."

Whatever else she thought about Harry, Maggie found that surprising. "By all accounts, he adored Adele and they had a very close relationship. Remember how she jumped to his defense when Phoebe accused him?"

"I think that's true. But it hardly rules him out," Dana argued. "Most murder victims are killed by someone they know. A spouse, or a relative. Even a friend. Investigators look to the closest connections first."

"When did Harry get to the cottage the night Adele was killed?" Lucy asked. "Maybe he heard or saw something?"

"He claims that after the market, he went out for a few beers with friends, then went to bed early. He said he slept through the night and didn't hear a thing," Dana reported. "He also said that yesterday morning, he went straight to the market. He said Adele liked to sleep late and he never bothered her before eleven or even noon, unless it was an emergency."

Maggie looked up from her knitting. "So, he left for the market yesterday morning, believing his aunt was alive and well?"

"That's what he claims," Dana concluded. "The last Jack heard, the police were ripping the property apart, looking for any possible clue."

"I know he couldn't go back to the cottage last night. Phoebe told me," Maggie said.

"Where did he end up?" Suzanne asked.

"I'm not sure," Maggie replied.

"I hope he didn't make a run for it, feeling the heat. That never ends well." Suzanne brushed a crumb off her dark blue eyelet dress. One of Maggie's favorites in Suzanne's ample wardrobe.

Dana laughed. "Suzanne, you should write detective novels, the hard-boiled variety."

"Just sayin'. I don't know if the kid is guilty or not, but it's no joke when the police pin you as their prime suspect. Believe me."

Suzanne had been in that hot seat not too long ago, when her office rival had died at her desk under mysterious circumstances. Maggie could tell Suzanne was thinking of her ordeal and about to speak of it.

But Maggie heard footsteps in the shop and waved her hand to hush her friends. "Phoebe's coming."

Phoebe appeared at the screen door, dressed in pajama shorts, a T-shirt with a mermaid on it, and fuzzy slippers. Her nighttime ponytail had flopped to one side of her head, adding to her dozy look. "You're all here early. Did I miss a memo?"

"We were just talking about Adele," Maggie admitted.

Phoebe glanced at Dana. "I guess Jack knows what's going on with the police. They mobbed Adele's house, like someone was giving out free TVs."

"So we heard," Maggie replied in a circumspect tone. Phoebe would hear everything Dana had related, sooner or later, but maybe it had been best that she'd missed the first report. She and Harry's aunt had enjoyed a pleasant relationship. The gritty details would definitely upset her.

Before Phoebe could reply, a blue-and-white cruiser pulled up and parked in front of the shop. Maggie recognized Detective Reyes as she got out of the passenger side. The driver, a uniformed officer, got out of the car as well and followed her.

"It's Marisol Reyes. What does she want?" Suzanne said.

"We'll soon find out," Maggie murmured. She rose and headed to the top of the porch steps. "Good morning, Detective."

Out of the corner of her eye, she noticed Phoebe backing toward the screen door and twisting the edge of her T-shirt.

"Mrs. Messina." Detective Reyes glanced around the group. "I just came by to speak to Phoebe."

When her gaze fell on Phoebe, Maggie felt the sudden impulse to step between them, but managed to hold herself back.

"Here I am," Phoebe said in a small voice.

"I understand you're a friend of Harry McSweeney?"

Phoebe pursed her lips, as if biting back her reply. "I guess you could say that. We dated for a while, but we broke up a few weeks ago."

Detective Reyes nodded. "Any idea where I can find him?"

"He was looking for someplace to stay last night," Maggie cut in. "Did you ever find out where he landed?" she asked Phoebe.

Detective Reyes turned to Maggie with a quelling look. One that said, *I'll ask the questions. Not you.*

"Why do you want to know?" Phoebe sounded defensive. *Not a good tactic,* Maggie thought.

Detective Reyes remained composed. "It's important that we speak with him. If you know where he is, it would be best if you tell me."

Phoebe squinted; her head tilted to one side as she weighed her choices. Before she replied, the screen door opened.

Harry appeared. Maggie could barely hide her surprise and neither could her friends.

He stared around with a sleepy expression, dressed in black jeans that hung low on his hips, and nothing else. His lids were still heavy and his curly dark hair in disarray. He stared at Detective Reyes, like a deer in the headlights.

"Mr. McSweeney. I was just asking about you." Detective Reyes paused to give Phoebe a look. Mostly amused. Maggie was relieved to see that. "Some new information about your aunt's death has come to light. We'd like to talk to you. At the station."

Harry sighed and looked down at his bare feet. *If he really had magic powers, he'd disappear right now in a puff of smoke, or a sparkly cloud,* Maggie thought.

He swallowed hard and took a deep breath.

"Can't you talk to him here?" Phoebe stepped closer to Harry. "You can go in the shop. It will be, like, totally private."

"I'm sorry. That won't do," Detective Reyes said.

Harry shrugged. "All right. If I have to. But I told you everything I know last night. Can I get dressed first?"

"Of course. Officer Clunes will come with you." Her tone was unfailingly polite, though it didn't matter one bit if Harry minded or not. Did she expect Harry to make a run for it, as Suzanne had suggested? Or do himself harm?

Maggie doubted Harry was considering either option. Though, she had to admit, she never expected the police to be looking for him this morning. Or for him to be found at her shop.

Phoebe touched Harry's arm before Officer Clunes led him inside. They exchanged a glance.

Maggie had hoped Phoebe would keep a safe distance from Harry, and from Adele's murder investigation. But apparently, that horse had left the barn.

Once Harry and the police officer disappeared inside, Detective Reyes said goodbye and retreated to her car. Maggie and her friends sat in stunned silence. All eyes on Phoebe.

"It's not what you think. He had nowhere to crash, so I let him stay over. On the couch," she clarified, staring straight at Suzanne.

Suzanne raised her hands in surrender. "I didn't say a word, honey."

"We believe you, Phoebe." Dana's calm tone defused the moment.

"We are not the problem. Detective Reyes is," Lucy said. "Now she has the wrong impression about you and Harry."

"Which is?" Phoebe asked curiously.

"That you're still his girlfriend. Which means, they'll start asking you questions about Adele's murder, too." Lucy sounded upset and concerned. Which was the way they all felt about that new twist, Maggie was sure.

Phoebe went pale as paper. "She was murdered? They know that for sure?"

Maggie let out a breath. They'd forgotten that Phoebe had missed Dana's briefing.

"The police determined last night that there was foul play." Dana rose and put her arm around Phoebe's shoulders. "That's why we're so concerned about you. And Harry."

If the investigation zeroed in on Harry, and the police believed Phoebe was his romantic partner, they could suspect Phoebe of involvement in the crime. Maggie quickly pushed the thought from her mind. It was too dreadful to contemplate.

The screen door opened and Harry appeared, Officer Clunes footsteps behind him. Harry was dressed in the same black jeans and a light blue T-shirt, his thick hair combed back from his forehead, a style that made him look even more Adonis-like, Maggie thought.

Phoebe stepped forward and grabbed his hand, as if to hold him back from leaving the porch. His dark gaze met hers, and he forced a smile.

"Call me as soon as you can," she said.

"It will be okay. Don't worry. I didn't do anything and I loved my aunt. I'd never have harmed a hair on her head. What can happen to me?"

The words were brave, but his tone faltered out of fear or guilt. Maggie had no way to judge.

"Can you tell my cousin, Martin, what's going on? He was going to check in today at the Lord Jeff. I sent him a text but he hasn't answered yet."

"Will do," Phoebe promised.

"Let's go, Mr. McSweeney." Officer Clunes prompted Harry and they walked to the police car. They watched as the officer helped Harry into the backseat. Then the car started up and drove away.

Phoebe stood at the porch rail, like a sailor's wife, watching her beloved set off on a dangerous voyage. "This is so unfair. Harry might be a flirt and a bad boyfriend and even bend the truth here and there," she conceded. "But no way is he a murderer. He'd never hurt his aunt Adele. She was like a grandma to him. She was his only family. This is like a complete travesty or something. I can't believe it."

"He was on the property when Adele died. The police just need to eliminate him from their investigation," Dana said.

Maggie hoped that was all the police wanted from Harry.

"No one has accused him of killing Adele," Lucy reminded Phoebe.

"Not yet. But they will." Phoebe sat in a heap, her chin in her hand. Maggie had never heard her sound so fatalistic.

"If he's done nothing wrong, the investigators will see that and move on," Maggie assured her.

"That's the way it should work," Phoebe countered. "But we all know, a lot of the time, that's definitely *not* the way it happens." She looked straight at Suzanne. "Right, Suzanne?"

Suzanne seemed about to agree, then stopped herself. Maggie was relieved to see that. Their outspoken friend had been wrongly and unfairly accused and it had taken some time for the investigators to see she was innocent. But that wouldn't happen with Harry. At least, Maggie hoped it wouldn't, for Phoebe's sake.

"My situation was much different. I found the body and someone was framing me," Suzanne reminded Phoebe. "Harry won't have all those complications."

Dana cast Phoebe a sympathetic look. "Does he have a good lawyer?"

"People my age don't 'have' lawyers, Dana. That's a middle-aged thing." It was rare for Phoebe to snap at anyone, and she instantly looked repentant. "Sorry . . . but it's sort of true?"

Dana had taken no offense. "You're right. Dumb of me to even ask that. Let me see what I can do," she offered, and quickly picked up her phone.

"Wait a second. Before we rush to the rescue." Suzanne gazed around at the group, as if the solution was obvious. "What about Adele's son? He should step up and help Harry. For goodness' sake, he's family. Harry just told you to call him."

"Second cousin," Phoebe countered. "But I guess that's true."

Maggie agreed with Suzanne and was not all that eager to rush to Harry's rescue. Even for Phoebe. "I think he's a cousin once removed?" She always forgot how that cousin thing worked. "But he's still family and we are not. And Harry wants you to get in touch with him."

"Absolutely. I'll call right now. He should know that Harry is in trouble."

Maggie agreed, but also wondered what sort of relationship Harry and Martin had. All things considered, Martin might see Harry as a rival for his mother's affection. And for her estate, if there was anything there to inherit.

Phoebe grabbed her phone and headed for the shop. The call would be a private one, it seemed. Dana stood up and handed Phoebe a slip of paper. "Here's a lawyer who might help Harry. Maybe Martin should get in touch with him?"

Phoebe looked grateful. "I'll tell him everything and find out what he's going to do. If he won't call an attorney, I will."

She slipped inside and Maggie waited a few moments until she was out of earshot. Even then, she spoke in a low tone. "It might be nothing. The police may just be trying to rule him out."

Lucy looked doubtful. "I got a more intense vibe from Detective Reyes. I think they found something."

"I think so, too." Dana's gaze darted to the screen door. "I think the boy needs an attorney present when he's questioned this morning and I hope this cousin steps up."

"Even if he does, that won't be the end of it for Phoebe." Lucy gazed around the circle. "She's very involved again. You heard her."

Maggie sighed. "She is, no question. It's too late to convince her to step back, even for her own good. Once the police start building a case, I'm afraid they'll start looking at her, too."

"You sound as if you think he's guilty." Suzanne stared at her with a wide-eyed gaze.

"I don't mean to. I don't think he is but . . . I'm not sure of anything yet." She paused and considered her words. "Phoebe believes he's innocent, but we all know that she's trusting to a fault. Once she forms a bond, she can rarely see someone's shortcomings. Frankly, I don't feel nearly as sure as Phoebe does that Harry is totally innocent."

Maggie could tell by their expressions that her friends felt the same way.

Chapter 10

Phoebe had offered to meet Martin McSweeney at the police station, but he thought it would be best if he stopped by the shop to give her an update on Harry's situation. Phoebe watched for him from the window for hours; he finally arrived about eleven.

"The police say it's all routine, but I'm concerned about the boy. It was good a thing you called and recommended that lawyer. I don't know many people in town anymore and I didn't know where to turn."

Harry had been questioned and agreed to giving his fingerprints, though he was not yet charged with any crime. Detective Reyes had told Martin it would take at least an hour or two. Or more. Maggie knew there was no way of predicting.

Martin McSweeney patted his upper lip with a folded hanky. He looked warm in his navy blazer, a patterned sports shirt underneath, but also like the type of person who would rather be uncomfortable than ruin the effect of a carefully planned outfit. He was as well-groomed and as neatly attired as his mother had been untidy and unfashionable, Maggie noticed, down to his soft, Italian leather loafers.

"I hope they don't keep him long. It's really not right.

There must be laws against that," Martin continued. "The boy is grieving. He's liable to say anything."

"I hope not," Phoebe piped up.

He nodded and sipped a glass of ice water Maggie had poured for him. Martin had a full, round face, his ruddy complexion in contrast with dark straight hair, combed back, to camouflage a thin spot on top. His large brown eyes glowed with warmth and concern for his younger cousin. Maggie could see a vague resemblance to Adele in his features, especially when he spoke.

"Do you know what the police want to ask Harry about? Did they find something more last night at the house, or in the cottage?" Maggie asked.

"They've told me very little. I plan to pin that detective down this afternoon and get the whole story. As soon as they're done with Harry."

Maggie didn't like the way he said, "done with Harry." But it was just a figure of speech, she reminded herself.

She recalled that she'd not voiced her sympathies yet about Adele. "I was very sorry to hear about your mother. I only knew her a little. She was an unusual woman. She will definitely be missed in the community."

He replied with a small, pained smile. "Thank you, she *was* unusual. Some would say eccentric. She was her own person. We have to grant her that. I should have visited more often. I regret that now. But I guess a lot of daughters and sons feel that way when this happens. I did try to come east a few times a year, but it wasn't easy for me."

Maggie wasn't sure what he meant. "Hard to get time off from your work?"

Martin had told them that he was in cybersecurity and ran his own firm in San Francisco. Perhaps the projects and his clients were demanding, but he was the boss and could make his own schedule, she reasoned.

"Coming back here, to Plum Harbor, I mean. I don't

have happy memories of my childhood. My mother and I got along fine, but my father was a difficult man. Hard, and bitter. A bully. I don't know how my mother put up with him."

Maggie had never known George McSweeney but had no reason to doubt his son's account.

"I left home as soon as I could," he added. "I know my mother felt bad about that, but she didn't blame me."

"I know how that is," Phoebe said.

He glanced at her and shrugged. "It had to be. The truth is my father threw me out. He wanted me to be . . . a different sort of man. More like him." He scoffed and shook his head. "He couldn't stand having me for his son. He thought it was my mother's fault, that she'd spoiled me or something. He insisted I could change, if I wanted to. That was just ignorant."

Maggie considered his carefully chosen words. Martin may have been saying that he was gay and his father couldn't accept that. But no matter why his father had bullied him, it was cruel to treat any child that way. Totally deplorable. No wonder Martin had left home, like so many misunderstood adolescents, rejected by their families. Her heart went out to him.

"That must have been very hard. Some young people end up losing their way entirely after that sort of home life. You should be proud that you've done so well for yourself, Martin."

Martin seemed to appreciate her understanding. "I always knew my mother loved and accepted me for who I am. She tried to stand up to him, but my father hurt her. He wouldn't let my mother and me have any contact. We communicated in secret, when we could, until he finally passed away."

Maggie was moved by the story and surprised. She'd

never guessed that Adele was dealing with such a turbulent family life.

"Why didn't she leave him?" Phoebe asked.

"I really don't know," he replied quietly. "I told her to leave a million times. I even sent her money and airline tickets. But she wouldn't budge. Her strange loyalty to him, to this place, was a mystery to me. I don't think I ever made peace with that decision of hers."

Adele was gone and could never explain it to him. If she'd even understood the reason herself, Maggie realized.

"But after your father died, you could visit her. Right?" Phoebe asked.

"I did. I'd planned to come here next week. I was on Cape Cod for a conference when the police tracked me down. I was going to stop to see her on my way home. I was going to surprise her," he said sadly.

"So you weren't that far when they called," Maggie said.

"Just in Brewster." He paused. "I was looking forward to seeing her, but I still stayed in a hotel whenever I came. I don't know how she lived the way she did. I tried to help her. I know she struggled to make ends meet and I sent her money every month, whatever I could. I even offered to have people come and clean up the place, but she wouldn't hear of it." His expression was partly disbelief and partly disgust. "It was like living inside a trash bin, I thought."

"Harry had the same problem," Phoebe said. "He could never go in her house because of his allergies and his asthma. I'm sure he told the police, but maybe you should remind them?"

"Of course I will," Martin promised. "I'll get a letter from his doctor. I'll talk to his attorney about that."

"Good idea. If it's necessary," Maggie clarified.

Martin sighed and stared out at the garden. "If only I'd

come sooner to visit her. Maybe this wouldn't have happened."

"Don't dwell on that," Maggie advised. "I'm not sure anyone could have prevented it."

He checked his watch, a slim, gold timepiece. "I should get back to the station. I'll let you know if there's any news."

Phoebe stood up when he did. "Maybe the police let him out by now."

Maggie doubted that, but didn't say. So much depended on what the police had discovered to prompt this new line of questioning. She was itching to find that out.

Martin smiled at her. "His lawyer promised to text me, but you never know."

"Can I come with you?" Phoebe asked.

"I'd be happy to have your company." Martin's expression lit up at her offer and Maggie felt her heart sink. Moments later, they left the shop together, heading off to help Harry.

She watched from the window as they got into Martin's rental car and wished that she'd spoken up. But what could she have said? Phoebe wasn't even due to work at the shop. Thursday was one of her market days. But she obviously had no interest in anything but helping Harry. There was no holding her back.

"It was jewelry. Real jewelry, not that cheap stuff she sold at her booth. Mounds of it," Dana told them that night at their meeting. "Hidden in bags of cat litter."

"Nice touch. You can't make this stuff up," Lucy said.

"I wouldn't even try." Dana was almost finished with her second pair of socks, working with a fine silk and bamboo blend that would take her longer to knit up. Though not by much, Maggie knew. Her reading glasses slipped down her slim nose and a wisp of blond hair fell across her cheek.

They'd finished their dinner, and with dessert on the table, had started to knit. Jack had told Dana more developments during the day about the investigation of Adele's death. Which included a big find in Adele's house on Wednesday night, which had resulted in Harry being dragged down to the police station so abruptly on Thursday morning.

"Most of the jewelry has already been linked to home robberies in town, reported over the last few months. But the police couldn't make any solid connection between the robberies, or the treasure trove, to Harry. Luckily, he had a good attorney there, Paul Schneider. Harry must be very grateful to Martin. And Phoebe."

"I'm sure he is. Which worries me," Maggie admitted. "It was actually his cousin, Martin, who made contact with Mr. Schneider and is paying his fee, I understand. Phoebe just passed along the information. I hope Harry makes the distinction, but I doubt it."

"And she contributes her ample concern. We can't discount the value of that," Dana said.

"Where is Phoebe?" Lucy looked up from her stitching. "She's not coming tonight?"

"Last I heard, Martin was taking her and Harry out for dinner. I doubt she'll be back in time."

"Martin sounds like a good egg." Suzanne had not advanced much on her first sock. Maggie was fixing a little mess she'd made in it, while Suzanne helped herself to another dollop of dessert. The chocolate mousse Suzanne had whipped up at home last night was decadently rich, but worth every calorie.

"We only spoke a few minutes, but he seems to be well-meaning and concerned about Harry." Maggie quietly yanked out a few rows of Suzanne's work. After all these years, she was not an able knitter but had to get extra credit for trying so hard.

Lucy caught her eye. "Seems to be? You don't sound entirely convinced."

Maggie avoided her gaze. "I'm just overly suspicious. You know that." She sniped a strand of yarn and tossed it aside. "When you consider who had motive to kill Adele, can Martin be ruled out that easily?"

Lucy seemed surprised. "The police must have ruled him out quickly. He wasn't questioned the way Harry was."

"No, he was not. Not so far, anyway. There was just something about him. Maybe he's just too nice, and forthcoming?" she said finally, knowing that wasn't a logical reason at all.

"Maggie may have a point," Dana cut in. "In addition to the stolen goods stashed in the cat litter, Adele's financials were another surprise. She had several big savings accounts. In different banks."

"You mean to say she was living like a bag lady and had piles of cash tucked away?" Suzanne put her dish aside and patted her mouth with a napkin. "That is certifiably nutty."

"Aberrant behavior, but not unheard of. You could call it a scarcity mentality? Feeling like you never have enough, so you need to stockpile," Dana explained. "Some people have been traumatized by a financial setback, or lack of food or resources at some point in their life. Growing up in a household where the adults argue or express distress about money issues can scar children this way. Storing up money or food, and material goods, or just about anything, lends a feeling of safety and security."

Maggie smoothed Suzanne's knitting on her lap, wondering if this lonely little sock would ever get done, or was destined to be another of Suzanne's UFOs—unfinished objects.

"Martin told us that their family life was unhappy. Sounds like his father was abusive to Adele and his son, and completely controlling. That must have extended to money issues."

"Definitely," Dana replied. "An abusive husband tends to hold the purse strings, to guarantee that his wife has no resources to escape the tyranny."

Suzanne shook her head. "I know that happens a lot, but even so, I always find it hard to understand why women stay. Especially after the kids are gone."

"It's complicated, Suzanne. It's not just a matter of wanting to leave," Maggie replied. "Sounds like she had no money, or support from friends or family to help her escape at that time, and make a new start. Her confidence was probably completely worn down and she was afraid to take those steps to freedom. She must have rationalized that it wasn't so bad, managing day by day?"

"Poor Adele, who would have ever guessed." Lucy sounded sad at the revelation. "She always seemed so chipper. She must have had some bright spot in her life?"

"Maybe by the time we knew her, she was just relieved that George was underground," Suzanne said, "and that put a permanent smile on her face."

Maggie had to laugh. "And she had her cats."

"The cat obsession was all projection." Dana had been checking her stitches and suddenly looked up. "She was giving what she yearned for—care, protection, nurturing. That reminds me, there's something I didn't tell you yet." She paused and dropped her work on her lap. "There are two wills. It's hard to say which will hold up in court."

"Two wills? There's an interesting wrinkle." Maggie sat up and looked over at Dana. "But how can be there be two? I mean, how can they both be valid? Doesn't the newest document always take precedence?"

"Usually, but it can get tricky. There's one will she drew up a while ago. It splits her estate between Martin and Harry," she began to explain.

Suzanne shook her head and made a little sound. "I bet Martin didn't like that. He was her son. Harry is just a nephew."

"Grandnephew," Maggie reminded her.

"If he didn't like that one, he probably despises the second," Dana continued. "It bears the most recent date. It was handwritten, but it's witnessed and notarized, so it could hold up in court. It specifies gifts of money for Martin and Harry. But the bulk of the estate will go to a rescue group to take care of her cats, and other strays."

"Wait a second, that pack of flea-bitten felines inherits all the loot?" Suzanne sat up in her chair, looking shocked. "I bet Martin didn't like that."

Maggie agreed. "Especially when he learned of those hidden bank accounts. I wonder when he heard this twist. After her death? Or had Adele told him her plan before she'd died?"

"It would be interesting to know the timeline there," Dana agreed. "I'm sure Detective Reyes will ask him."

Lucy took a sip of wine. "Judging from the way Adele lived, he probably didn't expect to get anything when she passed on, except the proceeds from her house and property."

"A knockdown if ever I saw one," Suzanne noted. "And the plans for new construction would include soaking the property with that animal hospital cleaner we used on Phoebe's stall."

Maggie had to smile at the notion, but her thoughts quickly turned back to Martin. "He may have found out about his mother's secret fortune at some point. Maybe she hinted at it in some way?" Maggie speculated. "I will add that when Martin spoke to Phoebe and me about Adele, he seemed to have no idea that she was secretly wealthy. He told us that he knew she struggled and often sent her money. As much as he was able."

"That would make the truth sting even more, don't you think?" Lucy asked. "After he hears that Adele had truck-loads of money, he finds out that her cats get most of it. That news could upset a person. Especially if they feel they've been shortchanged or mistreated in their child-hood. Maybe he confronted her and it got out of control?"

"Accidents happen," Suzanne added in a more serious tone. "You could easily push a frail old gal like Adele down without even meaning to kill her."

"I was thinking the same. Detective Reyes must be, too," Maggie decided. "We all thought Martin was com-ing from a distance, but it turns out he was just at a busi-ness conference on the Cape, in Brewster. He told us he'd planned to visit Adele this weekend, on his way home."

Lucy turned her work over and examined the stitches. "Maybe he dropped by Plum Harbor before that. Brew-ster is definitely a drivable distance, here and back, overnight."

"Wait—Martin doesn't have an airtight alibi?" Suzanne stared around, as if worried she'd missed something. "Dana, I thought you said the police eliminated him?"

"So far, seems they did. I suppose they could go back and check his story closer. There might be security cam-eras at the hotel where he stayed that would show if he left and returned during the night." She paused and took a sip of tea. "I'll ask Jack if he can find out anything about that."

Maggie's mind jumped back to a question she'd forgot-ten to ask earlier. "How did Adele come by all that stolen jewelry? Do the police know?"

"Don't tell us that daffy Adele was the mastermind of a robbery ring. I'd really plotz if I heard that." Suzanne laughed at her own imagining.

Dana grinned. "The police don't think that was the scenario. More like the house robbers who stole the stuff sold it to her, for pennies on the dollar. She, in turn, sold it to unscrupulous jewelers, or vendors at flea markets where the pedigree of goods is not that closely monitored. Then pocketed a hefty markup for herself."

Suzanne sat up straight in her chair. "She may have done those deals right in the farmers' market. Instead of buying worthless trinkets, some of her customers were selling her hot jewelry. Who would have noticed?"

"That could have been going on," Maggie agreed.

"So, she was making money on moving the stolen goods back into the retail flow?" Lucy asked.

"Exactly." Dana shrugged.

"Do the police think she was selling it from her stall?" Suzanne asked.

"I'm not sure. She'd be taking a big risk. Someone in the community might recognize their stolen possessions."

"That would be a risk," Maggie agreed. "The jewelry opens up a whole new line of investigation. Maybe some shady character that she dealt with killed her? They may have argued over money or something like that."

"I've heard that a lot of houses are robbed by kids who need money to buy drugs," Suzanne said. "They come in looking for anything they can sell or swap to support their habit. Trying to keep drugs out of the schools is practically all they talk about at PTA meetings lately."

"Sad but true." Maggie sighed. "Sounds as if Adele was dealing with a desperate group. When a person feels pushed against the wall, they are likely to lash out."

"This jewelry stash raises more questions than it answers," Lucy complained. "Do you think it connects in some way to Jimmy Hooper's murder? Maybe he found out what Adele was up to. The stalls were right across from each other. Maybe he blackmailed her? Which would explain the cash that was found in his workbench," she reminded them.

Maggie had resumed work on her own project, but she didn't like the way her first few stitches were sitting on the needle and yanked them out. Was Suzanne's wayward knitting contagious? *Perhaps I should have washed my hands*, she reflected.

"Blackmail doesn't seem like Jimmy," she said finally. "He was such a straight arrow. I imagine if he'd seen some illicit business going on, he would have reported it."

"But he was in dire need of money to save his farm," Suzanne reminded her. "I don't think we can count that out."

"Maybe not." Maggie started the row again. "Jimmy and Adele must have known each other. From the market, and the Hooper Farm is not that far from her house. Have the police found any connection between them?" Maggie asked Dana.

"Not that I've heard of, but I'm sure they're looking for one." She took her glasses off and wiped them with a tissue. "Did you ask Martin if she knew Jimmy? I'd be interested to hear what he had to say."

"I didn't think of it. But I really should have. I'll mention it to Phoebe. Maybe she can find out." She completed the row to her satisfaction and turned her work. "It would be interesting to see his reaction when Jimmy's name . . . and death . . . are mentioned," she added.

"I'm going to do some research online," Lucy offered. "About Jimmy and Adele. And Cousin Martin," she said, meeting Maggie's gaze. "You never know what might turn up."

"Good idea. See what you can find. I feel as if the solution to this riddle is staring us in the face, but we just don't see it."

"We can't see the forest for the socks?" Suzanne piped up.

Maggie had to smile, despite the poor wordplay. "Something like that. These new revelations about Adele are a lot to consider."

She knew her friends felt the same.

On Friday morning, while Maggie was still mulling over the possible implications of the stolen jewelry and other tidbits Dana had related the night before, she heard Phoebe coming down from her apartment.

"I'm sorry I missed the meeting last night. I meant to get back in time." Phoebe juggled tote bags and a wide-brimmed straw hat. It looked like she planned to go back to the market today. Maggie thought that would be a good thing and might take her mind off Harry's troubles.

"We got to talking over dinner," Phoebe explained. "Harry's cousin, Martin, is a really great guy."

Maggie was in the back room, at the oak table, sipping coffee and paging through a new issue of *Vogue Knitting*. The photos put her in the mood for fall knitting.

"He seems to care a lot about Harry. I'm sure you were all relieved that the police let Harry go. That was something to celebrate."

"Was it ever. What a nightmare." Phoebe rolled her eyes. "Harry only stayed at that dumpy cottage one night. What a fluke. If Robbie hadn't thrown him out of their apartment, he'd be totally in the clear," Phoebe insisted. "The police didn't even find the jewelry in the cottage. It was in the house. It was such a lame excuse to drag him back."

Flimsy, Maggie agreed. But Detective Reyes was looking for any connection between Harry and the crime. And any

reason to keep questioning him. Flimsy, lame, or other-
wise.

"What does Martin think about the jewelry? It was
stolen property," Maggie reminded her.

"He was stumped. He had no idea where it could have
come from. Detective Reyes asked him about it, too. Just
casually, not in a big interview or anything. He thought
there was some mistake. Like, maybe his mother didn't
know it was stolen? Or she was holding it for someone, as
a favor?"

"That's possible, but not very likely." Maggie didn't
want to sound harsh but she had to be honest. "Of course
Martin doesn't want to think badly of his mother."

She'd continued paging through the magazine as they
spoke and found a photo of three women modeling ponchos, the patterns all attractive choices. She folded back
the page to mark it. "So, Martin and Harry get along
well?"

"Seems so. They had a lot to catch up on. They haven't
seen each other in a long time." Phoebe pulled out a tube
of sunblock and began slathering it on her bare arms and
all the pale skin exposed by her sundress. "They both
loved Adele. It made me sad to hear them reminisce."

"I'm sure." Maggie recalled one of the questions that
had come up last night. "Do you know if Adele and Jimmy
were friends? Did Harry or Martin ever mention it?"

Phoebe paused applying the lotion, then shook her
head. "I never heard anything about that. I'll ask Harry, if
you want."

"I am curious. Will you see him today?"

"I'm not sure. He won't be at the market. He's too upset
about his aunt and all this legal stuff. He can't go back to
the cottage, either. Adele's property is still a crime scene.
Not that he even wants to go back there. Martin got him a

room at the Lord Jeff. They want to plan a memorial for Adele, but not until all the craziness dies down. The police still have her body."

"Oh, right. It hasn't been all that long. A full autopsy takes a while." Another question came to mind. "Did anyone mention Adele's will? She was far better off than she appeared. There's a surprising amount of money to pass on."

Phoebe's eyes widened. "Really? Who gets it? Martin?"

"I think you'll like this part." Maggie smiled as she prefaced her reply. "There are actually two wills, but the most recent specifies that the bulk of Adele's estate will go to her cats and toward setting up a sanctuary for strays, in general."

Phoebe's grin spread from pierced ear to pierced ear. "That's outrageous. What a badass thing to do. That Adele was totally cool."

"In that regard she was," Maggie agreed.

Phoebe stowed the sunblock in her pack and yanked the drawstrings closed. "Nobody said a word about that." She looked up at Maggie. "Maybe they just didn't talk about it in front of me. Family business and all that?"

"Possibly," Maggie replied. "Have a good day at the market. I hope your stall is so busy and your making so many sales, you have no time to think of anything else."

Phoebe hitched the backpack straps over her shoulders and tied the sun hat under her chin. "I don't think it will be. But I can fret down there as well as here, right?"

Maggie smiled at her logic. "I wish you weren't fretting at all. You've helped Harry a lot. Let the police do their job now. That's what they're trained for."

Phoebe looked shocked, then nearly laughed out loud. "Did you really say that, Maggie? This has to be the first time you've ever trusted the police to figure something out."

Maggie felt her cheeks flush. She knew her advice was hypocritical.

"Harry did not harm Adele," Phoebe insisted. "If the police keep badgering him, I'll figure out who killed her. By myself, if I have to."

Maggie met her determined gaze and bit her lip. She wasn't nearly as sure of Harry's innocence, but couldn't admit that to Phoebe. Not yet.

"This stolen jewelry opens up a whole new line of inquiry. Let's hope Detective Reyes leaves Harry alone for a while."

Phoebe looked satisfied with that reply. "Fingers crossed. See you later."

"Have a good day. Sell a lot of socks." Maggie watched her a moment from the shop door, then heard her cell phone ring. She dug it out of her purse, but not in time to speak to the caller, who had left a short message.

Maggie hit the playback button and heard Carrie Hooper's voice. "Hi, Maggie, just getting back about all that yarn I found in the attic. It's packed up. Give me a call when you can. Thanks."

Maggie was about to call back, but heard a tapping sound on the big picture window. She turned to see Lucy's face, framed by the faces of her two dogs, who were smearing the window with their hot breath and wet noses.

When she opened the door, a gust of warm air countered the shop's air-conditioning. "Come in, come in. It's too hot to sit on the porch today."

"Dogs, too?" Lucy asked in a small, hopeful voice.

"If it's too hot out for us, it's certainly too hot for anyone in a fur coat." Maggie stepped aside so the trio could enter.

Maggie walked to the back room and her visitors followed. The dogs settled quickly under the table with water and biscuits while Lucy helped herself to coffee.

"Phoebe just left for the market," Maggie reported. "I hope working at her stall will take her mind off Harry."

Lucy rolled her eyes. "I doubt that's enough to do it."

Maggie glanced at the magazine again, then put it aside. "She's convinced he's innocent. Let's hope she's right." She looked up at Lucy. "Are you busy later, around five or so? Would you take a ride to Hooper Farm with me? Carrie Hooper came across her mother's stash and she wants to donate it. I'm sure she'd drop it off here, but if we pick it up, I can chat her up a bit and find out if her father was friendly with Adele. That sort of thing?"

"Good idea. Count me in. I love farms." Lucy's enthusiasm was almost childlike. "I'm honored to be invited as your partner on this mission, Mag."

"You're always my first choice. You know that." She paused and winked. "Just don't tell the others."

"Sure. But I bet you tell all of us the same thing."

Before Maggie could deny it, her phone rang again. Phoebe this time. Surprising, since she'd just left.

Maggie picked up the call and put the phone on speaker.

"Maggie? Are you there? The weirdest thing is going on . . . The police are here. In Adele and Harry's stall. They're dressed in hazmat suits, and they've brought those sniffing search dogs."

Maggie and Lucy stared at each other, unable to answer. It seemed obvious the police were looking for something. "They must have a warrant to search the stall. Are they combing the whole market?"

"No one's said yet. So far, it's just that space," Phoebe replied in a cautious tone. "A police officer just carried out a big block of clay that Harry uses for his work."

"The clay? That's odd," Maggie murmured.

"Maybe you should close up and come back to the shop," Lucy suggested. "I'm sure that police activity is scaring all the customers away."

"I'll say. It's like a ghost town . . . no pun intended. But

I can't leave yet," Phoebe added. "That policeman who was with Detective Reyes yesterday morning?"

"Officer Clunes?" Maggie said.

"That's the guy. He told everyone to stick around. He needs to ask more questions."

It sounded serious. Another problem for Harry, very likely. But she didn't want to ratchet up Phoebe's worries.

"Maybe you could leave after you give a statement. See how it goes," Maggie suggested. "I'll pick you up. Just call."

"I'll keep you posted." Phoebe sighed. "I hope the police don't go after Harry again. I thought that was over."

Maggie had hoped so too, mostly for Phoebe's sake. But she wasn't truly surprised by this new turn.

"Martin is calling. I have to go," Phoebe said.

"Okay, dear. Hang in there. Let us know what happens."

The call ended and Maggie put the phone down.

"What do you think they're looking for?" Lucy asked.

"Sounds like they found something in the clay Harry uses to make his pottery. I guess we won't know exactly what for a while."

"If it's proof that Harry killed his aunt, game over for the boy wizard."

Maggie didn't want to say it aloud so plainly. But she knew Lucy had stated a strong possibility.

Chapter 11

Maggie closed the shop an hour or so early, and headed to Lucy's house, conveniently on the way to Hooper Farm. Lucy lived in an area of town called the Marshes, a patch of houses just a short walk from the town beach, and near a stretch of marshland and woods, most of it protected as a nature preserve. Despite the neighborhood's proximity to the water it was not in the least exclusive.

The winding streets were lined with small houses that had once been summer cottages. Most had been extended and even knocked down to be replaced by grander homes that were usually too large for the postage stamp–sized properties.

The cottage Lucy lived in with her husband and dogs was relatively unchanged from its original modest design, with the exception of a funny-looking dormer that stuck out from the roofline like the lid on a cracker box.

Lucy's aunt Claire had lived in the house most of her life. Unmarried and without children, she doted on Lucy and her older sister, Ellen, who had spent many of their childhood summers in Plum Harbor.

When the sisters inherited the house, years ago, they'd made a deal that Lucy could live there in exchange for a fair rent. As time passed and Lucy had married Matt, she'd arranged to buy her sister's half of the deed, which suited everyone perfectly. The cottage was far too quaint and uncomfortable for Ellen's taste, even as a summer place. She and her family lived in a mini mansion in Concord and preferred Nantucket or Martha's Vineyard for their seaside vacations.

But Maggie had always thought it was a lovely little house and was even more charming since Lucy and Matt had painted, redecorated, and updated it to their own taste.

Maggie pulled into the driveway and lightly tapped the horn. Lucy appeared in the front window. She waved and disappeared. Matt was weeding the big, raised garden, planted smack-dab in the middle of the front lawn. Maggie wondered what the neighbors thought of that.

A dedicated gardener herself, she envied the mini rainforest with its thick greenery—ripening tomatoes on tall vines, and bell peppers and zucchini growing happily in the shade of towering sunflowers that were just starting to bloom.

"Who needs the farmers' market with that garden?" Maggie called out to him.

He sat back on his heels and laughed, his dark eyes crinkling around the corners. His good looks reminded Maggie why her friend had fallen for him almost on sight.

"Good thing, too. I hear it's downright dangerous down there these days."

Lucy appeared, stopped to kiss his cheek, then held up her long cotton skirt as she ran to the car. Her dark blond hair was pulled back in a ponytail and she fanned her face with her hand as she jumped in the passenger seat. "I know AC is bad for the environment but it's so hard to do without it."

"I can stand just so much hot air blowing on me during

a long drive. I won't tell if you don't." Maggie raised the windows and hit the AC button as she pulled out of the driveway.

"Did you hear anything more from Phoebe?" Lucy asked.

Phoebe had texted Maggie shortly after her call to say that the police took Harry to the station again for questioning. His lawyer was with him, and Phoebe was going to meet Martin and wait with him for the interrogation to be over. Maggie had forwarded the update to her friends, but there'd been nothing from Phoebe since.

Maggie shook her head. "Not a word. Did you?"

"Nope. Dana hasn't heard any inside info yet, either." Lucy took out her phone and stared at it, as if that might make a message appear faster. "What do you think they found in Harry's stall?"

Maggie shrugged. "Whatever it is, the situation doesn't bode well."

Lucy sighed. "It really doesn't. I feel bad for Phoebe."

They soon reached Hooper Farm and Maggie turned in the gravel driveway, steering around assorted pieces of furniture that had been brought to the roadside—a battered student desk, wooden chairs stacked on each other, and a worn love seat with tufts of white stuffing exposed through tears in the fabric, like open wounds. Beside that pile stood an old barbecue and a bulky TV set. The silver antennae on top made it look like a big black bug.

"When's the last time you saw one of those?" Maggie asked as they drove by the castoffs.

"I can't remember. Someone's been doing some serious cleaning," Lucy said as Maggie parked her car.

"Carrie told me she needs to sell the house. It's a big undertaking to get this place in saleable condition."

They walked up the path and Carrie opened the front

door. "We're a little early," Maggie said. "I hope we're not interrupting."

"Not at all. Please come in. Sorry it's so stuffy," Carrie added, as she led them into the sitting room. "I've set up all the fans I could find, but they only seem to shift the hot air around."

Dressed in tan shorts and a souvenir T-shirt from Bar Harbor, she looked tired but exhilarated.

"You've made real progress from the last time I was here," Maggie remarked.

"Thanks, but it couldn't have looked much worse," Carrie said with a laugh. "Most of the furniture wasn't even fit to donate. I did hire some help for the clearing out, and I've lined up a painter and a handyman. They'll start next week, after I'm gone." She pushed a box aside with her foot. "China dishes" had been written on top in black marker. "I'll be back to check the work on the weekends, until it's ready to go on the market."

"When are you leaving?" Lucy asked.

"I doubt my to-do list will ever be done, but probably Sunday or sometime Monday morning? I need to get back to my office. There isn't much I want from the house. But I'll take my father's ashes with me." Maggie followed her glance to the fireplace mantel.

A dark blue china bean jar was set in the middle of the mantel, alongside a small vase of flowers. "My mother is laid to rest in New London. That's where her family is from. My father's remains will join her. We'll have a small ceremony soon, just the family."

"That sounds perfect for Jimmy. I'm sure he would have approved," Maggie said.

She smiled at the reply. "I think it's just right for him. He never liked a fuss, no matter what the occasion was."

"All of his customers at the market liked him so much," Lucy said. "I didn't know him well, but I admired him."

Carrie looked pleased. "That's nice of you to say. My father believed in his work, but he didn't think other people noticed."

"Speaking of the market," Maggie jumped in. "You must have heard about Adele McSweeney?"

"Yes, I did." Carrie's smile turned to dismay. "What a tragedy for her family. Believe me, I sympathize. I thought there might be some connection between her death and my dad's, since they both had stalls at the market. But now the police seem to think her nephew had something to do with it?" She shivered despite the room's warmth. "It's upsetting enough to hear about a murder, but I always think it's particularly ghoulish when a family member is involved."

"The police are only questioning Adele's nephew." Lucy's tone was even and matter-of-fact. "They're looking into many possibilities. What sort of connection did you think there could be between Adele's death and your father's?"

"Were they friends, do you know?" Maggie asked.

Carrie brushed her damp bangs off her forehead. "I can't think of any connection. I thought the police might find one. She was a nice lady. She used to visit when my mother was sick and sometimes bring us dinner or cakes. She liked to be helpful in the neighborhood. But that was a long time ago. I don't recall my father mentioning her recently."

Maggie shrugged. "I was just curious. I'm sure the police have asked you all these questions by now."

"They did. But I don't think they've come up with any link between the crimes yet. To tell you the truth, I've been so focused on the house and figuring out my father's business affairs, I've barely kept up with anything else. I clean all day and chat with my brother on the computer at night about my father's business matters. Brad is an accountant and lives in Tucson."

She'd stepped to the window to adjust one of the fans that was making a funny noise. "Would you like a cold drink?" She glanced from Maggie to Lucy hopefully. "There's ice tea in the fridge."

Maggie waved her hand. "That's very kind. If you show us the things you want to donate, we'll be on our way."

Carrie led them from the living room into a large kitchen, which looked just as Maggie had expected: old wooden cabinets covered with thick white paint, a white enamel stove and stained countertops, and a faded linoleum floor.

She led them through the kitchen into a sunroom with old-fashioned louvered windows. Maggie noticed a door that opened to the back of the house.

"I packed it in those boxes, under the window. It's mostly yarn, but there's a box or two with needles and other knitting supplies." Carrie pointed to the pile. "Thank you so much for taking care of this for me. I've been driving all over the county, giving away anything salvageable. You've definitely saved me a trip or two."

"It's not a problem at all. We're happy to help." Maggie bent to pick up a box. "There's so much here, I'll split it between at least two nursing homes. You've done a very good deed, giving all this away."

Carrie smiled as she also grabbed a box. "You should thank my father. I could hear him scolding if I even had a thought of throwing something out. 'Reuse, recycle, repair.' That was his motto long before it was a bumper sticker. My son said we should carve it on his headstone."

Maggie laughed. "It would be fitting. That was his gospel."

It took two trips to Maggie's car for the three of them to move all the boxes. Her hatch was filled so high she worried about seeing out the back.

"Your mother was a true knitter. We can't resist beautiful yarn when we see it, so we buy much more than we can ever use."

Carrie nodded with a wistful look. "She always wanted to teach me to knit, but I never had the time. Now I wish I had learned. She made such beautiful things for the family, when she was able. And always hoped her body would not betray her as quickly as it did. That yarn collection was proof of her optimism. Hopeful to the end."

Maggie felt moved by her words. She didn't know what to say. "At least you have the sweaters and such she created. I'm sure her love is stitched right in."

"Stop in the shop when you visit town again, Carrie. We'd love to see you," Lucy said.

"Yes, do. And good luck with the rest of your work here," Maggie added.

They said goodbye and Maggie and Lucy got into the Subaru while Carrie returned to the house.

"What do you think?" Lucy asked as Maggie put the car in reverse. Maggie knew Lucy was asking about Carrie, but couldn't address that subject immediately.

"I think I have too many boxes back there. Or I should be at least three inches taller." She craned her neck around as she slowly backed out of the driveway, checking side-view mirrors as well, but was still flying blind.

"Warn me if I'm going to hit anything," she told Lucy.

Lucy turned to watch the mirror on her side. "Don't you have one of those things that makes noise if the car is about to hit something?"

"I do. His name is Charles. Since he's not here, you'll have to step up."

Before Lucy could reply they heard the crunch of metal. Maggie quickly braked and put the car in park.

"Oh, dear. That didn't sound good."

She jumped out her side and Lucy got out, too. When they met at the back of the car, Maggie was relieved to see the collision had sounded a lot worse that it was. She'd struck down the old barbecue, resulting in a slightly dented license plate.

"No big deal. Let's prop it up and get out of here, before you do real damage." Lucy bent to help her move the accident victim toward the other discards. A warm breeze lifted the pile of ashes off the road and blew a puff on Maggie's clothes.

"Just what I needed." Maggie stared down at herself; her hands and legs were coated with black soot, along with her sneakers and the hem of her shorts.

"Carrie must have had one last barbecue before she tossed it." Lucy looked her over. "You might smell like a hamburger, or grilled chicken? Daisy will give you a nice greeting."

"Daisy loves me anyway. But you're right, best not rub greasy ashes into the fabric." Maggie found some wipes in the car and cleaned off her hands, shins, and shoes.

After she'd finally navigated safely to the road, she said, "It sounds like any relationship between Adele and the Hoopers was a neighborly connection, long ago, and mainly due to Penelope's illness."

"And it faded after Penelope's passing, like the rest of their social network," Lucy added. She was watching the green, open land pass by her window. "But there could have been a new reason for them to be friends. Or even adversaries?" She turned to Maggie. "I had an odd thought while we were sitting there. What if Adele killed Jimmy? Maybe he found out she was a fence for stolen goods and he was blackmailing her, like Suzanne said. What if they were in on something together, and had a falling-out?"

"It's possible. But she would have needed help to move the body and make it look as if he'd hung himself."

"The help of someone stronger, probably a man, you mean," Lucy replied. "Like Harry?"

"I didn't say that," Maggie replied quickly, though the thought had come to mind.

"Who else could have helped her?" Lucy seemed to be asking the universe, not just Maggie.

Before Maggie could speculate, she heard Lucy's phone ping with an incoming text. Lucy quickly pulled it from her pocket and stared at the screen.

"News from Phoebe?" Maggie asked.

Lucy nodded, but didn't reply as she stared down and read the message. As Lucy kept scrolling, Maggie got a bad feeling.

"Read it, please. I'm listening," she urged Lucy.

" 'The police found drugs hidden in the blocks of clay. Harry was arrested for possession. It's a large enough quantity to suspect that he's been selling the stuff, too. But no proof of that.' " Lucy turned to her, looking pale.

"No proof yet, she means," Maggie called out. She felt as if the top of her head might blow off.

"Or never," Lucy reminded her. "He still has to appear before a judge to be charged and enter a plea. That will take a few hours or might even happen tomorrow. His cousin, Martin, is working on arranging bail, if the judge will grant it."

"What a dreadful mess." Maggie felt so upset, she could hardly concentrate on her driving. "That changes everything."

"Wait, there's more," Lucy cut in. "The police want to question Phoebe. She's waiting to be interviewed."

Maggie's heart skipped a beat. She turned to Lucy, then swept her gaze back to the road. She took a sharp turn and headed straight to the village instead of Lucy's neighborhood.

"She can't go in there alone . . . Find my phone, it's in

my purse. Look up Helen Forbes in the contacts. Tell her I'll be responsible for the fees."

Helen Forbes had represented Maggie years ago, when she'd been accused of Amanda Goran's murder, and more recently had represented Suzanne when she'd been hounded by the police.

Lucy quickly dialed the attorney and explained the situation. Helen was up on the news known to the public about Adele's case, and the buzz on the legal grapevine, too.

"Don't worry. I'm leaving my office right now," Helen promised. "I'll make sure Phoebe doesn't go in the interview room alone."

"Thank you, Helen. Thank you so much," Maggie called out. "Tell Phoebe we'll be there very soon."

After Lucy ended the call, Maggie said, "I told Phoebe to steer clear of Harry. I wish she'd listened to me."

Maggie hated the way she sounded. Wasn't she always the one to say, "What's done is done?" and focus on a solution? But she couldn't help herself.

"That foolish girl," she added. "He's bamboozled her, again."

"Calm down. Do you want me to drive?" Lucy asked gently.

Maggie took a breath and lifted her foot from the accelerator. "I'm fine. It's just so distressing. It didn't have to be like this. No telling what the police will accuse her of now."

"They're just asking Harry's friends questions. That's to be expected. No one is calling Phoebe and Harry the Bonnie and Clyde of Plum Harbor."

"The *Plum Harbor Times* is not known for their clever headlines. Give them a day or so. They'll catch up."

Lucy touched her arm. "I know it's a muddle. But even if Harry is involved with drugs, that still doesn't mean he killed his aunt."

Lucy knew her so well. She'd never said aloud that she now thought Harry was guilty. But secretly, she did. She had to admit it. This last development had put her over the edge. She'd lost her objectivity, her ability to see the big picture. Her mind had tightened, like a fist. But she'd never see what was really going on that way.

"Yes, yes. I agree. I doesn't mean he killed his aunt," Maggie said finally. She took a deep breath. "But it gives the police a clear motive. A much better motive than stolen jewelry. Adele found out that Harry was dealing drugs, they fought over it, and he killed her. Maybe even by accident. None of us wants to think that, even if just for Phoebe's sake. But it might be true."

"It might," Lucy conceded. "But Phoebe will still insist that he's innocent. You know she will. If she was in the car with us right now, she'd beg us to figure out who really did it."

"That goes without saying. You'll forgive me if I'm not inclined right now to give Harry McSweeney the benefit of the doubt. My only concern is Phoebe, and whether or not the police drag her into this mess. There might be so much evidence stacked against Harry soon that not even Phoebe's kind heart can ignore it."

Chapter 12

"All's well that ends well?" Suzanne swirled a stream of syrup over her pancakes, then smeared a soft square of butter on top.

Lucy had been watching with interest. "She quotes Shakespeare one minute and makes a smiley face on her pancakes the next."

"Smiley faces cheer me up. You ought to try it."

Maggie was about to interrupt when the waitress returned with more of their orders. They'd decided to meet at the Schooner Diner, a Plum Harbor institution, just across Main Street from the shop.

Maggie usually wasn't free to have breakfast out on a Saturday morning, but Charles had stopped by with Daisy, hoping to tempt her to go to the beach. Instead, she asked him to watch the shop while she ran off to meet her friends.

Maggie decided her husband-to-be and their little dog couldn't do much damage this morning. She hoped she was right.

The line outside the diner on the weekend was always intense, but Edie Steiber, the diner owner, was a dedicated knitter and a regular at Maggie's shop. When she spotted Maggie and her friends in the crowd, she'd magically found a table amidst the clatter of silverware and rising voices.

Maggie felt a pang of guilt as they cut ahead of other customers, but Suzanne basked in the privilege. "Pretend you're an A-list celeb, Mag. It's easier that way."

The classic menu—eggs anyway you liked them, stacks of golden pancakes, from blueberry to chocolate chip, and crisp waffles topped with whipped cream . . . not to mention ham, bacon, or sausage dropped on every dish—was certainly not the food movie stars ate. Maggie didn't think so. Nor was it the least bit healthy. But all agreed comfort food was required this morning.

Maggie felt better from simply inhaling the rich scents of coffee and tasty things sizzling on the grill. Phoebe was the only one missing. After her ordeal at the police station the previous night, she needed to sleep in.

Dana was the first one served. She had cleverly crafted a nutritious dish and sprinkled a side order of blueberries and sliced banana over a bowl of oatmeal.

"I wouldn't say it's over yet, and certainly not for Harry," Dana said, stirring the concoction together. "He was arraigned last night and charged with possession of an illegal substance. It was all opioids, much in demand right now. The judge denied bail, even though his record is clean. The fact that the police are calling him a person of interest in both murder cases weighed heavily against him."

"But what did Harry say? Did he admit that the drugs are his?" Suzanne spoke quickly, choking down a bite.

Maggie leaned forward. The whole diner didn't need to know their private business. Or Harry's, for that matter.

"He insists he had no idea the drugs were there," Maggie replied, "and claims he never once used drugs, of any kind. He told the police that he's totally innocent and believes someone is framing him. Though he has no idea why, or who it could be."

"Phoebe told you that?" Suzanne asked. Maggie nodded and sipped her coffee. "I bet she believes every word."

"She does," Maggie said solemnly. "At least the police didn't hold her for long. Helen Forbes helped in that regard. They questioned everyone in the market and had drug-sniffing dogs check all the stalls. They didn't find anything more. Thank goodness."

"Phoebe wasn't the only one interviewed?" Lucy asked.

"All of the vendors at the market were questioned, but a few, including Phoebe and Robbie, were brought to the station for interviews because of their close relationships to Harry. They also rounded up some of Harry's other friends, artists who share studio space with him on the college campus. I think they searched the studio where he works on his ceramics, but didn't find anything more. Phoebe said they were trying to flush out someone who had bought drugs from Harry, or seen him in the act. Or even heard him talk about it."

"Did they?" Lucy peered up from her plate of scrambled eggs and nibbled on a toast crust.

"Phoebe doesn't know. Robbie was the only one she spoke to last night. I think Harry's problems are causing a rift between Phoebe and Robbie. Which is unfortunate," Maggie added.

Dana had worked her way through half the oatmeal and paused to sip her tea. "What did Robbie tell the police? They lived together. He'd be a likely witness."

"Robbie told Phoebe he'd never seen or heard anything that clear-cut or conclusive. But he did tell the police a few things that troubled her. Especially in regard to the night that Adele died. He now says he stopped by Adele's house to drop off some of Harry's belongings and he heard Adele and someone arguing. He didn't look in any of the windows, and claims he was too far away to tell if it was

Harry or not. But he told Detective Reyes it was definitely a man's voice."

A bite of pancake dangled from Suzanne's fork. "Why didn't he say that sooner? He had plenty of time to speak up."

Maggie shrugged and looked down at her plate. She'd ordered eggs Benedict, which was well prepared at the diner, but the sauce had gone cold. Eggs Benedict Arnold, she decided, pushing her dish aside. "Who can say? He told Phoebe he held back because he didn't want to make things worse for Harry. But now he felt pressured to tell everything he knew so he wouldn't get in trouble with the police himself."

"Maybe at first he didn't think Harry was guilty but now he does," Suzanne offered.

"That could be." Maggie stirred a dash of milk into her coffee.

"So, Harry's in hot water. Deeper than a lobster at a beach party." Suzanne shook her head.

"He is," Dana agreed. "But the police still can't place him in Adele's house, or at Hooper Farm. They have no physical evidence, or witnesses, that connect him to either crime scene."

"Except for Robbie hearing a man's voice," Suzanne reminded them. "We all know that could have been Harry."

"We do." Dana didn't sound at all happy about that sorry fact. "But for better or worse, they need a lot more to convict him." She turned to Maggie. "I'm concerned about Phoebe. She must be taking this very hard."

"She is," Maggie confirmed. "Charles and I waited at the station last night for her to be released, and she told us everything. She seemed just . . . bereft. I hope a good night's sleep will restore her spirits and give her some perspective."

"How did she leave it with the police? I hope they aren't

going to hound her now, too." Suzanne sounded concerned.

"She told the detectives that while she and Harry were dating, she never saw him engaged in any illegal activity. Or overheard suspicious phone calls, or conversations. It depends on whether the police believe her or not."

"Who wouldn't believe Phoebe?" Suzanne asked the others.

"She's so sincere. Though her die-hard defense of Harry might be misplaced."

"Her adamant defense of Harry and obvious loyalty might make the police doubt her testimony," Maggie said. "They might decide she's just trying to cover for him."

Lucy blew on her coffee. "Now Harry is being pressed from two directions. The investigation of his aunt's murder, and these drugs charges. And we can't discount Jimmy Hooper's murder, if the police consider him a person of interest in that case, too, and can link Adele and Jimmy in some way."

"That makes it three directions. Unhappily," Maggie said solemnly. "I hope Phoebe doesn't continue to help him. It will only keep her under the microscope. But I can't tell her what to do."

"None of us can. Let's see how these investigations unfold," Dana suggested. "The police need to follow up on a lot of new information. I don't think Harry's fate is sealed yet."

"Not yet, but things are moving fast," Suzanne said. "If that kid doesn't catch a break, he could end up behind bars. As long as there's a breath in my body, Phoebe will never end up as one of those women visiting a guy in jail for twenty years." Suzanne sounded serious. As if she believed it was a real possibility. "Ever watch *Prison Wives*? It's so depressing."

Lucy's eyes bugged out. "What cable package do you get? You watch shows I never heard of."

"You know what I mean," Suzanne murmured.

Maggie thought it was a good moment to change the subject.

"Anyone see our waitress? I could use more coffee."

"Me too." Lucy was rooting around in her tote bag and pulled out a yellow file folder. "As promised, I nosed around on the internet. So much more fun than doing real work. I did find a few interesting items."

Suzanne's dismal vision of Phoebe's future was swept aside and they leaned closer to hear what Lucy had to say. "First, about Martin McSweeney." She picked up the top sheet of paper in the pile.

"He is who he says he is, a software engineer who lives in San Francisco. He owns a company, CyberShield. The firm specializes in information security."

"That's impressive. Big bucks in that field, for sure," Suzanne said.

"Yes, and a lot at stake for the clients," Lucy added. "The security of one of his clients was breeched and they sued. The judge ordered CyberShield to pay millions in damages, enough to put the company in Chapter Eleven."

"The chapter every entrepreneur wants to skip," Suzanne cut in.

"The company is appealing the decision," Lucy continued, showing them another short news article. "But with all the bad publicity and legal fees, he's got to be pressed for capital."

"Despite the custom-made sport shirts and expensive loafers," Maggie noted.

"Financial pressure is certainly a motive," Dana agreed.

"Classic," Suzanne said. "If he knew his mother had socked away a small fortune, and he *believed* he was going to inherit at least half of it."

Lucy nodded. "Until those sneaky cats persuaded her to cut him out and leave it all to them."

Dana was the only registered cat lover at the table, but did not take affront. "I'm sure the cats didn't forge her signature. Dogs can be just as crafty, when you get down to it."

Dana's big Maine coon cat was both crafty and crazy, and they could no longer have meetings at Dana's house because the cat perched on an armoire or the curtains and attacked their knitting. But Maggie didn't want to sidetrack everyone by reminding them of that.

"It does give Martin motive, depending on when he found out about the new will. And if he knew about the hidden bank accounts. I suppose with his computer expertise, he would have been able to hack into his mother's financial records, if he wanted to," Maggie mused. "But the police must have looked into his background and possible motives, first thing."

"These are a lot of ifs," Lucy began, "but what if he knew Adele was loaded, and he was unaware of the second will? What's Harry's situation in regard to collecting an inheritance if he goes to jail? Would his share go to Martin?"

"Good question." Dana sat up with attention. "If he's only found guilty of the drug charge, he won't lose his inheritance. But in Massachusetts, a person is disqualified from collecting an inheritance if they're found guilty of first or second degree murder, or manslaughter of the decedent, meaning, the person who named them in a will."

"In that case, I think we can assume that if Harry is found guilty of murdering his aunt his share of Adele's estate would go to Martin.

"And maybe the cats," Dana added. "But he most likely wouldn't get any."

"But so far," Suzanne said, "Martin seems eager to help Harry, not throw him to the wolves."

"It appears that way," Maggie agreed. "But he was just on Cape Cod the last week or so, within striking distance of all the strange things that have been going on here. It does make you wonder." She paused, considering her words. "I'm just not sure we should rule him out as quickly as the police did."

"Me either," Lucy agreed. "And I do have one more thing to show you," she added, picking up the folder again. "It's more a bit of nostalgia than anything that might help." She slipped a piece of paper to the center of the table. "I found this at the local newspaper, on their microfilm."

"Now, that's real digging," Maggie commended. "It's hard to remember a time when every moment wasn't documented on the internet."

"I found a few mentions of Jimmy over the years in the local paper, donating produce to a food pantry and a newspaper interview about his organic farming. He started up the market with a group of other farmers, over ten years ago." Lucy showed around copies of old newspaper articles. "But this one has a great photo. June thirtieth, nineteen eighty-nine. A little over thirty years ago." She slipped the sheet of paper to the center of the table.

Maggie read the headline aloud. " 'Community Unites to Aid Farmer's Wife.' " She quickly glanced at the report. "It's about a fundraiser for Penelope Hooper. To help with their medical bills that were mounting up. She'd been diagnosed a few years prior." She paused, thinking back. "I think I remember that."

"It looks like half the town is there, but I didn't see Adele. Maybe one of you can find her?" Lucy asked.

Maggie adjusted her reading glasses and examined the photo. There was the usual lineup of friends, family, and supporters in two long rows, with Penelope at the center.

Jimmy stood on one side of her, a big hand resting on her shoulder, and their two children, Carrie and Brad, stood on the other. He gazed down at his wife, his rough features softened by a soft, loving smile.

"It does looks like half the town is here," Maggie murmured. "I think I even recognize Warren Braeburn. A much younger version," she added.

She passed the photo to Dana and Suzanne, who were eager to see it, too.

"Carrie said Adele had been nice to her family while her mother was ill," Lucy recalled, "but she didn't describe a strong friendship. I suppose this picture might bear out that story, if Adele isn't even in it."

Dana passed the photo along and sat back. "It's hard to say one way or the other. Maybe she didn't attend for some reason, or maybe she stepped away when the photo was taken. She's listed as one of the organizers, but there are many."

Edie Steiber appeared, making the rounds with a pot of regular coffee dangling from one hand and a pot of decaf in the other. "You girls asked for more coffee over here?"

"I'd love some, Edie." Lucy held up her cup. As Edie leaned over to pour, Lucy moved her papers out of the way.

"Where in the world did you dig that up?" Edie laughed softly. "That photo must be a hundred years old."

"You recognize it?" Maggie said.

"Sure I do." She set one of the coffee pots down on the table and pointed with her free hand. "Look at the pretty young thing in the back row. With the Farrah Fawcett haircut? Don't laugh at me too hard. I won't jump you in the line anymore."

Maggie grinned up at her. "Don't be so hard on yourself. I think that style was a law back then. We all had to try it once."

"You too, Mag? I can't believe it." Lucy looked shocked.

"I plead the Fifth." Maggie felt herself flush.

"I won't tell if you don't," Edie promised. "But I do recall that shindig. We held it at the Elks Hall. Big turnout. We collected a tidy sum for the Hoopers. They were very pleased. She was a fighter. She lasted a long time. Poor thing." Edie sighed and plucked up a menu from the table.

Dana turned to face her. "We don't see Adele McSweeney in the picture. Can you remember if she was there?"

Edie cocked her head, a few strands of her trademark bouffant hairdo escaped from a multitude of hairpins. "Good question. It was a big crowd, it's hard to say. I will say Adele was a do-gooder, even with all her problems at home. Or maybe because of them? She took in every stray that crossed her path, cooked soup for sick people, did errands for the housebound. The Hoopers were on her rounds for a while. She'd bring over casseroles and cakes. All that stopped once Penny passed away, as far as I ever heard."

Maggie passed the copy of the news article back to Lucy. "It was interesting to see it, Lucy. Even if it doesn't move us forward."

"Good digging, kid," Suzanne acknowledged.

"Thanks. I do have something else that might push the ball down the field a bit." Lucy leaned forward and spoke in a quieter tone. "While I was in the newspaper office, I ran into a reporter I know, Emily Creeder. We got to talking and she told me that Jimmy asked to meet with her privately. He claimed that he had a good story for the paper. But she never found out what it was."

"Wow, that's big," Suzanne said.

"When did he contact her?" Dana asked. "Did she say?"

"Just a few days before he died. She got the feeling he

wanted to give her something, or show her something, in person."

"Like documents?" Dana asked.

Lucy shrugged. "Maybe. Something he didn't want to explain in an email or even on the phone. It could have been anything. He gave her no clue."

"Carrie said her father was a pack rat. There were boxes of old papers in the sitting room the first time I stopped by," Maggie recalled. "Come to think, those ashes that got on my clothes when I ran over the barbecue?" She looked at Lucy. "They brushed right off. They weren't from grilled food. It looked to me like ashes from burnt paper."

Suzanne raised her hand as if directing traffic. "Can you back it up a bit? You ran over a barbecue? I hope it had insurance."

Maggie glanced at her, feeling impatient. "I was backing out of Carrie's drive and the rear window was blocked with boxes. She had all this junk on the side of the road, waiting to be carted away." She sighed. "The point is, Carrie burned some documents or even photographs in that barbecue. I'm almost positive of it. Something that she found in her father's copious files. I'd love to know what it was."

Lucy looked down at the folder again. "This could all be connected. Emily told the police about Jimmy's call, but she has no idea if they followed up, or figured out what he wanted to tell her."

"It is intriguing," Dana agreed. "The investigation must be pursuing that angle, if the information was so confidential and significant enough to bring to a reporter. I'm going to ask Jack if he can poke around about that."

"Please do," Maggie said. "The question is, did Jimmy discover something so dangerous that it put his life at risk?"

* * *

Lucy stepped up beside Maggie as they crossed Main Street and headed the short distance down to the shop. "You look worried, Mag. Still thinking about Phoebe?"

Maggie smiled and shook her head. "Just wondering if my shop is still in one piece, with Charles and Daisy in charge. It seems intact from the outside at least."

Charles sat on the porch, reading the newspaper. Daisy, a soft brown ball of energy, was tied to his chair on a long leash. She'd found a shady spot under the wicker table, where she chewed a Nylabone. She dropped it quickly and raced across the porch to greet Maggie and Lucy.

"We're back." Maggie leaned down and patted the pup, whose tail wagged furiously, like a small fur helicopter.

"All quiet on the knitting front?" she asked as she kissed Charles on the cheek.

"Quiet as a graveyard. With yarn."

"That's the kind I want to end up in. Remember that, when the time comes," Maggie told him.

He smiled at her suggestion. "I just mean, I'm not sure why you stay open on Saturday in the summer, honey. We could be on the boat all weekend."

"We could," she agreed, sidestepping the familiar debate.

If Charles had his way, she'd sell the business and they'd sail all year long. The business and her house. But she caught herself. His ideal wasn't that extreme, but almost.

He stood up and folded his newspaper. "I love spending time with you. That's a good thing, right?"

The light in his eyes melted her prickly reaction. "It's the best thing." She kissed him goodbye. "Thanks for your help. I'll try to close early. I'll let you know."

"See you later." Charles seemed happy with the plan and took Daisy's leash in hand. "Almost forgot. There was one call. Jimmy Hooper's daughter, Carrie. She's coming by soon. She wants to drop something off. I left the message inside for you."

Carrie's name caught her attention. Lucy had been leafing through a new pattern book and suddenly looked up, like a meerkat popping up from her tunnel.

"Thanks. I'll go check on it." Maggie slipped into the shop, eager to see Carrie's message. Lucy followed. Charles had made out an official pink message slip in his neat, block print. It showed Carrie's name and phone number, and her reason for calling.

Maggie handed it to Lucy. "She's found another box of yarn. She's going to drop it off here around noon."

Lucy checked her watch. "Perfect timing." She reached into her bag and pulled out the yellow folder. "Let's show her the photo of the fundraiser. Maybe she'll say something interesting about it."

"Just what I was thinking," Maggie said.

They returned to the porch and took out their knitting while they waited. Lucy had run into a small challenge with her second sock, and Maggie helped her fix it.

Maggie heard a car pull into the drive and looked up. Carrie got out, waved, and then leaned in the backseat to pull out a box.

Maggie glanced at Lucy. "We'll need to be subtle. I don't want it to seem as if we're baiting her or anything."

Lucy nodded and focused on her knitting again. Or at least pretended to. The yellow folder had conveniently been left on the low table between the wicker furniture.

"Let me help you, Carrie." Maggie rose to meet her and took the box from her hands as she climbed up the porch steps.

"Hard to believe there was more than what you took away yesterday. But I found this one in the parlor last night."

"Thanks for dropping it off."

"Not a problem. I was curious to see your shop. It's charming."

Maggie smiled at the compliment. "It's even nicer inside. Would you like to take a look?"

"I'd love that, but some other time. I have a lot of stops to make."

Lucy looked up from her knitting. "Before you go, Carrie, I have something for you. I was at the newspaper office and came across a really nice photo of your family."

Lucy handed the page to her. Carrie looked pleased and curious. "How thoughtful. When was it taken?"

"Back in nineteen eighty-nine. At a fundraiser for your mother here in town," Lucy said.

"I remember that. I was about nine years old, I guess." She stared up a moment, calculating. Then looked down again. "My parents look so young."

"Yes, they do," Maggie agreed. "There are a few familiar faces in the crowd, younger versions. And a lot of familiar names in the list of people who organized it."

Carrie was still reading the article. "I never gave it much thought. You know how kids are."

She shrugged and looked up at Maggie. Carrie had just been a little girl and what she said was true. Maggie believed that the photo hadn't prompted any revelations for her. At least they'd tried. She glanced at Lucy, sensing she felt the same.

"By the way, you probably know this already," Lucy said in a more confidential tone, "but a reporter at the local paper told me that your father wanted to meet with her about a news story. He seemed to think it was important."

"Really?" Carrie looked surprised. "The police didn't tell me anything about that."

"Oh, well, sorry to speak out of turn. The reporter said she passed the information to Detective Reyes."

"What did my dad want to talk about? Did she say?"

Lucy shook her head. "He never told her. Not a hint. Only that he had a good story for her."

It might have something to do with the papers you burned in your barbecue, Maggie nearly said aloud. But of course, she couldn't go there. She would sound way too intrusive. Even a bit nutty. Carrie might complain to Detective Reyes, then where would they be?

"Now you've got me curious. I'll ask Detective Reyes. I hope the police identify my father's killer before I leave. At least my family will have some closure before his memorial." Carrie sighed and stared out at the street. "I did hear that Adele McSweeney's nephew was arrested. I heard on the news that he's a drug dealer. They say that's why he killed his aunt." She paused and picked up her purse. "You'd need ice water in your veins to murder your own flesh and blood, I think. But drug dealers are like that. The police think my father may have found out and the nephew killed him, too."

Maggie knew the police would explore that possibility but wondered if they had new evidence that linked Harry to Jimmy's murder. "Is that so? Have they found any proof?"

Carrie met her glance, then looked away. "I can't say. But sounds to me like that boy deserves to be locked up. Anyone who peddles drugs destroys lives. Lots of lives, not just one or two people. In that regard alone, he's a killer. Don't you agree?"

"Harry claims he's innocent," Lucy countered.

"What do you expect? I'm sure he also denies killing his aunt. And my father."

Carrie spoke with a cool expression, but her tone was

searing. The conversation was getting out of control. Not what Maggie had expected at all. Carrie hardly seemed the passionate type. But she was grieving her father. That could make anyone emotional.

"May I take this?" she asked Lucy. "I'm making a scrapbook for my family."

"Please do." Lucy smiled and handed up the page.

Maggie felt a pang. She wanted to study the picture again, with the aid of her magnifying glass and a strong light. The diner was so dim and the photo so grainy, she'd only caught the high points.

A customer wandered up the path. "Can you help me find an easy pattern for a baby sweater?"

Maggie could have hugged her. "We have piles of them. The pattern books are on the front table inside. I'll be right with you."

The customer entered the shop and Maggie jumped up from her chair to say goodbye to Carrie. Maggie and Lucy watched her walk to her car, but Maggie waited to speak until Carrie drove away.

"I wish you hadn't given her the photo."

Lucy looked like she might laugh. "Grumpy this morning, aren't we? Careful, you'll scare away your only customer."

Maggie ignored her teasing, though her friend had a point. "I wanted to look the photo over again. With care. But now I have to wait for another copy. Can you get me one on Monday?"

"It's a pain in the neck and takes a load of time," Lucy complained. Maggie's heart fell. "Good thing I made a few extras," Lucy added as she picked up the folder, leafed through the pages, and handed Maggie a fresh copy.

Maggie grinned. "I walked right into that."

"You did. But Carrie didn't play into our hands, did she? She must have seen Adele's name on the list of orga-

nizers. Maybe there's some other, more important link between Adele and Jimmy. Something to do with the market?" Lucy suggested. Then hurried to add, "Not that I'm
saying I agree that Harry is guilty of both crimes. And
more."

"I know what you mean." Maggie wasn't sure what to
think of Harry now. "I'm going to look over this photo
again. We could have missed something."

Lucy had gathered up her knitting and stuffed it in her
tote. "Aren't you forgetting about somebody?"

Maggie replied with a blank look.

"That woman who wants a pattern?"

Maggie sighed and shook her head. "Those pesky customers," she whispered. "Always interrupting at the most
inconvenient moments."

"I know you don't mean that. Most of the time." Lucy
shot her a clever grin.

Maggie didn't answer. This time she did mean it. She
could barely wait to examine the photo. Unfortunately,
she had to.

Chapter 13

Maggie was always amazed at how much personal information customers disclosed, once they started chatting about the projects they planned to make. "I had such happy news this morning. I had to run right over," the customer said as soon as Maggie walked into the shop. "I'm going to be a grandmother. Isn't that great?"

"Wonderful news," Maggie agreed heartily. This sale was going to take longer than she wanted it to.

"My daughter lives in Vermont. She's an assistant professor at the university in Burlington. The history department. I wished she lived closer, so I can help once the baby comes. This morning I decided, why not move up there? I'm divorced and retired. I can do as I please. I'll miss my friends, but I'll make new ones, don't you think?"

Maggie agreed with a quick nod, unable to squeeze in a comment as her customer continued. "—The winters are colder in Vermont, for sure. And I'll miss the beaches around here. So pretty. But I think it will be worth it. I know my daughter and her husband plan on more children and I don't want to be one of those 'big occasions only' grandmas. You know, the kind who only visit on graduations and holidays?" She looked up from the patterns Maggie had pulled out for her. "I'm usually not like this. So impulsive, I mean. Does it sound crazy?"

"Not at all. I know just how you feel," Maggie replied. "My daughter lives in the Midwest and I wonder what will happen when she starts a family. But if the mountain won't come to Mohammad, and all that?"

"Exactly." Her customer seemed very satisfied with Maggie's answer and finally focused on her shopping.

Wendy Ross, that was her name, described herself as a novice knitter, but she was clearly eager to express the love she already felt for the new baby in a knitted creation that would wrap the child in warmth and affection. No matter how the little sweater turned out, it would be perfect because it was stitched from the heart.

Maggie showed her a few basic patterns, the kind that did not make great demands, but could yield beautiful results with the right yarn, in the right color. Cute buttons in the shape of ducks or hearts always made a baby project look more advanced.

"This one is actually a single knitted section," she said, showing Wendy one of her favorite baby sweater coats. "It's folded over and stitched on both sides. I teach the project in a beginner class. Everyone does very well with it."

"I love it. Just my speed," Wendy agreed. "What sort of yarn should I use? The color has to be gender neutral. They want to be surprised. Isn't that funny? Used to be everybody was eager to know if it was a boy or a girl."

"Wanting to be surprised seems to be the current trend." It was interesting how trends came and went. Especially when it came to raising children.

A few minutes later, Maggie rang up a substantial sale of yarn, needles, a pattern, and a class registration for What to Knit When You're Expecting.

Phoebe came down just as the grandma-to-be was happily floating out of the shop, her supplies tucked into a complimentary Black Sheep reusable tote, which Maggie only gave out with a purchase of fifty dollars or more.

"She rated a tote? Way to go," Phoebe said as soon as the door closed.

"It was a good, solid sale. But the only one so far today," Maggie admitted. "Charles wants me to close early and go to the beach. He just sent another text. I'm definitely tempted."

Maggie wondered if Phoebe would join them. Or did she plan on going back to the market, as her persistent spirit might demand?

Phoebe had landed on the love seat and was fiddling with her cell phone, dressed in denim shorts, a T-shirt, and flip-flops, with her long hair still wet from a shower.

"How was the Schooner?" Phoebe asked.

Maggie guessed from her tone Phoebe wished she'd made the effort to join them. Maggie had tapped on Phoebe's door and tried to wake her, but only received a sleepy snarl in reply.

"The eggs Benedict were a little gloppy," she confessed. "Don't tell Edie. It was my fault. I was talking too much and the sauce got cold."

Phoebe looked up from her phone. "Talking about me. And Harry, I bet."

Maggie couldn't deny it. "We're concerned about you. Everyone wanted to know what happened at the police station."

"But not so worried about Harry. Do you all think he's guilty now of killing Adele? And drug dealing?" She sounded sullen, as if her friends had already disappointed her.

"We're all giving him the benefit of the doubt. There are a lot of moving parts in regard to all these crimes. Who knows how it will sort out."

Maggie's tone was firm, though that was as far as she was willing to go. Truth was, she hadn't heard anyone but Phoebe jump to Harry's defense.

Talking to Phoebe about Harry was always challenging, but this morning, Maggie knew the topic was a minefield. She remembered the article and photo Lucy had passed around at breakfast and took out her magnifying glass from the drawer under the counter.

"I'm glad that customer finally left, even though she was very pleasant. The whole time she was here, I was waiting to take a closer look at a photo Lucy found in the *Plum Harbor Times*."

Maggie sat on the love seat next to Phoebe, and picked up the photo from the coffee table. Phoebe leaned closer to see it.

"A photo? Of what?"

"There was a fundraiser for the Hoopers, years ago. To help pay for Penelope's medical bills. The article says Adele McSweeney was one of the organizers, but she's not in the photo. Edie Steiber is, though. Look—" Maggie pointed out their friend in the back row.

Just as she expected, Phoebe marveled at the young Edie. "Wow. That's Edie? She was hot off the griddle."

Maggie had to grin. "She was very pretty. No question."

"I wonder if that hairstyle will ever come back."

"I hope not," Maggie murmured.

"Look at that little boy with the round face and black hair. He's at the end of a row of kids sitting on the floor," Phoebe said. "I bet that's Martin."

"Martin? I didn't notice him before." Maggie peered over her shoulder. Sure enough, there was Martin McSweeney, in miniature. He looked shy and confused. He sat on the floor, cross-legged, hands neatly folded in his lap, as someone had instructed, no doubt. But instead of looking straight at the camera, his head was turned to the left, his attention drawn by something, or someone, just beyond the frame of the photograph.

"I think it's odd that Martin would be there without his mother, at that age," Maggie mused. "She must have been there, somewhere."

"Probably," Phoebe agreed. "Is it important?"

"I don't know. Probably doesn't prove anything one way or the other," Maggie admitted. She looked up at Phoebe again. "But you just reminded me. Lucy found out that Martin has some financial problems. Seems that his company is being sued for a ton of money. Inheriting Adele's estate right now would definitely help."

"Really? Geez, Maggie . . ." Phoebe's frustration was comical. "I sleep in one measly morning and I miss everything."

"I did try to wake you," Maggie reminded her.

Phoebe glanced at her and then back at the photo. "When he took us out to dinner his credit card was declined. The first card he used, I mean. He seemed embarrassed but I didn't think anything of it. It happens sometimes by accident."

"It does happen," Maggie agreed. Though the event seemed to fit with their theory about him.

Phoebe was holding the magnifier now. "Look who's standing near Edie, farther down the same row. Pickle Man, the prequel?"

Maggie peered through the glass and held her breath. "So it is. Thirty years younger, and fifty pounds lighter. And with hair on his head. Same mustache, though."

"Same sour puss, too," Phoebe muttered. She took a moment to scan the photo further. "I see Warren Braeburn, too." She pointed to the farmer and market manager, lanky and relaxed looking, back in the day.

"It looks like most of the local farmers and their families attended," Maggie said. "But that makes sense, considering the circumstances." Maggie set the photo aside. "Carrie stopped here this morning and we showed her the photo, too. She didn't offer any great insights. She said she hardly remembered the event."

As for her condemning opinions about Harry, Maggie thought best not to relate that part of the conversation.

Phoebe took the photo off the table. "Edie was very pretty, once upon a time. Penelope Hooper was, too," she said after a moment. "Jimmy wasn't much. He was so . . . beardy. He looked old even when he was young."

"Not your type?"

"Pul-eeze." Phoebe gave her a look.

"I think it's very easy to look at older people and never imagine that they were young once. With passions and attractions, living a full life."

"Some old people, maybe." Phoebe offered Maggie a sly smile. "I always think that stuff about you."

"Thanks . . . I think." Maggie's grin twisted to one side.

Maggie thought Phoebe was done, but she held on to the magnifying glass. "That's sort of funny," Phoebe said finally. "Penelope is wearing one of those big ugly pins. The kind Adele always wore. Was that the style back then?"

"Not really. Those broaches were more fashionable in the fifties and early sixties. Women would wear them on sweaters and coats," Maggie recalled. "Let me see."

Phoebe handed her back the photo and she checked Penelope's dress through the glass. The black-and-white photo was grainy, and the copy was hardly the highest quality. Luckily, Penelope's dress was a solid color and Maggie did spot a large broach, heart shaped, with a few stones inset. Manipulating the magnifier, she could even make out two tiny birds, one on either side. Finally, she looked up.

"It's a heart with lovebirds. Jimmy must have given it to her."

Her gaze fell on Jimmy Hooper again. She examined his expression under the glass. It had appeared, at first, that he was fondly gazing at Penelope, but now she noticed the line of his sight seemed to bypass his wife. He wasn't quite looking down at Penelope, he was looking to the left, in the same direction as Martin.

Were they both looking at Adele?

Phoebe's insistent voice cut into her thoughts. "We have to show Detective Reyes this photo. It could connect to something important."

Maggie sighed. "It might. Though I can't for the life of me understand what."

"But it might help Harry."

Maggie doubted that, but she wouldn't admit it.

She didn't doubt that the detective would call the photo interesting memorabilia but totally irrelevant. Then remind Maggie to stay in her lane, and stop wasting valuable police time.

Maggie had heard it all before. Over the years, she'd been ridiculed, scolded, warned off, and dumped upon with all kinds of flak from the local police. It hadn't stopped her yet. For Phoebe's sake, she could certainly put herself in harm's way one more time. Though she did not expect the tidbit to amount to much.

"I will call Detective Reyes, Phoebe. I'll call right now."

Phoebe stood by as Maggie dialed the detective, then listened to the call. Maggie felt her stomach flutter with nerves. She wasn't sure why. This was hardly the first time she'd contacted Detective Reyes with information that related to an investigation.

I'm just trying to be a good citizen, she reminded herself. *Not a nosybody and a snoop. We have helped her solve quite a few cases, though she'd rarely admit it.*

The call was brief, as Maggie had expected. It was hard to tell if Detective Reyes was actually interested in the photo and article, or just humoring her. She asked if someone could pick it up at the shop. She wasn't sure what time, but promised to send someone by the end of the day to get it.

"Not a problem. If I leave early, it will be in an envelope on the porch, with your name on it," Maggie told her.

Maggie was about to say goodbye and end the call, when Detective Reyes said, "I know you're a close friend of Phoebe Myers's and have an interest in seeing someone besides Harry McSweeney charged with his aunt's murder. But let this be the end to your involvement, Ms. Messina. Two people are dead. Maybe because they both saw or heard something they shouldn't have. I'd hate to see you or any of your friends in a dangerous situation. As it is, Phoebe and everyone working at the market should be on their guard. I hope she understands that."

Maggie knew Detective Reyes had a good point and wasn't just trying to scold her for being a busybody. Not this time, anyway.

"I understand, Detective. I really do. I'll remind Phoebe to be careful." They said goodbye and Maggie looked up at Phoebe.

"Well, that's that. The ball is in the detective's court now." Maggie put the phone aside. "At least she didn't brush us off. She's sending someone over to pick up the photo. That's something."

Phoebe didn't look so easily satisfied. "Hardly. The police haven't looked further than their nose for Adele's killer. Or for Jimmy's."

Maggie sighed. She could see how it appeared that way

from Phoebe's perspective. The trouble was, so far, all paths seemed to lead to Harry.

"Let's give it a day or two. The police might glean some new leads from the interviews they did at the market yesterday." Maggie fussed with a display of bamboo needles, though the shop was in perfect order since so few customers had come in lately to mess it up.

She was about to pass on Detective Reyes's warning, then stopped herself. No reason to make Phoebe more anxious than she was already. Surely she understood that everyone at the market had to be very watchful and cautious. Especially after her stall and online profile had been attacked last week.

"I think I will close early. It's just too beautiful outside to stay in here all day if there are no customers." She tried to catch Phoebe's eye. "Feel like the beach? I bet it's perfect there today."

Phoebe twisted her hair up with both hands in a bun and shook her head. "I'm going to the market. I've lost a ton of time the last two weeks. I can still catch some of the Saturday rush if I hustle."

Maggie knew that was true, though she also expected Phoebe was still tired from her ordeal at the police station and all the stress she had been through over Harry.

"If you really want to. I'll drop you off on my way home," Maggie said.

Phoebe accepted that offer, and they both got ready to leave the shop. Charles would be happy to see her home early. And Daisy, too. They'd relax at the beach today and be on the boat all day tomorrow.

While Phoebe gathered her things for the market, Maggie stuck the photo in an envelope for the detective. She decided to add a message about their observations, despite stepping out of her lane. With a line or two, she noted Adele's name in the article and her absence from the group, and also the way Martin and Jimmy were looking in the same direction, at a spot beyond the camera's sight. She also mentioned Penelope's pin and how it resembled Adele's favorite style of jewelry.

She slipped the note in and sealed the envelope.

A few moments later, Phoebe came down with her backpack and tote bags. Maggie led the way to her Subaru, though privately, she wished Phoebe wasn't so conscientious and responsible. Just for today.

The warning from Detective Reyes would make her worry about Phoebe all weekend.

"Phoebe . . . wait."

Phoebe froze in her steps, her first inclination to pretend she hadn't heard Robbie call her. But he was already running across the parking lot to catch up. There was no avoiding him.

"Hey . . ." He touched her shoulder and she turned to face him. "Didn't you see my text?"

"I must have missed it. My stall was so busy today."

"It was crazy at the truck, too. Food was flying."

If he knew she was lying, he was giving her a pass. As usual. He was really too nice to her. It got on her nerves sometimes, which was sort of witchy. But she couldn't help it. *Suzanne would understand,* she mused.

"I was going to stop at the truck, but it looked like you still had customers." Another fib, but she had thought about doing that for a second or two. All the food trucks except Mighty Taco were closed, but there were still a few people hanging out near Robbie's truck. Enough to give her an excuse for walking by.

"Oh, those kids. They're not customers. They come by for free food." Robbie shrugged. "I feel bad for them so I pack up the leftovers and give them out when I shut down."

Phoebe had noticed the scraggly group before, when

she'd come to his truck at closing time. They'd grab the
paper bags and dash into the dusk on banana bikes or
skateboards. The kind of kids who cut school or smoke
cigarettes and worse behind the football bleachers when
they're there. The kind who dare drivers to hit them when
they swoop around the road on their bikes and boards.

"That's nice of you. They look like punks to me," she
admitted.

"They're just a little lost. I was like that once, too. Until
I got into art. I can't wait till this food truck gig is over and
I find a real job again." He paused and caught her gaze. "I
know you're mad at me. I know why, too. I hate for you to
feel like that. Can we talk about it? Just for a minute?"

Phoebe felt herself flush. Robbie did have a way of reading her moods. It was flattering, she had to admit.

"I don't think there's anything to talk about. The damage is done, wouldn't you say?"

He sighed, his blue eyes begging for understanding. "I
had to tell the police the truth. I already *forgot* on purpose
the first time they asked me questions about the night
Adele died."

Phoebe tried to calm down and keep an open mind. It
was unfair of her to expect Robbie to lie to the police and
get in trouble for Harry. Something like that could cause
all sorts of problems for a person for the rest of their life.
Could she really blame him for that?

"Well, what did you say, exactly?"

"All I said was, I stopped at the house and left some
boxes on the porch. I heard voices, a man and a woman. I
never said it was Harry. I couldn't tell who it was. And I
didn't see anything." He shrugged. "I don't see how that
could get him in trouble. It's not proof of anything," he insisted.

"More trouble, you mean," Phoebe said tartly.

He looked down at her but didn't reply. His serious expression was starting to scare her. "I know you don't want to hear this, but I could have told the police a lot of other stuff about Harry. I just answered their questions yes or no, and managed to get out of there without going into details."

"Details? What sort of details?" She stared at him, feeling her stomach get all knotty. She hated that.

He looked away, as if he wasn't going to tell. Then he sighed. "Do you really want to hear this? I'm afraid you'll get upset."

Madder at him, he meant. "Tell me, Robbie. Or I'll get upset anyway."

"Okay, okay." He swallowed hard. "Let's see . . . where to start. For one thing, I could have told the police that lately, there were some really sketchy people coming around to see Harry. At weird hours, too. He'd say they were friends from the studio where he rents space, or from pickup basketball games at the park. But they didn't look like that to me. More the type that makes you worry if you left anything valuable in clear sight."

Phoebe sighed and crossed her arms over her chest. The disclosure was distressing but she tried not to show it. She was glad Robbie had not told that to police.

"Okay. Well. Maybe they were friends. That's definitely possible," she insisted.

"Absolutely. That's why I didn't say anything. It would just sound bad. Like, well, maybe drug deals, or something."

Did he really think that? She felt scared, then brushed it off, forcing herself to sound calm and normal. "Is that all?"

He sighed and looked away again. "There's something else. I never wanted to tell you this because you felt so bad about Harry after you two broke up. But I really think you should know. Seeing how you're risking a lot to help him, Phoebe."

Phoebe braced herself. "Just tell me already."

"Harry messed around with a lot of other girls while you were going out with him. It wasn't just that time you caught him."

Phoebe felt his words like a physical blow. It must have showed in her expression, she realized, from the way Robbie stared back at her.

Robbie pressed his lips together and shook his head. "I'm so sorry. I promised myself I'd never tell you. One part of me thought you should know the truth, so you could make a clean break with him. Another part knew it would really hurt. And I never, ever, *ever* want to hurt you, Phoebe. Not for anything."

Phoebe felt stunned. When she looked back at Robbie his eyes were glossy, as if he was about to cry.

Aren't I supposed to cry now, if anyone is? She stared at him, feeling her frown face coming on big-time. "Is that really true? I mean, *really*?"

His big glasses slid down his nose and he pushed them up again, his eyes wide with surprise from her question.

"Why would I make up something like that? I didn't even want to tell you." Before she could reply, he raised his hands, as if pushing away something invisible but very nasty. "Let's just leave it. There's no reason to talk about this anymore. I'm sorry I said that much."

"I am, too. But I did push you to tell me," she admitted.

He sighed and swallowed hard. She watched his Adam's apple bob in his throat. "The thing is, I want you to know that if you still believe Harry had nothing to do with all the stuff the police are accusing him of, I won't be the one to throw him to the wolves. He's one lucky guy to have you in his corner. But for your own safety, Phoebe, you should know that Harry is not the guy you think he is."

Phoebe felt light-headed, trying to process all that Robbie had just told her. Her first impulse was to shoot the messenger. At least to shout at him. But she had no energy or heart for that. It wasn't Robbie's fault. She knew that, too.

She touched her hand to her head, as a sudden headache split her brain in two, like a lightning bolt striking a tree. "Okay. Harry's not perfect. I got your point. The rest is going to take a while to process. The thing is, even if he is a liar and a cheat, and has some shady friends and all that, I still know he didn't kill Adele. Or Jimmy. And I believe him when he says he never saw those drugs before."

Robbie stared down at her with clear blue eyes, looking as if he'd just seen an avenging angel swoop down into the food court. "I won't lie to you and say I feel the same about Harry. I'm not sure what to think anymore. But if you really feel that way, after everything I just told you, I'll do what I can to help you help him. I promise. Because . . ." He paused. She wasn't sure if he was going to finish the sentence. Then he said in a rush, "Because, I might not care about Harry. But I sure care about you."

Phoebe was surprised by his reason. Then not surprised. They had to talk about this thing he had for her. But not tonight. No way. She was totally exhausted and had no idea how she was going to haul her sorry carcass all the way up Main Street.

"Well . . . he needs all the help he can get right now, that's for sure." She met his searching gaze. "I'm beat. I better get home before I crash."

"You don't have to walk with all that stuff. Let me give you a ride."

Phoebe was about to refuse, then nodded. He took her heavy bags, one in each hand, and headed back to his truck. She followed without arguing, then climbed in the passenger side and they drove off.

The sun was low and the temperature had gone down. Cool air blew through the doorway, offsetting the food smell. Robbie glanced over at her, but didn't try to start a conversation. He could sense that she didn't want to talk and that was fine with her.

He wasn't such a bad guy. She was way too hard on him. Maybe she'd never pushed a talk about just being friends because she wasn't sure that was the only sort of relationship she wanted. From time to time, she did think she could date him. He was actually cute in a nerdy sort of way. In time she could redecorate him. That wasn't the problem.

He was always there for her. Even when she wasn't particularly easy or pleasant to be around. She had to grant him that. He was as dependable as her women friends and that was saying a lot.

Unlike Harry, who would never be the dependable type, though she had never blamed him for it. Harry had usually been distracted and too busy with his own stuff to focus on her little dramas. But Robbie was totally tuned in to her. All that attention was a funny feeling. But maybe a good thing? And Robbie never found her little quirks annoying. To the contrary, he always seemed charmed.

He was definitely a healthier choice than Harry. She knew her friends thought so. If only she liked him more "that way." Wouldn't her life be a lot easier?

The things he'd said tonight about Harry were an adult portion. It would take a while to figure it out. She wasn't sure if she should share the disclosures with her friends. Though she usually shared almost everything. She hated for them to see Harry in a more negative light. But maybe Robbie was right. Maybe all this time, she'd been blinded by some fantasy, and had just seen the parts he'd wanted her to see.

Was it really true? Was Harry just not the guy she thought he was?

The truck stopped with a jolt, metal things rattling in

the back. Phoebe sat up straight, feeling as if she'd just woken up from a nap. They were parked in front of Maggie's shop and she turned to see Robbie smiling at her.

"Earth to Phoebe. I think this is your stop?" he said gently.

She laughed and grabbed her backpack.

"I'll get the other bags," Robbie said as he jumped out of the driver's side.

"That's okay, I can take them up." Phoebe grabbed her tote bags from the back of the truck before he could. But he still walked with her as far as the porch.

"Thanks for the lift."

"Any time, madam." He mocked a bow and made a flourish in the air with his hand. "Will you be at the market tomorrow?"

"Sure. I'll be there. Bright and early. Got to sell those socks. Even if the whole world is going down the toilet." She was trying for a little joke but it fell flat.

His sympathetic look touched her. She guessed that he really wanted to come up and hang out, but he was too nice to even hint at it. Not like a lot of other guys who would be pushy or wheedling, or making her feel guilty right now. *Is that a bad thing, either?* she had to ask herself.

"Okay. See you then." He smiled and stuck his hands in his front pockets, bobbing on his sneakers. "If you want a lift down or back, let me know. I'm just your Mighty Taco Uber."

That made her smile. "Good to know. Thanks."

She turned to go up the porch steps and he called to her. She turned and noticed his concerned expression.

"I was just thinking, Phoebe. Make sure you lock up good tonight. And be extra careful? Until everything is figured out?"

"Um. Okay." Phoebe paused, feeling she might laugh at

him. "You sound like Maggie now. Do you think I might be next?"

He looked surprised. "Of course not. Don't even say that. There's just so much weird stuff going on. We need to be alert. That's what the police said." He paused and took a few steps closer. "If Harry is not totally innocent," he added in a quieter tone, "he's been hanging around with some dangerous people. People who might think you could tell the police things that can get them in trouble, too."

Phoebe was about to argue, then realized what he said could be true. The police certainly thought she knew more than she did. Other people probably assumed that, too.

"Point taken," she said finally.

"Good. Because . . . well, I worry about you. You must know that."

His question rang out in the darkness. Phoebe wasn't sure how to answer. "Uh, yeah. I do."

He was standing even closer and from the look in his eye, she thought he was about to move in for a kiss.

But he suddenly stepped back and ducked his head, chickening out. Which she thought was sort of cute.

"Okay, then. Good night."

She smiled at him as she unlocked the shop door and let herself in. "Don't worry. I'll be fine. The shop has an alarm system."

"That's good to hear. Maybe I'll text you later anyway, to make sure you're all right?"

"If you really want to."

He nodded and waved and she waved back. Then she closed the door and locked it, the top and the bottom. She didn't want Robbie's warning to get to her. But it had.

She walked to the back of the shop and stepped in the storeroom to make sure the alarm was set. The red light was on and the screened read, "Armed." She'd make sure to tell Robbie if he did text.

She climbed the steps to her apartment, dumped her bags, and quickly switched all the lights on. Then she stood by the window, pulled back the curtain a bit, and peered out at the street.

Robbie's truck was gone. The sidewalks were empty but a bit farther down Main Street, the Schooner was ablaze with light. A few customers walked in and a few came out. The sight was reassuring.

Van Gogh emerged from some secret spot where he'd been sleeping. He jumped up and rubbed his nappy, warm head on her shoulder. Phoebe turned and stroked him under the chin, just where he liked it, until she heard him purr.

"Time for dinner. I know," she crooned to him. "And there are no scary people hiding out there, trying to get us. That's just plain crazy, right?"

Chapter 14

Phoebe dumped a can of cat food into Van Gogh's dish—chicken delight, his favorite—and gave him a bowl of fresh water. Then she fixed herself a dish of yogurt with strawberries, bananas, and granola on top. She liked to cook but didn't bother much for herself. Especially in the summer. Yogurt was fine for any meal, day or night. Avocado and toast was another fast favorite. Or leftover pizza, or pad thai. She didn't know why people made such a big deal about eating certain foods at certain times of the day. It was all going to the same place, as Maggie would say.

She'd been waiting for a text message from Martin with an update about Harry and automatically reached into the back pocket of her shorts for her phone, then felt surprised when it wasn't there.

She dug through her knapsack next, and then her knitting bag, finally emptying both bags out completely on her living room floor. But still couldn't find it.

She felt a pain in her chest and forced herself to take a few deep breaths. She totally hated misplacing her cell phone, it was like another body part. What an annoying thing to happen. The tote bags. It must have slipped into one of the bags that she used to cart her products back and forth from the stall. She emptied the totes out in a different pile in the living room, not caring about the mess. Then dug through the mounds of socks, hats, hair bands, and knitted bikinis, like a dog digging a hole. Still no phone.

She sat back on her heels, so annoyed and frustrated that she wanted to scream.

When did she use the phone last? She tried to remember. Right before she'd closed down for the day, she'd answered a text from Lucy. Had she checked her messages again, in Robbie's truck? She thought that she had, then stuck the phone in her pocket.

A super-dumb move, because it had fallen out of both spots before. Once, right into a toilet with disastrous results. She felt like smacking herself in the head, but it would only make matters worse.

You were distracted, she reminded herself. *It could happen to anyone. The stupid phone is probably sitting on the floor of Robbie's truck right now.*

She ran down the stairs and called Robbie from the shop phone, a landline, stationed on the front counter. After three rings, Robbie's voice mail picked up.

"Hey there, it's me. I can't find my phone. I must have dropped it in your truck. Could you check, please? I'm using the landline in Maggie's shop. I'll try you again later. Or first thing tomorrow."

She heard the beep and realized she'd left an annoyingly long message. She hoped that he heard the whole thing.

It felt so weird to be without her phone. She felt naked. Or something just like it. She stared at the cordless handset of the shop phone and decided to take it with her. Maggie certainly wouldn't mind. In fact, she would have said something like, "Clever girl, Phoebe. Very resourceful."

The black hunk of plastic was truly a primitive instrument. She might have to resort to her laptop to check her emails, or watch kitten videos on YouTube. Or shop on-line for yarn.

But it was probably just as well to cut down on screen time for one night. She felt suddenly beat. She flicked on the TV and found an old movie, which she'd always loved. One good thing to chalk up for the day.

Notorious, one of Hitchcock's best, in her humble opinion. She'd studied the movie in a film class but had watched it loads of times before that. She loved Ingrid Bergman's outfits and jewelry, especially in the party scene when she and Cary Grant find uranium in a champagne bottle. She loved how Cary Grant thinks that Ingrid is a bad apple, but falls in love with her anyway. And then he finds out he's all wrong when she's half dead from being poisoned, by Claude Reins's wicked mother, the old prune.

She settled in her favorite chair with her knitting and Van Gogh in her lap, a cup of ginger tea on the side table. Juggling the three was a challenge, but a small feat that she was good at.

The last thing she remembered was Claude Reins's horrified expression as he leaned over his mother, asleep in her sumptuous bed. "Mother, wake up . . . I've married an American spy."

Phoebe woke up and found the room pitch black. The TV was off, as well as the lamp behind her chair. She hadn't shut it. She was sure of that. Had the electricity gone out for some weird reason? It happened sometimes. She'd have to call Maggie and Charles would come and fix it for her.

She so hoped it didn't turn out to be one of those nights. Besides, instead of going to the beach, they'd gone out on their boat and were staying overnight. Maggie had sent her a text. Phoebe didn't want to bother them over a blown circuit breaker.

She felt Van Gogh's heavy, warm weight on her legs, and gently nudged him. His tail swept under her nose and almost made her sneeze.

"Come on, big guy. I need to figure this out." She was about to gently push his bottom when they both heard the sound of breaking glass. The cat leaped to the floor with a throaty snarl.

Phoebe froze in place. She strained to hear more. Was that squeak the side door opening? The hinge needed oil. Her heart was pounding so fast she could hear it throbbing in her ears.

She jumped off the chair and dashed to the kitchen table, feeling around for the big phone handset. She finally found it but knocked it to the floor, then crawled around under the table, grabbing for it in the dark. She could have sworn she heard heavy steps crunching through glass. Coming closer to the staircase. She pressed her hand over her mouth to keep from screaming.

Someone had broken into the shop. How could that happen? Why didn't the alarm system go off? She was sure it was set.

She found the phone and peered down at the numbers, luckily iridescent in the dark. She hit 9-1-1 and held it to her ear, unable to breath. The police would come in time. She'd hide somewhere. It would be okay. *Just breathe, Phoebe. Just breathe.*

No dial tone. She stared at the phone and shook it and pressed all the buttons, till she thought she might break it.

It was silent. Dead. Then she realized, the lines had been cut. The electricity and the phone line, too. That's why the alarm hadn't gone off.

Now what? She cowered under the table, confused about where to hide. Her apartment was the size of a postage stamp. With a loft ceiling. Van Gogh brushed by in the dark and she nearly jumped out of her skin. She grabbed the cat and ran to the bathroom, then locked herself in.

The lock was so flimsy. Not much of a challenge if someone wanted to break through it. She peeked out the window. She was far too high to climb out. She'd slide down the roof and break her neck.

She pulled open the cupboard and tried to see what was on the shelves. There was a little light from a streetlamp and she could make out a few shapes. She searched quickly for something heavy, something she could use to defend herself. There wasn't much—an eyelash curler? A pair of manicure scissors with round safety tips? A bottle of face cream and one of shampoo?

On the bottom shelf she spotted a bottle of chemical-free cleaning spray, lemon scented. *Someone might even like getting hit with this stuff,* Phoebe fretted. But for lack of anything better, she grabbed it.

Aim for the eyes, she ordered herself.

She climbed into the tub and pulled the shower curtain—which was printed with cats doing yoga—closed. Then huddled in the far corner of the tub, near the faucets. She was breathing so heavily she was sure the intruder could hear her all the way downstairs.

She stood very still and listened. Silence. She waited but still no sound.

Had the intruder left? Could she be so lucky? Van Gogh stared up, yellow eyes glowing in the dark.

Then she heard it—someone turning the handle on her apartment door. Luckily, she'd locked it. Truth was, she didn't always. The knob rattled a few times and then she heard the loud sound of someone throwing their weight at the door, to try to force it open.

She trembled and covered her mouth to seal in a scream.

There was silence again and she silently prayed the intruder had given up. Could that be possible?

Van Gogh arched his back and growled deep in the back of his throat, and then she heard it, too. A metallic, scratchy sound on the door to her apartment.

Someone was using a tool to pick the lock.

It wouldn't take long now. She was shaking all over. Even her teeth were chattering. She couldn't control it but forced herself to hold on. She crouched down into the tub, wishing she could suddenly shrink so small she could slip down the drain, like a bug. She hugged the bottle of cleaning spray to her chest, knowing it was useless.

The scratching stopped. She braced herself, waiting to hear the door creak open.

Instead, she heard heavy footsteps pounding up the staircase. A man's voice, shouting, "Get out of here! Get out! You . . . scum . . ."

Scuffling. Lots of footsteps, up and down. Bodies banging on the stairwell walls. More shouts, down in the shop now. Moving farther away.

It was quiet for a moment, then someone ran back up the steps and called her name. "Phoebe? Are you in here?"

It was Robbie. Robbie was here. She could hardly believe it.

She scrambled out of the tub and called to him. "Robbie? I'm hiding in the bathroom!"

She unlocked the door and ran out. He had the light from a cell phone turned on. The thin strong beam pointed straight at her.

"Thank God you're okay. You're not hurt, are you? No one got in here, did they? Please, tell me you're all right, Phoebe."

He ran across the room and took hold of her shoulders. Phoebe felt her legs go out from under her, but he held her up and helped her to a chair. Then he knelt down beside her and stared up.

She pressed her hand to her forehead. "What just happened? Did someone break in?"

He nodded solemnly. "They broke the glass on the side door and walked right in the shop. I thought you said Maggie has an alarm system."

"She does. It didn't go off. The phone and the electric lines must have been cut. And I dropped my phone in your trunk and all I had was this dumb Fred Flintstone landline and I couldn't even get a dial tone. I was terrified. I was going to defend myself with eco-friendly spray cleaner." She still held the bottle and waved it in the air.

He took it from her hand. "Don't wave a loaded bottle of that stuff around. It's dangerous."

She laughed for a moment, then felt her face collapse into a super-ugly cry. "Robbie . . . I was so scared. I thought someone was going to kill me." She gripped his shoulder with one hand, as her other hand covered her mouth.

His expression was grave. "Let's not even think about it."

She stared down at him. "What made you come back?"

He reached in his pocket and pulled out her phone, the purple case glistening in the shadowy light. "I got your message and I found the phone under the passenger seat. I thought you'd want to have it. Even if it was late."

Maybe he'd thought if he returned the phone at this late hour, her defenses would be down and something romantic would happen? He was still a guy. She couldn't blame him for that. No matter what his motivation really was, he'd still saved her. She could never thank him enough.

She swallowed hard, trying to get her bearings. "Thank you. Thank you so much. Thank goodness you decided to bring it back tonight. You totally rescued me. And Van Gogh."

The cat jumped on the kitchen table, attracted by the light. He playfully batted at the moving beam with his big paws.

Robbie laughed and lightly stroked Van Gogh's head. A lot of guys were good with dogs, but not too many were gentle enough to win over a cat, especially one like her cat. That had always been a test for Phoebe when she began dating someone new.

Van Gogh lay on the table, his paws folded under his chest, in his Buddha pose. He looked content to have Robbie pet him all night.

"He looks fine. He probably didn't even know what was happening." Robbie turned to her.

"Probably not. When I was crawling on the kitchen floor looking for this stupid shop phone, he thought it was a game."

Phoebe picked her own phone up, but wasn't sure whom to call.

"Maggie and Charles are on their boat. If I call, they'll insist on coming back in the middle of the night. But there's nothing they can do."

"True. Maybe you should call one of your friends? Lucy or Dana?"

Phoebe thought about it, then shook her head. "I guess we should just call the police. I mean, we have to make a report. Maggie would want me to do that right away."

Robbie nodded. "Definitely. While the details are still fresh in your mind and in mine." He sighed. "I wish there was some way to get the lights back on, but I guess whoever broke in cut the lines leading to the house so the alarm wouldn't sound."

"Oh, right. That must be it." Phoebe dialed 9-1-1 and spoke to the operator, reporting that she lived above a shop on Main Street and someone had just broken in. She answered the dispatcher's questions about the address, her name, and if she was safe. The dispatcher left the call for a moment, then said a squad car was on the way and would be there in three minutes.

"Do you want me to stay on the call with you, miss, until they arrive?"

"That's okay. My friend is here. He scared away who-ever broke in," she added. She glanced at Robbie and he smiled shyly, then fiddled with his eyeglasses. She thought he might be blushing. It was hard to tell in the dark.

While they waited for the police, Phoebe dug out a few flashlights from the storeroom, and Robbie brought in a big emergency light that he kept in the back of his truck. Phoebe thought it looked like a robot, a silver box with two large halogen lamps on top that looked like ears. The knitting shop looked like a nighttime construction site, but it was better than nothing.

Had someone crept into the shop to kill her? The ques-tion was chilling, but she couldn't shake it off. Maybe Robbie had been right. Someone wasn't happy that she was trying to prove Harry was innocent. Or thought she knew more than she did . . . about something?

She tapped her fingertips to her mouth, a little tic she had when she was thinking. She didn't even realize until she caught Robbie staring at her.

"Don't be nervous. I don't think the police officers will take long, but we need to tell them everything. This must be connected somehow to . . ." She thought he was about to say the drugs in Harry's stall, but he caught himself. "Everything that's going on at the market."

"I was thinking the same thing." Phoebe checked the

time on her phone. It was after one o'clock in the morning, but she felt wide awake, as if it was the middle of the afternoon.

"Later, when the police are done, I'll clean up the glass and patch the side door somehow. With cardboard and tape, I guess. But I don't think you should be alone here. I really think you should call someone, even though it's late. I'll drive you wherever you need to go."

Phoebe didn't want to be alone. But she didn't want to wake her friends up in the middle of the night. And terrify them once they heard why she was calling.

"That's okay. I'll be fine. I'll sleep down here, by Mr. Construction Light." She patted the big light as if it was a new friend.

Robbie answered with a goofy grin. "You'll sleep upstairs, in your bed. I'll sleep here in the shop with Mr. Construction Light."

"First you save my life. Then you offer to cripple yourself on Maggie's lumpy antique sofa? You are brave."

She was teasing but not totally.

"No big deal. Let's see how it goes."

She nodded in agreement. Van Gogh had followed them down to the shop and jumped up in her lap again. She automatically stroked his fur, her thoughts racing. She wouldn't get a wink of sleep. But it was good to know she would not be here alone. Even if her champion and bodyguard had turned out to be Robbie. *I'll never think of him as wimpy or nerdy again.*

Well, maybe once in a while, she amended, as she watched him fiddle with his glasses.

But not in a bad way. Not like I used to.

She glanced over at him. He sat on the wing chair, and ran a hand through his spiky hair, then grinned.

"We sure had a weird night, didn't we?"

She smiled, the shock settling in. "Totally weird. It was out there."

Phoebe felt like the ground between them had shifted in some significant way. They'd been through an adventure together, definitely. But she didn't want to think too much about what that might mean, or how it might change things between them. She had enough to worry about tonight.

Chapter 15

"You must have been terrified! I don't even want to imagine it. You poor thing. Why didn't you call me?" Maggie didn't mean to scold, but she was so upset. She didn't care a whit about the shop. From the moment the police had called, she'd been worried sick about Phoebe.

"You were out on the boat. What could you do? I didn't want to freak you out," Phoebe tried to explain.

"The police had no such qualms," Maggie said.

"It's protocol. You're the property owner," Charles said. It was not the first time he'd reminded her of the procedures the police followed after a break-in was reported. The officer in charge of the report had contacted Maggie by phone, after speaking to Phoebe, sometime after two in the morning. Of course, she and Charles could not fall back to sleep after that conversation. They'd hoisted anchor and motored home from Newburyport Harbor, where they were docked for the night.

They arrived at the shop just before six in the morning. Hardly Phoebe's favorite wake-up hour, Maggie knew, though she did amble downstairs in her pajamas when she heard Maggie call up to her, announcing their arrival.

Robbie was fast asleep on the floor, with Van Gogh

perched on his back. Standing guard, Maggie thought. The young man rolled over and blinked as the cat jumped down to the Persian-patterned rug.

"Oh. Hey. You guys are back. Great." He sat up and fumbled for his eyeglasses, which he'd left on the coffee table. Then he offered a sleepy wave as he sat up and pushed aside a pile of covers.

"Hello, Robbie." Maggie's greeting dripped with gratitude. "Thank you so much for staying here with Phoebe last night. I was worried sick when I heard what happened."

Robbie shrugged and yawned. "I wasn't going to leave her alone and she didn't want to bother any of her friends."

"I wish she'd bothered me." Maggie's tone was stern as she turned to glance at Phoebe. "If anything ever happens like this again, I want you to promise me . . ."

Phoebe raised her hands in surrender. "I will. I do. I promise," she rattled off. "Nothing happened. I'm totally fine."

Maggie did not agree. Phoebe had come perilously close to the very opposite of "totally fine." But there was no sense debating that point now.

"Let's have some coffee," Charles suggested. Recalling the electricity was off, they'd stopped at the bakery and picked up several cups of coffee and some soft cinnamon and raisin rolls. "These are still warm." He waved a white paper bag that emitted the tantalizing fragrance of fresh bread.

"Sounds good to me." Maggie watched Phoebe follow the scent like a tracking hound.

"I'm totally down with that. Then I better go." Robbie had stood up, and neatly folded the afghan. His baggy clothes did not look much different from usual, she noted, despite sleeping in them.

A short time later Phoebe and Robbie had related the entire frightening tale. Charles asked them a lot of questions, sounding very much like his former detective self. And wearing his detective's expression, Maggie noticed. The serious, focused look he'd worn the first time he'd walked into the shop, she recalled, that brought his handsome features into sharp focus—deep-set eyes, strong jaw, wide mouth, longish nose. She thought he was handsome, anyway.

Robbie showed him the side door, where the intruder had broken in. The shattered pane of glass was patched with cardboard and tape.

"I guess you can have that fixed easily. The lock seems fine. The guy didn't even bother forcing it."

Charles twisted the knob a few times to test Robbie's diagnosis. "It is working, but I think we should add a dead bolt here. I don't know why we don't have one." He looked back at Robbie. "So, you saw the person who broke in?"

Robbie nodded solemnly and swallowed hard. "Up on the stairs, near the door." He pointed to the narrow staircase that led to Phoebe's apartment. "It all happened so fast. I, like, grabbed the back of the guy's sweatshirt and sort of yanked him down the stairs? I didn't even know what I was doing," he admitted. "I just knew I couldn't let that guy get to Phoebe."

Robbie's cheeks grew flushed remembering, his breath a little short, as well. It had been a very frightening event for both of them.

"You say, 'guy.' You're sure it was a man?" Charles asked.

Robbie paused, considering the question. Then nodded. "It was a man. I'm practically positive, from his build. And he was pretty strong. A little bigger than me. He had on a sweatshirt, a dark color, maybe black? And a woolen ski mask over his face. That was creepy."

Charles's eyes narrowed, his thick brows drawing together. Maggie recalled that look, when he was focused on solving a problem. Finishing the daily crossword mostly, these days.

"Did the person say anything? Anything at all? Did he cry out when you grabbed him?"

Robbie shook his head. "Not too much. Just a lot of grunting when we were fighting." He glanced at Maggie and Phoebe. "We struggled on the steps a little and I finally managed a knee into his groin. He did cry out then and mumbled some really foul stuff. I won't repeat it in front of the ladies. Thinking back, it was almost like he didn't want me to recognize his voice?" Robbie shook his head again, still a bit in shock by the experience. "I got him off-balance and pushed him down a few steps. He sort of stumbled to the bottom and I guess I got lucky. He gave up, and ran out the side door."

Robbie swallowed hard and turned to Phoebe. "I didn't chase him. I was so worried about Phoebe. I just wanted to see if she was okay."

Charles nodded. "You did the right thing. You were very brave."

"He was brave. A real superhero," Maggie agreed. She suddenly recalled the conversation with her friends about who would make a better superhero, Robbie or Harry. Harry might look better in the outfit, but Robbie had certainly proven he deserved the title. "I wish there was something more we could do to thank you, Robbie."

Robbie looked embarrassed. He waved his hand. "No way." He glanced at Phoebe. "As long as Phoebe is okay, that's enough for me. I'm so glad now that I decided to bring her phone back last night, and didn't wait until this morning."

"Let's not even go there," Maggie said quickly. "I'm sure this has something to do with the market."

"I think so, too." Robbie glanced at Phoebe. "I've been watching my back and just last night, I told Phoebe to be careful."

"You did. And I made sure that everything was locked and the alarm system was on." Phoebe looked at him and sighed.

"There was nothing more you could do, Phoebe. This is certainly not your fault." Charles sat back in his chair. He was far more circumspect and slower to voice assumptions. But even he had to agree there must be some connection, Maggie reasoned.

"I'd be interested to hear what Reyes thinks," Charles added. "She's smart and she knows the whole picture. Things we don't know. Not even you, my dear."

Maggie stared back at him. "Me? I'm totally flummoxed. But since my property was involved, maybe she'll be more forthcoming than usual if I ask her a few questions."

Charles grinned and sipped his coffee. "Doubt it, but I know that won't stop you from trying."

Maggie didn't reply. Robbie stood up, preparing to go. He cleared his place of the empty cup and paper napkins. He'd been taught good manners, unlike a lot of other young people, Maggie noticed.

"I'd better catch a shower and get ready for work. Thanks for breakfast," he said.

"Don't mention it. Have a good day, if you can," Maggie called after him.

Phoebe walked him to the door, and Maggie turned to Charles, speaking in a hushed tone. "I wonder if any of us will have a good day. Or a restful night, for that matter, until the police find out who killed Adele and Jimmy."

*   *   *

News of the break-in at Maggie's shop spread fast among Phoebe's nearest and dearest. By eight o'clock Lucy and Suzanne had arrived to lavish their darling younger friend with concern and sympathy, and hear the details of her ordeal. Dana was running late, but texted to say she'd be there very soon, and hoped they could wait for her.

Maggie wondered what that request was about, but when she replied with a question mark, Dana didn't answer.

The electricity was still off and it was far too stuffy in the shop without the air-conditioning, so they sat out on the porch. Phoebe had showered and was wearing a sundress and sandals. She'd mentioned something about visiting Harry in jail today with Martin.

Maggie sincerely hoped that outing didn't come about. At the very least, she hoped Phoebe didn't mention it in front of Suzanne. The last thing she wanted to hear this morning was another rant about *Prison Wives*.

"Robbie thinks someone wants to scare me, because I'm trying to prove Harry is innocent," Phoebe tossed out. "Someone who's really guilty and thinks I know more than I do," she added.

Maggie knew that wasn't exactly what Robbie thought but Phoebe wanted to think that was the reason. But the intruder could have been after her for a variety of reasons. Still, she hesitated to argue about it.

"This is just another bizarre piece in a mishmash of mayhem," Suzanne announced. "All we know for sure is that lanky, gawky Robbie is a prince in disguise. I hope you noticed, Phoebe?"

Phoebe looked self-conscious. She bit her lower lip to keep from smiling. "I don't know about the prince part, but he did run in the shop to save me. He could have just called the police when he realized someone had broken in."

Before Suzanne could use the opening to give Robbie more rave reviews, Phoebe said, "There's Dana. Finally. Why did she want us to wait for her? I have to go soon."

"I have no idea. You can ask yourself," Maggie said as she watched Dana stroll up the brick walk with a bounce in her step. Wearing a beige linen shift with a slim leather belt and sandals, she looked cool, comfortable, and professional, dressed for office hours.

Phoebe was the first she greeted. "Thank heaven you're all right." She gave Phoebe a tight hug. "That was some scare. How do you feel now?"

Phoebe shrugged, reluctant to be in the center of attention again. "I'm good. I'll just sleep with the light on for a few nights . . . and maybe the TV. Maggie is putting bigger locks on all the doors. I'll be fine."

"The alarm system is going to be updated, too, ASAP," Maggie assured her. "I feel terrible about this."

"Maggie, you're the last person I'd blame for what happened last night," Phoebe said.

Maggie knew that but she couldn't help feeling some responsibility. "I've never worried much about the shop's security in this town. But with all that's going on lately, I feel as if no one is safe. Especially anyone who works at the market."

"Understandably." Dana took a seat next to Phoebe. "But maybe when I tell you what I just heard from Jack, you'll feel a bit more at ease."

Suzanne's brown eyes grew wide. "Spill it, Dana. I knew you would bring us something juicy."

"You won't be disappointed, either. This is good." She took a breath and sat back. "The police have taken Carrie Hooper in for questioning. She was packed and ready to leave town this morning."

Suzanne sat back, looking shocked. "What prompted

that turnaround? I thought they'd eliminated her from the suspects list, right off the bat."

"They're not questioning her in regard to her father's murder," Dana explained. "It's about Adele. She told the police that on the night Adele was murdered, she'd been on a long video chat with her brother, sorting out their father's business affairs."

"That's what she told us, too," Lucy said, "when Maggie and I visited to pick up some boxes of yarn she wanted to donate. She didn't specifically mention the night of Adele's murder, but did say she was cleaning all day and conferencing via computer with her brother every night since she arrived. Right, Maggie?"

Maggie nodded. "I remember. I didn't think much of it at the time. Seemed she was quietly complaining about all she had to do after her father died."

"They were videoconferencing every night. That part wasn't a lie," Dana said. "But on the night Adele died, her story fell apart. When the tech forensics expert took a close look at the transmission of their call, she found a window of dead air time. The computers were connected but there was no activity or communication between them for at least an hour or more, corresponding to the time frame of Adele's murder. Police in Tucson questioned her brother. Without him knowing why they were questioning him, I might add. It didn't take long before Carrie's alibi unraveled."

"You mean the computer was on, but nobody was home?" Suzanne asked.

Dana nodded. "Exactly. Carrie was gone from Hooper Farm just long enough to visit Adele, and end her life."

"That gives her the opportunity," Lucy said. "But what was her motive?"

Before Dana could answer, Maggie said, "Adele and Jimmy were having an affair. At least, at one time." She thought of the photo from the fundraiser and felt sure now. "Remember the photo? Martin was staring somewhere off camera. When I thought about it, he had the look on his face that a child only has when they are separated from their mother and looking to her for reassurance." She paused while her friends considered her theory.

"When I looked at the photo closer with my magnifier," she added, "Jimmy was gazing in the same direction. With a different sort of warmth and affection in his expression. Both Martin and Jimmy were looking at Adele."

"Brilliant," Lucy said. "I knew that photo would yield some important information. In the hands of the right person."

"It is brilliant. If it's true," Suzanne said. "Did Carrie confirm this love triangle, Dana?"

"Her brother, Brad, did. Carrie told him that she'd found letters in her father's desk from Adele. Her brother said she'd been very upset. He was, too. As children, they hadn't known a thing. Adele and Jimmy were good at keeping their secret."

"If Edie Steiber didn't even figure it out, they were masterful," Maggie agreed. "When Carrie realized how Adele and her father had betrayed her family, she must have paid Adele a visit. Maybe she didn't even intend to kill her."

"But she did," Lucy concluded. "And was very happy to see Harry being accused of the deed. Still, there are no witnesses, and we haven't heard of any definitive evidence at the crime scene, like fingerprints. Or else, the police would have to eliminate Harry."

"And I bet Adele's love letters were the last blast for the old Hooper barbecue," Maggie suddenly realized. "Too bad I didn't save any ashes from my clothes. There may have been some evidence there."

"So?" Suzanne turned to Dana. "How can they charge her? Did she tell her brother she was going to visit Adele?"

"Carrie had some harsh words for Adele, but told her brother that she never wanted to see her again." Dana turned to Lucy. "The photo you found was the key. There was something in it even we didn't see. Well, we saw it," she corrected. "But we didn't understand its significance."

"What was it? Do you know?" Lucy asked.

"The broach Penelope was wearing," Dana told them.

"Phoebe noticed that when we looked at the photo with a magnifying glass. She noticed that Jimmy's wife was wearing a broach that looked just like the kind Adele always wore. I mentioned it to Detective Reyes in a note when I passed her the photo."

"What about the broach? I still don't get it," Suzanne cut in.

"Remember that odd detail about Adele's body that the police were keeping secret? We suspected it was a message from the killer of some kind? It was not disclosed in news reports, or known beyond the investigation team. The thing is, Adele's body was found with an ornate pin stuck directly into her heart. The police weren't sure what to make of it. She was known to wear the same type of jewelry, though the coroner did notice that the angle the pin entered her flesh was unlikely to occur during a tumble down the cellar steps. Still, that scenario wasn't impossible. So, they really weren't sure if her killer had added that touch, or not. But the pin that was stabbed into Adele is identical to the one Penelope is wearing in the old photo, taken at the fundraiser."

"Are they sure?" Maggie asked. "I mean, what if Jimmy had given Adele the pin after his wife's death?"

"What a guy!" Suzanne railed. "He gives his side dish his dead wife's jewelry? Aside from being super tacky, that's truly twisted."

"It would have been all that and more," Dana agreed.

"But Jimmy didn't give Adele the pin. A recent inventory of Jimmy's safe-deposit box includes the pin. Unlike most of Adele's jewelry, it was made of fourteen-karat gold and precious stones. The police are fairly certain Carrie found it when she closed her father's bank accounts."

"What did Carrie tell the police? Did she admit to killing Adele?" Phoebe asked.

She had not said a word so far, and Maggie could only guess what she was thinking. If Carrie killed Adele, Harry was in the clear. For this accusation anyway.

Dana met Phoebe's dark gaze with a look of sympathy. "She hasn't admitted it yet, honey. Her brother's information was helpful, but without witnesses, or physical evidence to place her at Adele's house, it's a challenge to charge her with the murder."

"There must be some other way they can place her at the scene." Maggie's mind was churning. "But if she did visit Adele with the intention of ending her life, I'm sure she was careful not to leave any fingerprints or DNA."

"She is smart. Maybe too smart to get caught," Dana agreed, sounding downhearted.

"Seems pretty simple to me. Anyone who sets a toe in that house was instantly covered with cat hair. You couldn't avoid it. It rolls around like sagebrush. It was in the air, like . . . like weird, fuzzy clouds," Phoebe insisted. "That's why Harry couldn't have killed his aunt. He would have needed to go in with diving gear."

Maggie had heard that defense of Harry before, though she doubted it would hold up in court. But now it seemed as if it was true. Harry had not killed his aunt. Phoebe was the only one who had remained steadfast, never doubting his innocence.

"That is a good point, Phoebe," Maggie said. "I'll mention it to Detective Reyes if she calls me back. Though I'm sure they'll search Carrie's car and Jimmy's house now, as well. Of course, the DNA from the cat hair follicles will need to be traced back to Adele's cats. But they're safe and well cared for at the cat rescue center. That step shouldn't be a problem."

Phoebe jumped up from her seat. "I'm going to call Martin. He probably doesn't know any of this. If the police think Carrie killed Adele, maybe the judge will let Harry out on bail."

"His lawyer can definitely appeal based on this turn of events," Dana agreed. "It's worth a try."

Phoebe needed no more encouragement than that to grab her cell phone and disappear into the shop.

"He still has the drug charge hanging over his head, and is a person of interest in Jimmy's murder," Maggie said quietly.

"Well, one alleged crime down, two to go. At least there's some progress," Lucy murmured.

"Some," Maggie reluctantly agreed.

Dana's phone alarm went off. She quickly shut it and grabbed her purse. "I have to get back to the office, but I'm glad I had a chance to give Phoebe this news in person. Even though the police still need to dig up enough evidence to charge Carrie."

"We can't break out the champagne yet," Maggie replied. "I hope Phoebe understands that, too."

"Let's say the police do *pin* Adele's death on Carrie. Pun intended," Lucy countered. "Even if Adele's murder has no connection to the market, I still think that Jimmy's murder does."

"I agree. But how?" Maggie still had no clear idea of what that connection might be.

Chapter 16

The electric power and the telephone line running into the shop were restored by midday and a locksmith had come and gone as well. Maggie had already called the alarm company for a quote on an updated system that couldn't be knocked out so easily. She'd fallen so far behind in technology and social media know-how; she didn't even try to keep up lately. But this issue was important, more than she'd realized.

If only there had been a video surveillance camera hooked up outside, or some other gadget that could have helped the police identify the intruder. Had it been someone known to her, or to Phoebe? Robbie had mentioned that he felt the intruder had not wanted to speak aloud, for fear of his voice being recognized. But that was just a feeling Robbie got about the encounter, afterward. And it had all happened so fast.

Who would have reason to hurt Phoebe, or at least, scare the living daylights out of her? Had she unwittingly witnessed something going on at the market? Some sight that put her in grave danger?

Robbie was possibly right. If Harry was involved with drugs—though Phoebe would not believe that about him, either—that meant he was involved with people who would go to any lengths to avoid exposure. They possibly thought Phoebe had more knowledge about Harry, his activities and sources, than she really did.

That's what truly scared her. By the end of the day, Maggie had persuaded Phoebe to come to her house for dinner and stay the night. And later, to stay at her house until the new alarm system was installed.

"Maggie, please. You can't adopt me just because someone broke into the shop. For one thing, I'm too old for that move."

Maggie laughed. "Age has nothing to do with the legality of adoption. I know you love your comfortable little nest, but I'd feel a lot better if you'd stay over with us a few days. Just until the new alarm is installed. I'm getting one with all the bells and whistles. This place is going to be like Fort Knox."

"Guarding a lot of yarn and knitting needles," Phoebe reminded her. "Can I bring Van Gogh? He gets along with dogs fine."

Lucy's dogs went berserk if they even spotted the cat in the display window. She didn't know how her little dog, Daisy, would react to a cat. But it seemed she was soon going to find out. If she wanted Phoebe safe and sound at her house for a few days, Van Gogh was a deal breaker.

"Absolutely," Maggie said. "Daisy needs to socialize with cats, too." The thought had just come to her. She hoped Charles would agree, though she wasn't going to check with him beforehand.

Maggie felt so much better having Phoebe stay with them and knew that she'd be sorry to see her go on Wednesday, when the new alarm system would be installed. Phoebe was the perfect houseguest and delightful company. Charles enjoyed having her over, too.

Daisy and Van Gogh were a different story. The little

dog was endlessly curious about the cat, and clearly wanted to play. Van Gogh was not amused. Every time Daisy tried to make friends, Van Gogh would yowl and leap to higher ground, or dash under the sofa. Daisy would wait patiently for him to emerge and got swatted on the nose once or twice. She was such a good-natured pup; she wouldn't give up.

On Wednesday morning when Maggie and Phoebe arrived at the shop, they found Dana on the porch checking her cell phone. Maggie had texted her friends the night before and asked if they could stop by the shop first thing, but Dana was even earlier than usual.

She offered a cheerful wave as they met at the top of the steps. "I have some news. I wanted to tell Phoebe first. Carrie Hooper was charged last night with Adele's murder. You were right, Phoebe. In addition to the pin, they found strands of hair in Carrie's car and on clothing, which were matched to some of Adele's cats and place Carrie at the scene. Carrie hasn't said much yet, but Detective Reyes thinks she'll give a full confession soon. Jack heard that Carrie's feelings for Adele are so vehement, she may have grounds for temporary insanity."

"Wow, that's big." Phoebe stood with her mouth hanging open a moment, before a wide smile lit her face.

"That *is* big. It was nice of you to tell Phoebe first," Maggie added. "Do they have any more insight into Jimmy Hooper's death?"

"If they do, it's not on the grapevine. Jack hasn't heard a thing about that investigation for days."

"Well, I have some news," Maggie said, feeling suddenly shy. "But I want to wait for Suzanne and Lucy."

Dana's brows jumped up, her eyes alight with curiosity. "No inside scoops for early birds?"

Maggie laughed. "Sorry, not this time."

Maggie made coffee and brought out a dish of carrot muffins that one of her customers had brought to a Tuesday afternoon class. She also had a bowl of peaches that she'd been saving in the storeroom to make a pie. But she'd have no time the next few days and decided to set them out, too. A healthy choice, as Dana would say.

Lucy and Suzanne soon appeared, both eager to know why they'd been summoned.

"What's the rumpus?" Suzanne dropped into a wicker chair and helped herself to coffee. "Hmm, nice spread for a Wednesday morning. Are we celebrating something?"

"Carrie Hooper was officially charged with Adele's murder," Phoebe announced. "I'm celebrating that."

Lucy and Suzanne were both suddenly alert. "Wow, that's news," Lucy said. "But I'm not surprised. She was the sort of person who had a patina of normalness. I got the feeling that if you scratched the surface a bit, she was very tightly wound."

"I got the same vibe, come to think," Maggie agreed. "The day we showed her the photo of the fundraiser, she nearly blew. It must have been hard for her not to admit she'd taken revenge on the woman who had invaded their family."

Dana nodded in agreement. "When a parent betrays a spouse, it's very painful for the children. Carrie was far too young to understand the factors that created the situation. Penelope was so sick and Jimmy must have felt overwhelmed and in need of support. By all accounts, Adele's husband was cold and abusive. It's not surprising the two found comfort in each other."

"I can see that, too," Maggie agreed. "I'm not condoning it, but I don't want to judge anyone, either. Obviously, the realization about the affair was very painful for Carrie. She had a far different perspective on the situation."

"Anyone would freak out in her position," Suzanne

said, "if you learned that your father was playing around with a neighbor while your mom was sick. And right under everyone's nose." Suzanne shook her head. "But she didn't have to kill poor old Adele. The whole thing is very sad. I feel bad for Carrie, too."

"I think we all do. Even Phoebe?" Lucy glanced at their young friend, who had the most at stake in the situation. "But that's not why you asked us to come here, Maggie. What's up?"

Maggie had a flicker of nerves, considering the news she was about to share, though she knew it was very silly to feel that way.

"Charles and I have finally set a wedding date. And agreed on how we want to celebrate."

She braced herself but not soon enough. Her friends bounced in the wicker seats with glee, making her fear the furniture legs would come loose. Then they all jumped up at once and pounced on her, with hugs and kisses and excited squeals worthy of an entire cheerleading squad.

When it was all over, she took a deep breath and straightened her clothes. "So glad you approve."

"When is it, where is it, what's the dress code?" Suzanne asked eagerly.

"So far, I can only answer two of your questions." Maggie named the Sunday afternoon of the first week of October as their ideal date, though they were willing to be flexible.

"We haven't figured out the location yet, but we're thinking of a medium-sized gathering, around fifty or so? We're looking for a restaurant in the area that can accommodate us. As for the dress code, I'd say put on your gladdest rags, Suzanne. This is a special day."

"Is it ever. I'm so excited. I can't wait." Dana leaned over and squeezed her hand. "But you must let us help. Anything at all. Don't be shy."

"It's barely six weeks from now," Lucy calculated. "Not much time at all to prepare."

"Or diet," Suzanne declared. "As of this minute, I'm officially starting mine." She returned a muffin to the platter, and picked out a peach instead. "I'll be busy planning a spectacular bachelorette party. But I'll help with the wedding, too."

Maggie cringed. "Back to that again? Do we have to use that word? Can't we call it a girls' night, or some such?"

"You call it whatever you like. I'm sticking with bachelorette. It's so darn cute." Suzanne shot her a saucy grin. "Got to run. Time to make the donuts. Sugar-free." She was about to toss the peach in her tote, then put it back in the bowl. "No offense, but this one looks a little wormy. Maybe you should toss it."

With her big sunglasses in place, Suzanne bounced off the porch and into her SUV. Dana left soon after. By the time Phoebe emerged from the shop after calling Martin, only Maggie and Lucy were left.

Maggie noticed right away that Phoebe looked glum. "Did you speak to Harry's cousin?"

She sighed and flopped in a chair. "He said Harry's lawyer is pushing for a new hearing, but even with Carrie charged for Adele's murder, he doesn't think the judge will let Harry out on bail. It's not just the drug charge. He's still a person of interest in Jimmy's investigation."

Maggie had expected that to be the answer. She glanced at Lucy, who mirrored her concern.

"Jimmy and the drugs in Harry's clay . . . it all goes back to the stupid market." Phoebe was upset, her voice fraught with frustration. "I wish somebody knew what was going on there. Detective Reyes doesn't seem to have a clue."

Maggie blinked, Phoebe's outburst jolting something in her brain. She knew it was only an expression and Phoebe hadn't meant the words literally, but "doesn't have a clue" reminded her of the only possible clue they'd come across about Jimmy.

"What about the list we found in Jimmy's hat? I wonder if Carrie ever passed it to Reyes," Maggie mused.

Phoebe sat curled in the wicker rocker, her chin in her hand, looking like a grumpy fairy. "I wish we had that stupid list. Maybe we could figure something out with it that the police didn't notice yet. I saw the broach on Penelope, didn't I?"

"A great catch. No question," Maggie replied. Though she did think it had been a lucky catch, as well. What were the odds that Phoebe, or any of them for that matter, could spot something on that list they hadn't seen before? Something significant?

She reached into her knitting bag and found her phone. "It just so happens I took a picture of the list before I passed it along."

"What made you do that?" Lucy sounded surprised.

"I don't remember why, exactly. It seemed a good idea at the time."

"Maggie . . . I love you." Phoebe jumped up and kissed Maggie on the head, then grabbed her phone and checked the photo. "I'm going to write this out on a big pad, so we can brainstorm."

Maggie wasn't sure how productive that would be, but it was good to see Phoebe optimistic again. She slipped into the shop for a moment and returned with a yellow legal pad and three sharp pencils.

"Here's the list." Maggie handed Phoebe the cell phone. "You read it aloud and I'll write it down."

"Five pounds peaches," Phoebe began. "Six pounds beets. Eighteen pounds clams. Twenty-two pounds string beans. Thirty-five pounds cucumbers." Phoebe looked up a moment. "Then the last line, which is sort of blurry, but we think it says, two Button apples."

"Never mind the blurry apples," Lucy said. "No one grows clams on a farm like Hooper's. Though I have heard of oyster farms."

"I noticed that last time, too." Maggie stared at the pad. "Carrie said her father didn't grow a lot of this stuff. He definitely didn't grow apples."

"And there's a numerical order," Lucy noticed. "The quantities go up from small to large. Except for the apples. That's interesting, too. Why would he list them in size order?"

"It could just be the way his mind worked. When I make a shopping list, I go aisle by aisle in my head. I know the layout of the supermarket by heart," Maggie admitted with a wry smile. "Sad, right?"

"Sad but convenient." Lucy swiped the pad from Maggie's hands. "Phoebe, do you have a map of the market? One that shows where all the stalls are?"

"I think there's one online." Phoebe had already grabbed her laptop off the side table and tapped a few keys. "Here we are. There's a map of the market in Rockport, and here's Plum Harbor." She turned the screen so they could see it. "These are the stalls. The sidebar has a key matching the vendors to the stall numbers."

Nobody spoke for a moment as they studied the screen. Lucy held the pad up. "I'll read the list, and you check the number on the map, Phoebe. Five pounds of peaches."

"That's Wilbur Family Orchard."

"Six pounds of beets."

"Another farm stand, Godwin Farm." Phoebe stared at Maggie and then at Lucy.

"Go on," Maggie urged. She wasn't ready to make any conclusions yet.

"Eighteen pounds of clams," Lucy said.

"Number eighteen is Yankee Chowder. That could count as clams, right?"

"How about number five, Pickle Man, right?" Lucy asked.

"That's . . . Honest Suds. Bath soap and pure cleaning products," Phoebe read from the description online. She sighed, looking stumped. Maggie felt that way, too. "Wait a minute. It's soap now, but it used to be the Pickle Man's spot. Before he complained and Warren moved him to a spot with more traffic."

"Which was well after Jimmy died," Maggie reminded them.

"When Jimmy was alive, Pickle Man's stall was number five, right?"

"Exactly. All of the amounts match the vendor's stall numbers," Lucy said. "It was Jimmy's code. Simple, too. I don't know why we didn't see it sooner."

"But we do now. That's what counts. The only item on the list that's unaccounted for now are the two apples," Maggie reminded them.

Phoebe checked the screen and frowned. "Stall number two sells shoes made from recycled plastic bottles. Nothing to do with apples, buttons, or anything close." She turned to Maggie. "I never even heard of a Button apple. Is there such a thing?"

"I never have, either. I suppose it could be a rare variety. There are so many types. McIntosh, Macoun, Fuji, Pink Lady?"

"Granny Smith," Phoebe added. "Wait, I'll Google it . . ."

As Phoebe tapped the keyboard, Lucy said, "Braeburn. That's my favorite." She turned to Phoebe. "And a guy named Warren Braeburn runs the market, right?"

"I just realized that, too." Maggie felt so dumb. "How did we miss that one?"

"Not so obvious to me," Phoebe said. "Did you ever see him? He's way too big to be called a button."

Maggie picked up her phone and looked at the photo of the list again. She stretched the image with her fingers as far as it would go. "It doesn't say, 'button.' It says 'rotten.' Two *rotten* apples."

She looked up at her friends. "So, Warren is one of them. I wonder who the other is?"

"And what are the rotten apples up to?" Lucy asked. "Whatever it is, Jimmy must have found out, and it got him killed."

"Maybe these other vendors are in on it, too?" Phoebe said.

"Or victims of some scheme," Maggie added.

Phoebe had noted the name of each vendor next to the numbers on Jimmy's list. "No surprise about Pickle Man. He has sketchy and creepy written all over him. But the Wilbur Family Orchard?" Phoebe shook her head. "I love to go apple picking there."

"Me too," Maggie said. "I bought these peaches from their stand just the other day. Suzanne said this one is bad." She picked up the peach Suzanne had rejected and examined it. "It looks okay to me." She passed it to Lucy. "What do you think?"

Lucy looked it over, then sniffed. She used her senses like a dog sometimes, Maggie had noticed, perhaps from hanging out with Tink and Wally so much. It was cute.

"It's not wormy. It's just not perfect. It looks like a real peach. Organically grown. Not the kind you find in the supermarket. Apples are even more fake-looking, like they're coated with car wax."

Maggie nodded. "Very true. I'll have to remind Suzanne that next time she criticizes my fruit bowl."

Lucy placed the peach back with the others. Her hand

lingered and she picked up the whole bowl and set it in her lap. "Did you buy all of these at the orchard stall?"

"I did. They came in a cute little paper basket. I couldn't resist."

Phoebe leaned over, craning her neck to see. "What are you doing, Lucy? What are you looking at?"

Lucy was taking the pieces of fruit out of the bowl, one by one. Examining each, then sorting them into two groups on the table. "A little experiment. Bear with me."

When she was done, she sat back. "I could be imagining this, but I'm not sure all of those peaches are locally grown and organic."

"Wilbur Orchard is faking it?" Phoebe asked.

"Maybe," Lucy replied. "Even a few commercially grown peaches, slipped in with the rest, would help their bottom line. Especially if they buy them wholesale."

"Their profit margin would be greater," Maggie agreed. "Produce is a lot cheaper if it's grown on a conventional farm."

Phoebe touched her hand to her head. "Whoa, this is big. Maybe Jimmy found out and he was some sort of whistleblower."

"That's why he wanted to meet with the reporter," Lucy said, suddenly understanding.

"This has got to be the reason Jimmy was killed. And it has zero to do with Harry," Phoebe added happily. "It was probably Warren. I bet he killed Jimmy."

Maggie took a breath. She needed a moment to get her emotions and thoughts under control. "I think we're definitely onto something. The vendor products and stall numbers on Jimmy's list match, which seems proof that this list is a record of some kind, that Jimmy felt was so important he hid it in his stall. But you all know what happens next. The police love to poke holes first, and consider that it *might* be a valid clue later."

"That's exactly how it goes," Lucy agreed. She glanced at Phoebe. "In other words, it will take a while to find out if this information helps Harry. Carrie passed this list to Detective Reyes. She may have already noticed the match-up, and looked into it, and come to a dead end. We don't know that, either."

Phoebe sat back and snapped the lid closed on the laptop. "In other words, don't get your hopes up, Phoebe."

Lucy smiled softly. "We know how much you want Harry to be cleared of all the accusations. Let's just keep our fingers crossed?"

"I'm going to tape mine together. Even if I can't knit for a while." Phoebe raised her crossed fingers.

A moratorium on her knitting? What a tribute, Maggie thought. Phoebe was really willing to go the limit for this guy.

Suddenly, Phoebe said, "Hey, maybe Harry noticed some of this stuff going on, too. Someone framed him with the drugs, just to mess him up and get him out of the way?"

Maggie doubted that, but she didn't want to dismiss the notion too quickly and risk hurting Phoebe's feelings. "It's possible. But even discredited, Harry would still be able to tell the police what he knows. Has he told them anything like this, so far?"

Phoebe looked deflated again. "Not that I've heard." She looked straight at Maggie. "Are you going to tell Detective Reyes that we decoded Jimmy's list, or should I do it?"

"I have been pestering her a lot lately," Maggie admitted. "Though that photo definitely helped her zero in on Carrie."

"Not that she'll be quick to acknowledge it," Lucy noted. "I think Phoebe should talk to her this time. She knows all the players at the market, and I'm sure she'll give a very convincing presentation."

"Thanks for the thumbs-up." Phoebe stood up and slipped the laptop under her arm. "I'll go right now, before I go to the market."

With all that had happened the last few days, Maggie didn't think Phoebe would go back to the market. The very idea made her nervous, though she knew she was being overly protective.

Phoebe could come to no harm there in the broad daylight, with so many people around. *Don't even voice your concern. You'll only make her anxious,* she told herself.

"Want some backup?" Lucy offered.

"I'd give you a lift to the police station," Maggie offered, "but I'm expecting someone from the alarm company."

"I'll be fine, guys. Chill. I hate going back to the station, but this is important."

"It is, Phoebe. I'm proud of you." Maggie picked up her phone again. "I'll text you the photo of the list, in case Detective Reyes doesn't have it handy."

"Good idea." Phoebe stepped inside the shop to grab her totes, knapsack, and sun hat. Then hopped off the porch with a bright wave.

As she disappeared down Main Street, Maggie turned to Lucy. "I worry about her at the market, after what happened on Sunday night," Maggie confided. "What if these insights about that list *are* significant, and someone there finds out that Phoebe brought the information to the police?" Maggie hadn't thought of that before. "Maybe we should catch her? And send the information to Detective Reyes some other way?"

Lucy sighed and patted her hand. "Phoebe's smart

enough not to blab about this all over the market. Detective Reyes can easily keep her name out of it. Carrie is the one who gave the police the list. Phoebe is just passing along our observations and theories."

Lucy's take on the situation calmed her. "True, and if anything comes of it, the police will take all the credit, I'm sure." She sighed. "I still think I'll send a text to Detective Reyes, and ask her to keep Phoebe's name under her hat."

"If you really want to. But I think she'd be the first one to realize Phoebe could be at risk."

Maggie agreed, recalling the detective's warning a few days back. "I hope Detective Reyes takes this seriously. Even if she's already looked into that list."

She'd often assumed the police would have some response or reaction, or make assumptions that seemed perfectly obvious to her. And they totally failed to do so.

Her gaze rested on the fruit bowl, filled again. "Must be that keen artistic eye that helped you spot the difference in the peaches."

"Keen eye, my foot. I hope I didn't let my imagination run wild and set Phoebe up to be laughed right out of the police station." Lucy held a peach up to the light and looked it over, as if to check her theory. "Fruit usually has stickers, organic or not. But these have none, as if they were just picked off a tree. I suppose with the market atmosphere, that helps them get away with the trick? If there is one," she added on a more cautious note.

"But the list and the stall numbers match. That's enough to indicate that the list means *something*. Even if our guess is off base," Maggie reminded her.

"And there's Warren Braeburn. I hope Detective Reyes calls him in for questioning."

"That's the first thing she should do," Maggie insisted. "I wonder who the other rotten apple is? I hope the police find out before . . . well, I hope they find out a lot of things," she amended. "I'll be very happy when all these questions are answered, once and for all."

Lucy patted her shoulder. "We all will. That's for sure."

Maggie didn't want to seem as if she was checking up, but couldn't resist calling Phoebe a few hours later to find out what happened at the police station. For one thing, she wanted to send a message to the detective about protecting Phoebe's identity, but didn't want to follow up until she knew the information had been delivered.

"So, how did it go at the station?" she asked Phoebe. "Did you get to see Detective Reyes?"

"It was so frustrating. I waited for like an hour and she never came out and they wouldn't tell me where she was. So, I ended up talking to this other detective. A guy named Detective Oliver?"

"Oh, him. He was on Suzanne's case," Maggie recalled, and did not have a very positive memory of the man.

"He said he was working on the case, too, and anything I had to tell Detective Reyes I could tell him. But he seemed, like, super bored, and hardly listened to me."

Maggie's heart sunk. Phoebe had been so hopeful that their insights about the list would help Harry, but it sounded as if she hadn't made much headway.

"Did he even try to understand about the amounts on the Jimmy's list and the numbers of the vendor stalls?"

"He never even heard about a list. He flipped through his case files right in front of me, and he couldn't find it. Which made the entire conversation so confusing. I had to go back and explain about the hat and how we found it under the floor of my stall, which used to be Jimmy Hooper's, etcetera and so on. . . ." Phoebe sighed. "He kept looking at me like I was a real nutjob."

"Oh my, that does sound . . ." She was about to say, *like a disaster*, but didn't want to make Phoebe feel any worse than she already did. "A lot more difficult than we expected," she said finally. "Was he rude?"

"Not really. He did seem super impatient, which made me nervous and I forget what I planned to say. The only thing he seemed to tune in on was how Jimmy's list matched the numbers of the vendor stalls. I guess that's something. Is there's some way to check if he even tells Detective Reyes? There must be some police rule that he has to, right?"

"I'm not sure. I'll ask Charles." Maggie had an idea that she hoped would lift Phoebe's spirits a bit. "What if Harry's attorney brings the information to Detective Reyes's attention, too? Why don't you contact Martin and tell him what we figured out? Then we'll be sure that it goes on record."

"Great idea, Mag. I should have thought of that myself. I was so busy saving the day. Wait a sec. Someone wants to buy something . . . Duh . . . I'm sort of asleep at the wheel here."

Phoebe left the line for a moment. Maggie could hear her talking with a customer. At least she was making some sales for all her trouble there. When she came back, Phoebe said, "Martin had to go back to California. I think he left this morning. But we'll figure it out. Either way, Harry's attorney will hear about the list, and Braeburn, and Pickle Man, and all this stuff," she added in a lower tone.

"Good plan. You have a good day." Maggie set her phone down and sighed. Did Harry McSweeney have any idea how hard Phoebe was fighting to clear his name? Did he even deserve it?

Only time would tell.

Even though Harry's attorney also gave the police the information about the list, there was no sign that the team investigating took it seriously. Dana's husband, Jack, had heard nothing about it from his contacts at the station, and Phoebe did not hear or notice any further police activity at the market.

The mood at their meeting on Thursday night seemed shadowed by Phoebe's dashed hopes and defeat. She was trying so hard to help Harry, but seemed blocked at every turn.

"I know it feels as if it's taking a long time for the police to put the pieces together, but we need to be patient," Dana said, after she'd sadly admitted that Jack still had not heard a word about the list, or any police interest in it.

"Tell that to Harry. He's stuck in a crummy jail cell. Everyone is giving up on him. Even his cousin, Martin, went back to the West Coast. He said he'll return for the trial."

"Sounds as if Martin thinks Harry is guilty. Of something," Lucy said.

"Doesn't it? He seemed so supportive at first." Phoebe yanked on a strand of yarn, trying to break it, instead of using scissors. She certainly knew much better than that, but she was so upset.

Maggie passed her a pair of scissors. Her heart went out to Phoebe, and even to Harry. She was starting to lean toward his innocence. At least in regard to Jimmy's murder. The drugs were another question altogether.

"What's going on with the wedding plans, Mag?" Suzanne's chipper tone was totally at odds with their low mood. "That bid to change the conversation is a little obvious, right?"

"It is. But we already know subtlety is not your strong suit," Maggie replied with a kind smile. She thought it was a good idea to move on to another topic. Hashing over this list situation any more was not going to move the needle, that was for sure.

"Charles and I are going to visit a new restaurant in Rockport tomorrow. It checks off all the boxes on our list: water view, elegant but contemporary atmosphere, and good reviews of the menu. And it sounds like the right size for our guest list."

Lucy looked up from her knitting. Her socks were just about done. Maggie loved the bright color combination. She'd cleverly used a lot of leftovers from her yarn stash.

"Sounds perfect to me. Rockport is such a picturesque spot. Great for wedding photos. I'm seeing the newlyweds in a cozy embrace, against a background of crashing waves on granite rocks."

Maggie laughed. "I'm seeing an accident waiting to happen with that pose. We're well beyond balancing on slippery rocks to catch the perfect shot. But we'll definitely try for some beachy-looking photos. That would suit us just fine."

There were many more suggestions and questions about her wedding plans from her friends. Maggie nearly grabbed a notebook and pen to remember them all. She knew they meant well, and it was a much more pleasant subject to discuss than their preoccupation with Jimmy Hooper's murder.

Maggie closed the shop at five on Friday, then changed into a dressier outfit for her evening out. Charles picked her up right on time. He was nothing if not punctual. The ride to Rockport was not long and a very pleasant trip on a summer evening, along winding Route 1A.

They didn't talk much. Maggie liked that about Charles, he sensed her moods and gave her space when she needed to unwind.

As the signs for their destination began to appear, he reached over and covered her hand with his own. "Worried about something, Mags?"

"Not really. Just the usual mind chatter." She forced a smile. This was supposed to be a fun evening, a special night for just the two of them.

"Does that chatter include worrying about Phoebe and the murder investigation of a local farmer?"

She had shared with Charles all that she and her friends knew, or thought they knew, about the case. He tended to get upset about her meddling in police business, though he often pretended to be oblivious, just to keep the peace.

"I do worry about Phoebe," she admitted. "She's so . . . vulnerable until this whole mess is figured out. At least the new alarm system is in. That makes me feel better."

"You've done what you could for her. I know she appreciates it. The police will find Jimmy's killer soon. But Harry and the drugs . . . I don't know about that."

She knew that tone. Charles did have a good guess at the outcome of Harry's situation. He just didn't want to say.

She squeezed his hand. "Let's just enjoy our night out. This is an important decision for us. If we like the atmosphere and the food, we'll talk to a manager about having the wedding there."

He glanced at her and smiled. "My plan exactly."

The restaurant was attractive but low-key, painted stone gray with a dark blue awning that seemed a fitting match to the wide view of the water and rocky coastline right behind it. A valet met them at the entrance to park their car. Maggie felt Charles's hand on her back as he opened the door for her.

"This is nice," she whispered, "I like it already."

It took a moment for her eyes to adjust to the dim light within. It was a few hours before sunset, but the sun had already wandered closer to the horizon and the water view from the long row of windows at the back of the dining area was stunning.

A hostess stepped up to meet them and checked their reservation. "Would you like to sit inside or out this evening?"

Charles turned to Maggie. "Your call. What do you think?"

It was still quite warm outside, but it would cool down soon and the stone terrace and umbrella-topped tables looked inviting.

"Let's go out. We'll see the sunset. It could be a nice spot for the cocktail hour, if the weather cooperates." *At our wedding,* Maggie meant. "Maybe we should move the date up to September just to be sure of that part?"

Charles laughed. "If you could figure it out, I'd marry you tomorrow. You know that."

"I do know. But thank you for saying it." Maggie smiled, feeling loved and appreciated. What more could anyone ask for? Floating on a happy cloud, she followed the hostess to the door that led outside.

She'd only noticed him from the corner of her eye. A man at the bar, who wasn't even facing in her direction. Though something about him seemed familiar, his build perhaps? The way he was dressed, a crisp blue blazer, khaki trousers, and Italian loafers, no socks. She paused and glanced over her shoulder, then felt a jolt of surprise.

Martin McSweeney? It *was* him. No question. Sitting alone at the bar. The bartender served him a drink and Martin took a sip. Then glanced at his watch, and then leaned to the side, to glance at the door.

For some reason, she didn't want him to see her. She quickly turned forward and continued walking. As she stepped outside to the restaurant terrace, she felt sure he hadn't noticed her. His attention was obviously focused elsewhere. He seemed to be waiting for someone.

What was he doing in Rockport? He'd told Phoebe that

he'd left for the West Coast days ago. Had he felt so pestered by her texts and phone calls about Harry, he'd just lied to avoid her? That could have been it.

Though the sight of him and the fact that he had lied about his whereabouts made her uneasy. They arrived at their table, and took their seats. Charles leaned toward her once the hostess left.

"Something wrong? We can get another table if you don't like this spot."

Maggie looked up, jarred from her thoughts. "Not at all. The table is perfect. Look at that view. Perfect for wedding photos."

Lucy was right. The backdrop of the wide blue sea and rocky shore line would make for a spectacular wedding album. She was thinking like a bride now. It was positively shocking.

She opened her menu and glanced at the selections, but couldn't really focus. She took her phone out and set it on the table, as unobtrusively as she could. Should she let Phoebe know that she'd just seen Martin?

What good would that do? It would only hurt her feelings and might even cause a rift between them. That wouldn't help anyone right now.

Martin had a perfect right to stay in the area. And a right to keep his reasons for that private, whatever they were. She glanced across the table at Charles, deep in thought as he considered his choices.

She could practically hear him scolding her. *There's a point when your admirable curiosity and interest in human nature crosses the line into downright nosiness.*

Very true, Charles, she answered silently. She took her phone and shut the ringer off, then slipped it back in her purse.

I won't go there, she decided. *This night is just for me and Charles.*

Chapter 17

Phoebe usually closed her stall by seven, but there were still plenty of customers roaming the market on Friday night as darkness began to fall, a hint of the busy weekend to come. With one eye on her customers and the other on her cell phone, she kept up with the texts flying between her friends. Dana had kicked off the round of rapid-fire messages.

BREAKING NEWS! Police picked up Warren B. No scene in Plum Harbor. He was at the market in Rockport.

Just what we thought. Some vendors are passing off non-organic foods as organic and he's been blackmailing them. And taking bribes for better stalls and misc. market perks.

He admits Jimmy knew and planned to go public. But totally denies killing him.

Lucy was the first to respond:

That's BIG. I bet he knows even more than he's said so far.

Suzanne was next:

Agree. That guy's rotten to the core, forgive the pun?

And I think he's lying. He probably did off Jimmy.

Phoebe tapped an answer quickly:

Totally agree with above. I bet he killed Jimmy. Or one of those shady vendors did. Which puts Harry in the CLEAR. TOTALLY.

Do not forgive bad pun, Suzanne.

Then she added an emoji doing an eye roll. And one with a scream.

Dana replied:

Could be true. Detective R is not done talking to him.

Yet. Will keep you posted!

PS—where's Mag? Not on this chain yet?

Phoebe had noticed that, too. Then remembered. She texted back:

Mag and Charles are checking out a special restaurant in Rockport. Could be a good spot for their wedding.

A screen full of okay signs, smiley faces, and hearts appeared. Phoebe did wish that Maggie knew the news about Warren. But she didn't want to call and disturb her dinner. She would check her phone soon enough, Phoebe decided. She would certainly be pleased to see their suspicions about Braeburn turn out to be true.

Phoebe looked around at the neighboring stalls, wondering if any of the other vendors knew yet about the market manager. The stall across that belonged to Harry was closed, of course. And the one to her right that sold handmade clothing was as well.

But to the left, the flowering plants and herbs stall was open and so was Honey Girl. Phoebe caught Samantha's eye as she took down a display on a front table. They waved to each other, but Phoebe decided not to run across and relay the news. Everyone would find out soon enough and the fact that she knew so quickly might result in unwanted attention. From unsavory people who were involved in this scheme.

What would happen to the vendors who were in on the scheme with Warren? Would the police raid the market, like in the movies? Or just deal with the business owners separately, in a quieter, less obvious way?

She suddenly felt uneasy and decided to close. The stream of shoppers had dwindled. It seemed a good time to go.

She heard a text come in and picked up her phone. She hoped for more news from Dana, but it was just Robbie, checking to see if she was still around.

Hey, are you still here? Want a lift back to town?

We could grab a bite somewhere. Anything but Mexican.

A scream face emoji made her laugh.

If you're not too tired? he texted next.

That was Robbie, no pressure. Always giving her an easy out. Phoebe stared at her phone, not knowing how to answer. His heroic rescue last week had made her feel a lot closer to him, and even a little more attracted, she had to admit.

But she still wasn't sure if she wanted to be more than friends with him. And she didn't need Suzanne's broad hints to see that Robbie really wanted their relationship to move in a romantic direction. She couldn't make up her mind and didn't want to raise his hopes.

There was too much going on right now, for one thing. But maybe that was just an excuse? She wondered if she was being fair, or just stringing him along because it felt good to have a guy so into her. Especially after breaking up with Harry.

And Robbie seemed willing to wait forever for her to decide. Not like some guys, who jumped all over you and asked if it was okay later.

Phoebe had to admit, some tiny part of her felt loyal to Harry, though she wasn't sure why. Maybe just because he was in trouble and she had a thing about rescuing people and stray animals? Just like Adele, she realized.

She wondered if Robbie knew about Warren. Probably

not. He would have mentioned something in his text. *I'll tell him when I see him,* she decided, then quickly tapped back a message.

Sounds good. Just closing up. Meet you at the truck.

He quickly replied with a row of bright yellow smiley faces. He definitely was her biggest fan. Who could complain about that?

By the time Phoebe closed her stall and walked toward the food court, the sun was low in the sky, casting long shadows on the market. The paved square where the food trucks set up every day was adjacent to the village green and surrounded by tall trees.

Robbie's truck was the last one left in the space. The service window on the side of the truck was closed, but the back doors hung open. She saw Robbie walking back from the dumpsters, pushing the handcart he used to carry trash bags.

"Hey. Perfect timing," he called.

Phoebe smiled and waved, but before she could shout back, a blurry shape zipped out of the shadows, brushing so close she felt a breeze pull at her clothing. She jumped to the side just in time to avoid being knocked down by a teenage boy on a low, stripped-down bike.

The sort of boy she'd seen hanging around the truck at night, waiting for the bags of food Robbie gave out. He headed straight to Robbie and stopped short, then stood with the bike balanced between his thin legs. He pressed his face close to Robbie's as they spoke.

Phoebe stood still and couldn't hear much of the conversation. The boy's words were rushed and low and she could make out the tone of his voice, carried in the thick, humid air, half-pleading, half-cocky.

She saw Robbie shake his head. He started walking toward the truck again, but the kid blocked his way. "Hey, man. Give me a break . . . What's going on with you?"

The boy sounded scared and angry. He tried to stick something into Robbie's T-shirt pocket, but Robbie shook his head and pushed his hand away.

Robbie moved past him, his eyes downcast. "Get out of here. I mean it."

Phoebe had never seen that look before. Or heard him use that tone. Was he afraid of the boy? She thought he might be. The boy was scrawny, but he looked tough. A lot tougher than Robbie.

Robbie climbed in the back of the truck and shut the doors from the inside. The boy had followed. He waited a few moments, staring at the closed doors, then banged on the door with his fist and called Robbie foul names. When the doors remained closed, he turned on one wheel and sped off into the shadows, shouting obscenities, like puffs of smoke from a tailpipe.

Phoebe had stood stone still watching the scene. Once she was sure the boy was gone, she walked the short distance to the truck. Robbie appeared at the driver's side. He walked over to meet her and took her bags.

"What was that about? That kid on the bike nearly ran me over. He was acting so crazy."

Robbie shook his head. "He just wanted free food. But he was too late. Most of the kids who come looking for freebies are okay, but he's a bad one. I hope he doesn't come back."

Free food. That made sense. Phoebe thought the little wad of whatever the kid had tried to stick in Robbie's apron pocket looked a like scrunched-up bills. But in the dim light, she couldn't be sure. Maybe he was trying to pay Robbie for a leftover taco?

If he was that hungry, why not buy some food some-where else? The kid's reaction made sense to her. But she was too tired to comment on it.

"I've had enough of this place for one day." He sighed and smiled. "Let's get out of here. Let's do something fun."

Phoebe nodded and climbed into the passenger seat. She never gave much thought to Robbie's job and how hard it was to run this truck, all by himself, day in and day out. Hot, too. He was always so upbeat. It was the first time she'd ever heard him even vaguely complain.

Because you're so self-centered when you're with him, madam. It's all about Phoebe, Phoebe, Phoebe. You barely give his problems a thought.

He'd started up the truck and steered it out of the lot, then turned to her and smiled. "What are you thinking about? You have a mysterious look."

She felt embarrassed and quickly faced forward. "Noth-ing special. I've had enough of the market today, too. Hey, did you hear about Warren?"

Robbie turned to her. She could tell from his reaction that he had not heard the big news yet. "What about him?"

Phoebe paused. She wasn't sure how much she should or even could say. A lot of the information Dana learned from her husband, Jack, was confidential. Especially when it got into the weeds with details like Warren admitting to accepting bribes from vendors and that sort of thing.

But a lot of people in town must have heard by now that Warren is being questioned by the police, so that much is fine to relay, she decided.

"I heard that he's being questioned by the police."

Robbie looked surprised. "Wow, that's big. When did this happen?"

"Sometime today. I'm not exactly sure when."

Robbie was staring straight ahead at the road. "They must be asking him about Jimmy Hooper. Is that what you heard?"

Phoebe had an impulse to disclose the information Dana had passed on, but stopped herself. "I didn't hear why the police brought him in. Just that they wanted to question him." She'd been looking out her window and turned to him. "It does seem logical they'll ask about Jimmy. And all the weird stuff going on at the market. I mean, he's the manager, right?"

"Absolutely. I'm surprised they haven't questioned him sooner. I think he knows a lot more about Jimmy than he's said so far."

"I do, too," Phoebe agreed. "Maybe we'll find out now what really happened."

Robbie didn't answer for a moment. "If Warren killed Jimmy, that would let Harry off the hook. At least for Jimmy's murder."

"Yes, it would. It might explain the drugs, too. Maybe Warren wanted to frame Harry and planted the drugs in his stall, just to stir up the pot."

Robbie nodded, his eyes still on the road. "I never thought of that. You might be right." He glanced at her and offered a small smile. "But do you mind very much if we don't talk about Warren . . . and Harry and all that stuff tonight? I really need to chill."

What was he trying to say? He didn't want to talk about Harry possibly being free and clear, and competition for her affections again? Phoebe suddenly felt a wave of sympathy. He did try so hard to make her like him. She really needed to give him a chance.

"So, what do you feel like eating? Pizza? Sushi? Indian?" Phoebe asked. "I picked last time. And the time before that, I think," she admitted with a grin.

He smiled back. "I'm not sure. When you're smelling food all day, it sort of takes your appetite away."

Phoebe thought that must be true. But he usually liked sushi and she wondered if the Japanese restaurant delivered. Maybe this was the night they could hang out at her place and watch a movie?

And she'd let their relationship move to new ground?

It was a big step and she felt the takeout suggestion stick in her throat.

She pulled out her phone to look up the restaurant, but the truck took a sharp turn and she dropped it on the floor.

"Not that again. At least this time, I know it fell." She leaned over and felt around on the truck floor, near her feet.

Robbie glanced at her. "Are you okay? Want me to stop?"

"It's fine. I think I've got it." She felt the hard edge of the phone and grabbed it. But also felt something else next to the case and picked that up, too.

A small, plastic envelope with white pills inside. The same kind of pills that were found in Harry's stall. Pills that someone had put there, to frame him.

She quickly slipped the tiny bag into her pocket, and busily wiped her phone with a tissue.

Robbie offered a wincing smile. "The floor in this truck is totally gross. Sorry."

She shrugged. "No big deal."

Phoebe's brain was suddenly flooded with startling revelations. The nasty kid on the bike wasn't bothering Robbie for free food. He'd come to buy drugs and Robbie didn't want to deal with her standing right there. Or maybe, he'd stopped doing business altogether with the police all over the market lately.

He must have planted the drugs in Harry's clay to frame him, and tried to make the police think that's why Harry had killed his aunt. And he'd probably trashed her stall and trolled her online, to make Harry look bad, too. And make her angry with Harry. Robbie had learned a lot about computers while earning his degree in textile design and was definitely capable of the tech side of that mess.

Who knows what else he'd done?

Jimmy said there were two rotten apples at the market. She suddenly realized she was sitting next to the other one.

Phoebe felt frozen in her seat; cold sweat dripped down her body. She swallowed hard and hoped he didn't notice her sudden panic. *Hang on, Phoebe. You can't freak out and give yourself away.*

Just get him to drive to a restaurant, make an excuse to slip away, and call the police.

"So, did you decide what you want to eat?" she asked, trying hard not to sound like a squeaky mouse.

He sighed and glanced at her. "You're being so sweet. And I really want to hang with you. You know that. But I have the most awful, splitting headache. The truck was so hot today. I'd better go home and stick an ice pack on my head. Or I'll end up with a migraine. Do you mind if we do it another time?"

"Umm . . . sure. I mean, not at all." Did she sound too relieved? That wouldn't be good. "I feel so sorry about your headache," she added quickly. "But I totally get it. I'm wiped tonight, too."

A wave of relief washed over her. Phoebe stared out her side of the truck, struggling to hide her reaction.

Robbie had just turned up Main Street. In a few minutes, she'd be safely locked in her apartment, protected by ten new dead bolts and the new alarm system.

Then I'll call the police.

She heard a text come in and she fumbled to check it. Her hands were shaking so much she feared she might drop the phone again.

It was from Maggie. She'd caught up on the news about Warren and had heard even more from Dana.

Shocked to hear about Robbie. I bet you are, too. We can pick you up if you feel uneasy about being alone at the shop tonight. At least until the police find him.

Make sure you set the alarm. Call when you get this, okay?

Phoebe's mouth went dry. Her stomach knotted with dread. She quickly scrolled through her messages and realized that she'd missed a big update from Dana.

When she saw it, she had to bite her lip to stifle a scream. Dana wrote:

The police are looking for Robbie. Warren just named him as Jimmy's killer. Phoebe—Please let me know you saw this.

"Is everything all right?" Robbie glanced at her; his familiar, gentle smile suddenly looked so sinister in the shadowy light.

"It's just Maggie. No big deal. She and Charles are nailing down their wedding plans."

He turned back to the road. "You looked worried. I thought it was bad news."

"Not at all. But I'd better text her back." Phoebe quickly tapped out a message, copying all her pals. She was careful to turn the phone so Robbie couldn't see.

With Robbie now. Almost at the shop.

Pray that I get out of this truck in one piece.

She hit SEND and slipped the phone in her pocket. If he tried to kidnap her, at least the police could track her whereabouts with her phone signal.

Don't even go there. You'll be free of this psycho in a

few tiny minutes. He's obviously planning on a quick get-away.

They had come to the shop and she forced herself to stay in her seat until he stopped the truck. With no doors on her side, the idea of jumping out was almost too tempting.

"Thanks for the lift. I hope your headache goes away."

"Wait, I'll pull in the driveway, so you don't have to carry your stuff so far."

He usually helped her carry everything up to the porch. But of course, he didn't have time for that tonight.

"That's fine. Park anywhere. I can handle it. I really need to work my biceps more, you know? Flabby arms are so noticeable in the summer."

Phoebe knew she was rambling but couldn't help it. She was so eager to get away from him, she thought she could barely stop herself from leaving all her stuff and running straight to the front door of the shop.

Robbie parked the truck at the curb but left the engine running. He turned to her, his expression curious. And suddenly suspicious.

She avoided his gaze and picked up one of her bags from the floor. "Hope you feel better. See you tomorrow, I guess."

She had one foot out the opening, her toe practically touching the grassy strip next to the sidewalk, when a police cruiser came flying down the street, headed straight at them. No siren, but the light on top was flashing.

Robbie's eyes went wide with shock. Another cruiser roared up, from the opposite direction. He grabbed her arm, and yanked her back into the truck.

"Not so fast, Phoebe. Maybe we should have that date, after all."

Phoebe made a move to jump out, but Robbie was much stronger than he looked. He squeezed her arm so tight she nearly cried out. Before she could wiggle free, he hit the gas and the truck leaped forward, back onto Main Street.

The police cruiser pulled around in a quick, tight turn and suddenly sat perpendicular to their path, blocking their getaway.

But Robbie steered up over a lawn, knocking down a fence and bashing into a car, as he navigated a wild path around the cruiser. All the damage in their path barely slowed him down.

Phoebe screamed and pressed her hands over her face, certain that they were going to have an accident.

"Relax. We'll be fine. The police will think twice about taking me down by force, if I'm hanging with my girl-friend."

His hostage, he meant. Phoebe felt her body tremble. She was too terrified to speak. Or she would have shouted at him,

I'm so not your girlfriend. We're not even friends any-more, okay?!

The truck was moving so fast, she felt her body pressed to her seat. The bypassed police cruiser had spun around and was in pursuit again, along with the second car that had been approaching the shop from the other side of the street.

Both had sirens screaming and lights whirring, but the noise only made Robbie's focus stronger and the truck moved even faster. They came to the village green and he rode up over the sidewalk again and across the grass, then bumped down over the opposite end. The police cars fol-lowed, but fell behind.

Robbie turned up a narrow winding side street that had few streetlights. Phoebe was so disoriented; she couldn't place where they had ended up. But she did notice that the sirens were farther in the distance, which filled her heart with dread.

Robbie laughed to himself and swerved down another long dark road, this one lined with trees. She recognized it, Mariner's Way; they were headed to the Marshes, where Lucy lived.

There was a large tract of vacant land in that area of town, a nature preserve of thick, overgrown woods and stretches of marsh grass. A short bridge over an inlet led to the entrance. A car couldn't drive through those woods and the big, bulky truck certainly could not fit. She guessed Robbie had some idea of escaping on foot.

And taking her with him.

Phoebe couldn't hear any police cars near them now. Where were they? Talking to each other on their radios, like in the movies? Why wasn't anyone popping out of the woods to save her?

She racked her brain for some way to get out of the truck before it was too late. They were moving much too fast for her to jump. She'd break her neck or worse. She needed to slow the truck down. But how? She was much too far to reach the brake with her foot.

She had an idea, but wasn't even sure it would work. It was worth a try and there was no time to lose.

"Give up, Robbie. The police have us surrounded by now," she insisted, though there was no sign of that. Just the opposite, in fact. "We're going to have an accident," she shouted.

He grinned, clearly enjoying her panic. "Why not? I'd rather go out with a bang than get arrested. Dealing drugs and a murder charge—that's a bad combination."

She swallowed hard, shocked by his admission of guilt.

Then turned in her seat, to put her plan in motion.

"What are you doing?" He grabbed her arm a moment. So tight, it wasn't hard to look teary-eyed. If he really had any feelings for her at all, somewhere in his wicked little heart, she prayed he would take some pity now.

"I'm just putting my seat belt on," she said in a tiny, submissive voice.

"Be my guest. I doubt it will help by the time this ride is over." He released her and turned his gaze to the road. "We're almost at the bridge. Feel like a dip? I think it's high tide tonight."

Just a few yards ahead, the short, narrow bridge spanned an inlet. Robbie was so crazy and desperate now, he might steer the truck right over the edge.

Phoebe couldn't answer. She sucked in a terrified breath and quickly clipped her belt. He wanted to end his life and was taking her with him. She didn't like that plan at all. Not one little bit.

Pretending to fix her seat belt, she slipped her hand to the side and grabbed the stick shift.

Robbie turned to see what she was up to, but before he could react, she pushed the transmission into reverse. Then, she hunkered down and crossed her arms over her head, preparing herself for the truck to crash.

The truck gave a horrible whirring sound, and suddenly changed direction. Robbie tried to push it back into drive but the damage was done. The top-heavy truck flew backward, sliding from one side of the road to the other. He shouted all kinds of obscenities, pulling on the wheel and working the stick shift, but the truck wouldn't respond.

Pots, pans, and all sorts of cooking equipment flew toward them from the back of the truck.

Phoebe pushed herself toward the opening on her side. They were still moving too fast to jump out and she dared not open her seat belt.

She reached out and yanked on the wheel, trying to aim the truck into the woods. A crash on land was definitely better than flipping into the water.

He struggled to pull the wheel back, but it was too late. The truck bumped over the shoulder and a huge tree trunk filled their view. Phoebe felt her body jerked in all directions, her belt barely holding her in her seat. She bent low and protected her head with her arms as best as she was able.

A clump of scraggly bushes slowed the truck before the rear fender plowed into the tree. The big truck leaned toward the driver's side as the sound of crunching metal and shattering glass roared all around her.

And then it was suddenly still.

She heard sirens rushing closer and let out a long breath.

Then lifted her head and dropped her hands from her face. She tasted blood on her lips and her neck felt like a wet rag that had been wrung out to dry.

Robbie sat slumped in the driver's seat, his forehead pressed to the steering wheel, his eyeglasses broken in two.

He mumbled incoherently and struggled to sit up. She could see he was alive, but appeared to be semiconscious. He hadn't gotten his wish, thank goodness.

She wasn't sure how, but she'd saved herself. Through the haze of pain setting in, she felt proud of that.

Police officers had crashed through the woods and suddenly swarmed the truck, vague silhouettes and shouting voices behind powerful beams of light. She lifted her arm to shield her eyes and felt a stabbing pain. They called to her, and she tried to answer, her lips bruised and swollen.

One of them reached in and lifted her out. She fussed, thinking she didn't need so much help, then realized she was too shocked and weak to support herself, and her left arm ached something awful.

She felt her body set down on a stretcher and stared up into a web of leafy branches and fragments of the clear night sky. A thin blanket that seemed to be made from tin foil was pulled over her body. Back at the truck, she heard voices as Robbie was pulled out, too.

An ER tech gave her a quick exam, and asked a lot of questions about where it hurt, if she knew her name, the date, where she lived, and all of that.

Then the stretcher was carried to an ambulance parked nearby. Just before she was lifted inside, the ER tech said, "You're a lucky girl. That could have been a lot worse."

She felt like she might laugh, then wondered if shock and hysteria had set in. "Tell me about it. I was *seriously* thinking of dating that creep."

Chapter 18

"A hard cast for three weeks and then I'll have a soft one for three more." Phoebe held up her injured forearm, which was covered in pink plaster. "I can't go back to the market. But at least I can knit," she added, wiggling her fingers.

"Thank heaven for small favors." On Saturday afternoon, Maggie and her friends gathered on the shop's front porch. They sat in a circle with Phoebe in the center, surrounding her like guard dogs, or hovering guardian angels, Maggie thought, though thankfully, the danger was past.

But just barely. Phoebe had spent Friday night in the hospital, for observation after the accident. Her main injury was a fracture in her lower right arm, some bruising, and a sore neck from the crash.

Robbie had not been so lucky. He'd ended up with two broken legs, broken ribs, a punctured lung, and a severe concussion. He was still in the hospital, though his injuries had not prevented the police from charging him with Jimmy Hooper's murder, and possession and dealing in illegal substances.

"All I can say is, when I'm wrong, I'm wrong. I admit

it." Suzanne sat back and tossed her hands in the air. "That Robbie totally scammed me. That kid must have a double personality or something weird like that going on. Don't you think, Dana?"

" 'Something weird' covers it as well any medical terms I can offer," Dana agreed. "I wonder if his attorney will use mental instability as a defense, or to mitigate his sentencing. I suppose it's a possibility."

Phoebe looked uneasy at the mention of Robbie. But that was to be expected, Maggie thought. At least until she got past the shock of her experience.

"I hope I'm not called to be a witness at a trial. But if I am, I could give a jury an earful. I mean, about the things he said when we were on our wild getaway. I already told the police." Phoebe was trying to cast on stitches for a new project, Maggie noticed. She claimed she was able to knit, injury and all, but it was definitely a challenge.

"I'm sure you'd step up and do your civic duty, Phoebe," Maggie said. "But it sounds as if he's confessed to everything. Dealing drugs at the market and Jimmy's murder, and he won't go to trial. Isn't that what you heard, Dana?"

Dana had taken out her knitting but hadn't touched it. "Yes, he gave a full confession with little prodding. The police first got Warren to admit to the scheme at the market, where some stalls were selling fake organic products and he was paid to keep quiet."

"Excuse me," Lucy cut in. "Using the list from Jimmy's hat, that we supplied and decoded?"

"A crucial clue, for sure," Dana agreed. "But I don't think Detective Reyes will give you and Maggie credit. At least, not officially. It was enough to squeeze a confession out of Warren and deal with all the vendors Jimmy named. They all have a lot to answer for."

"So, once Warren was accused of Jimmy's murder, it didn't take him long to point the finger at Robbie?" Suzanne asked.

"That's up for debate," Maggie said. "If Warren had come right out with it, Phoebe wouldn't have ended up in such a perilous situation."

"But how did it actually happen? Why did Robbie end up murdering Jimmy? He wasn't in on the scheme in the market, too, was he?" Suzanne asked.

"No, he wasn't," Dana replied. "But he knew about it. And Jimmy figured out Robbie was dealing drugs from the truck. Warren tipped off Robbie, who went to Hooper Farm. Just to persuade the farmer to look the other way. Robbie offered him a fat bribe, of course," Dana explained. "Warren had already given Jimmy a few thousand dollars to keep quiet about the market scam, so he believed Jimmy's silence was up for sale. Warren didn't know that Jimmy was holding on to the money for evidence and waiting until he had enough proof to go to the newspapers, and the police."

Lucy looked up from her knitting. "That was the cash the police found in Jimmy's workbench?"

Dana nodded. "Warren's fingerprints and a DNA test came back positive, confirming it. But it seems on the fatal night, Jimmy refused Robbie's bribe. Robbie's drug dealing disgusted him. It made Jimmy terribly angry. They had words, which made Robbie snap."

Dana paused to take a breath. Maggie had imagined a few situations that would account for Jimmy Hooper's murder. But the real story was far more dreadful.

"Robbie's dark side came out," Lucy said. "The side Phoebe saw last night."

"Exactly. He choked Jimmy with a lamp cord, then hung him by a rope from the loft in the barn. He put a chair underneath and kicked it aside, to make it look like suicide. He would have gotten away with it, too. It was easy to believe that Jimmy may have taken his own life, with all his debts. But the medical examiner found injuries that were inconsistent with that method of suicide."

"How gruesome. And to think how Robbie hid all that malevolence behind such sunny smiles. Always offering a helpful hand, and saying the nicest things to everyone." Lucy looked stunned, reflecting on how Robbie had tricked them.

"Not to mention the tacos," Suzanne recalled. "Just goes to show, there's no such thing as a free lunch. I never really liked his food. The churros were pretty good though."

"I liked the tacos. And the churros. I liked him, too," Dana admitted. "As a psychologist, I feel especially fooled. And embarrassed, that I didn't see through him."

"I feel like a plain, garden-variety sucker," Lucy chimed.

"Join the club, ladies," Phoebe mumbled. "Suckers Anonymous meets here."

"Now, now. We all fell for his act. You can't blame yourself, Phoebe. None of us should. Not even you, Dana. You saw him so infrequently and hardly under ideal circumstances to analyze his personality." Maggie did consider herself an excellent judge of character, but this revelation had knocked her down a peg or two.

"Thanks, Mag. I suppose that's a possible excuse." Dana sounded as if she hadn't entirely let herself off the hook. "He was living in two distinct realities, you might say. When he was playing the role of 'nice Robbie,' he was so immersed, he believed it himself. And was able to convince us, too."

"Until he had to be Robbie the drug dealer," Maggie added. "What about that other reality? Did he give any explanation for it?"

Dana shrugged. "Just that he needed money, and it was a lot easier and faster to pay off his student loans selling meth and opioids than working two minimum-wage jobs. I don't think Robbie started off without a conscience, or moral compass. But he'd lost his way somewhere, though who knows when or why."

"So, there was no connection at all between Jimmy's murder and Adele's?" Lucy asked.

"It doesn't seem so," Maggie observed. "But if Jimmy had not died, his daughter Carrie would have never gone through is papers and discovered his affair with Adele. And never sought her revenge."

"Very true. One death led to the other." Dana paused for a moment. "There was another connection, too. Though it didn't cause Adele's murder. Some of Robbie's customers paid with stolen goods and he was passing the jewelry to Adele, for resale. Right under Harry's nose, too. So that accounts for the stolen jewelry found in the cat litter. He may have even been at Adele's house the night she was killed and claimed that he heard Adele arguing with someone. But it wasn't the voices of a woman and a man, as he told the police. If he heard anyone with Adele, it must have been Carrie."

"Figures," Phoebe said. "So, are you all willing to admit now that I was right about Harry?"

Phoebe's tone was as strong and decisive as Maggie had heard in a while. A good sign, she thought.

"That goes without saying," Maggie replied for all of them. "I admit, as the evidence mounted up, it was harder and harder to believe he was completely blameless."

"Because Robbie was so diabolically clever at framing him," Lucy pointed out. "He obviously hid the drugs in Harry's clay. Probably before Adele was even killed."

"He did," Dana confirmed. "He admitted to it, finally. Though at first, he tried to make the police think that Harry was an accomplice of some sort in the drug dealing."

"That rat." Phoebe was incensed all over again by that detail.

"I'm not surprised," Lucy said. "Remember that morning when Phoebe argued with Harry, and Robbie told Harry to leave their apartment? He must have planted the drugs beforehand, knowing Harry would take the incriminating evidence with him when he moved out."

Maggie thought back to that day, and the disturbing incidents that had sparked the argument. "And he must have trashed your stall and posted all the complaints about your products on social media, Phoebe. Just to make it look like Harry was taking revenge."

"Because he was so crazy in love with you and wanted to have you for all for himself," Suzanne cut in, putting a more romantic spin on the situation.

" 'Crazy' is the operative word there." Phoebe made a face that made Maggie laugh. "He does have enough computer knowledge to have pulled that off. But I never once suspected him." She shook her head with disbelief.

"It gets even worse," Dana added, looking at Phoebe. "He also admitted to breaking into Maggie's shop. There was no intruder coming up the stairway, about to break down your door. It was all Robbie, play acting. Just another attempt to make you bond with him. He created the danger, and then saved you from it."

"That is just too twisted and creepy. But when I looked back at all the weird things that happened, I realized Robbie had to be the intruder. He probably stole my phone that night, and made me think I dropped it in the truck. I still get a shiver thinking about it."

Phoebe covered her face with her hands as best as she was able with her cast on.

"We don't have to dwell on that anymore, do we?"

Maggie said briskly. She hated to see Phoebe relive these

frightening moments. "I have to admit, I did wonder at times if Martin McSweeney was tangled up in this mess. I even suspected he had broken into the shop and was trying to get to Phoebe for some odd reason that I couldn't understand. I was even more suspicious when I saw him last night in Rockport, after he'd told Phoebe he'd gone home to San Francisco. Did you know why he did that?" she asked Phoebe.

Phoebe sat up, preparing to explain. "Martin called this morning to see how I was doing. And he did admit he'd stuck around, in secret. It's sort of private. I'm not sure I should tell everyone."

Maggie's curiosity was piqued. "Your discretion is admirable. But you know it won't go any further."

"Well, when he was on the Cape at his business conference, he met someone he really likes and he wanted to see that person again. But he's in a relationship, so it was a little awkward."

"Oh . . . I get it. Nothing sinister." Maggie sat back. Maybe she was too suspicious, as Charles sometimes warned.

"More like plain old unfaithful? But he was glad he was still around to see Harry when he got out of jail this morning. Totally cleared of all charges," Phoebe reminded them.

"That must have been a happy reunion," Lucy said. "Poor Harry. He's been misjudged and treated badly by just about everyone."

"We all feel sorry for Harry." Maggie quickly turned to Phoebe. "But now I'm worried again. Do these tribulations weigh in his favor romantically?"

She felt uncomfortable being so blunt, but she had to know.

Phoebe cocked her head to one side, her smile mysterious.

"He's coming to visit later. Just as a friend," she in-sisted. "We're going to take it very slowly."

Maggie was relieved to hear it. "That sounds wise."

"But I will get a 'plus-one' invite to the wedding, I hope?"

Maggie was surprised at the question, then laughed. "Absolutely. And the choice of an escort is yours alone."

"My cast should be off in time," Phoebe calculated.

"I hope so," Maggie said. "And we'll all be recovered from these dark, unfortunate events. I'm so relieved this is all over and we can get back to some serious knitting again."

Lucy laughed at her. "And plan your wedding, and enjoy it?" she added. "Did you forget about that part?"

Maggie smiled, feeling caught. "That too, of course. You know me. I have my priorities."

Epilogue

Maggie had to marvel at the weather on her wedding day: Indian summer on the first weekend of October. Practically unheard of in New England. But there you were, the wide blue bowl of sky above was sparkling and clear, the temperature perfect for an outdoor celebration, against a breathtaking ocean view.

"We couldn't have picked a better day," Charles declared when they arrived at the restaurant.

"We're very lucky," she agreed, and meant that in many more ways than just the weather.

For one thing, her daughter, Julia, had arrived a few days ago to help with the last-minute details and simply help Maggie relax and enjoy the wedding pregame—trying on clothes and choosing the right jewelry, and hosting the rehearsal dinner.

Maggie had forgotten what a production getting married could be. Despite opting for the simplest route possible.

Julia touched her shoulder as they got out of the car. "How are you doing, Mom? Are you okay?"

"I'm good, dear. Good to excellent," she added, with a grin.

They walked out to the terrace, where final touches were being added to the decorations, and tables. Maggie had been very particular about the flowers, and had chosen arrangements of white hydrangeas, tinged with pink, trumpet lilies, and touches of lavender. The floral designer had also decorated with swoops of white voile and white ribbons, but not too much. Maggie had made sure of that.

"It looks great," Julia declared.

"Very lovely. A dream come true," she whispered, glancing at Charles.

"Mine too." He leaned over and kissed her cheek. "I have groom things to do," he added, excusing himself.

"And I have some maid of honor things to do," Julia said. She smiled and Maggie followed her glance. "I think your pals can take care of you for a while?"

Maggie turned to see her friends waiting for her, clustered on the far side of the terrace to stay clear of the bustling staff.

"I think so, dear. Don't worry about me." Julia kissed her cheek, too, and strolled off to talk to the musicians, who had just arrived.

Maggie turned back to her friends. Dressed for the occasion, they looked like a beautiful bouquet of flowers, each so distinctive and unique, and lovely, in their own way.

"Maggie!" they called. "You're here, finally!"

A light breeze ruffled their dresses and fancy hairstyles as they ran up to meet her.

The sight brought a wide smile, her love for them welling up unexpectedly, and almost making her cry.

"Hey, what's going on? Are those tears?" Dana said quietly as she offered a tissue.

"Happy tears." Maggie dabbed her eyes carefully, worrying about her makeup.

"Get it over with now, so we can work on your mascara before showtime," Suzanne said. "Luckily, I have some waterproof Thunder Lash in my purse."

"Might as well have your eyelashes laminated," Lucy murmured. But even Lucy, usually artifice free, had added a few dashes of cosmetics today. *As it should be,* Maggie thought.

"Are you ready, Bride?" Dana asked her.

Maggie smiled. "Ready as I'll ever be. I've got my vows right here, along with lipstick, comb, breath mints, and my phone."

She patted the tiny bag that matched her raw silk ensemble, a cocktail-length dress in dusty pink. Sleeveless and square-necked, with a short matching jacket, the lines were very flattering and the heels, which she wore so rarely her poor feet were in shock, added to the polished looked. Even Suzanne had approved. "Very bridie. In your own way, Mag," she'd said.

"What else do I need?" Maggie asked. "Besides a send-off from my best pals, I mean," she asked as they linked arms. Even Phoebe joined in, cast-free, just in time for the festivities.

How lucky they all were to have Phoebe there today. She didn't even want to think of how the summer's harrowing episode may have turned out. Not for a moment.

Today was for celebrating. Her heart overflowed with gratitude for so much good in her life—wonderful Charles, who would share the rest of her days; her darling daughter; and dear friends, who brought so much laughter, affection, and even adventure into her life.

"Thank you all so much for being here. Where would I be without you?"

"Oh, Maggie . . . you don't have to thank us. That's silly." Lucy's smile was contrasted by her bright, teary eyes.

"We wouldn't miss this day for the world," Dana insisted.

"Not for the entire galaxy," Phoebe added.

"I'll tell you where you'd be, if I'd had my way," Suzanne answered. "Happily wed to Charles at least a year ago. And you," she added, turning to Lucy, "would be expecting a baby by now."

Lucy sighed and didn't answer. Maggie couldn't help notice her amused expression.

"I didn't want to steal Maggie's thunder but . . . who says I'm not?"

Everyone stared at Lucy, and then at each other. Without exchanging a word, they huddled in a group hug, then hopped up and down, unmindful of fancy dresses, high heels, makeup, or any other trimming the day had demanded.

This is what true joy feels like, Maggie realized. *Let's celebrate what we can, when we can, with everyone we love.*

Notes from the Black Sheep & Company Bulletin Board

Dear Knitting Friends,

It's hard to believe that it's mid-October and autumn, in all her glory, is sweeping through New England. It seems we're knee-deep in fallen leaves and knee-deep into knitting season, too. How did that happen?

The summer flew by so quickly. And not without excitement here in town. I mean the mysterious passing of farmer Jimmy Hooper and Adele McSweeney, of course. May they both rest in peace. We feel much more peaceful, too, ever since those crimes were solved—once more with the help of my intrepid knitting circle, I will add. But that's just between us. I don't want to step on any official toes....

There have been much happier distractions for me lately. As many of you know, I was recently married to my longtime partner and sweetheart, Charles Mossbacher. We've decided to postpone our honeymoon, since this is a busy time of the year for the shop. But we are mulling over plans to travel to Italy or Greece in the spring.

Right now, we're enjoying the brisk weather and getting cozy in the evenings by the fire. What knitting project says cozy better than a pair of hand-knit socks? Our group got a jump on preventing cold toes and started stitching socks this summer, with amazing results. I've put a few pairs on display in the shop window, for you to admire.

Here's a link to a vintage collection of over twenty free two-needle sock patterns that will keep you busy all winter. And don't miss Phoebe's class, Save-the-Earth Socks, featuring fibers made of recycled materials, which she'll teach at the shop very soon. Sign up ASAP; this session will fill up quickly.

Happy autumn and happy stitching to all,
Maggie

PATTERN LINK: https://freevintageknitting.com/
patternbook/socksbk57.html

ZUCCHINI & CARROT PATTIES WITH YOGURT DILL SAUCE

These tasty, baked vegetable cakes are perfect as a side dish with fish, chicken, or most entrées and fine on their own as a vegetarian meal. Baking, instead of frying, keeps them diet friendly. If you'd like to push the calorie count even lower, omit the shredded cheese and add more fresh herbs, or just a tablespoon or two of Parmesan.

Preparation:
Heat the oven to 375 degrees.

Line a large cookie sheet with parchment paper, preferably one without sides. Lightly coat with cooking spray, or use a pastry brush to spread a few drops of olive oil over the paper.

Ingredients:
2–3 medium zucchini (about 2 cups grated)
1 medium yellow onion (about 1 cup diced)
3 large carrots (about 1 cup grated)
3–4 garlic cloves
2 tablespoons olive oil

1 egg, beaten
Any combination of fresh herbs, about 3–4 tablespoons combined:
    Chopped flat leaf parsley
    Chopped basil
    Chopped dill
1 tablespoon dried oregano
1–1¼ cups cheese, shredded (cheddar, muenster, mozzarella, Jarlsberg, or a blend)

2 tablespoons or slightly more, sea salt (for zucchini
    preparation)
1 teaspoon freshly ground pepper

Prepare zucchini: This step will keep the batter from being
watery and will keep the cakes from falling apart.

Wash and cut off ends of zucchini. Scrape away some skin,
but leave some on. Grate on the thick side of a cheese
grater to make 2 cups. Slightly more is fine.

Place zucchini in a mesh strainer over a bowl, and mix
with 1 tablespoon of salt. Let stand for 10 minutes so that
salt draws off water.

After 10 minutes, you should see water in the bowl. Press
down on the mixture so that the vegetable releases even
more moisture.

Spread a clean kitchen towel on the counter or a cutting
board (or heavy-duty paper towel) and place shredded
zucchini inside. Roll it up and squeeze out even more
water.

Move the zucchini to a large mixing bowl.

Wash and scrape about 2 or 3 large carrots. Shred on the
wide side of a cheese grater to make one cup. Add grated
carrots to the zucchini.

Dice onion and garlic into small bits. Heat oil in a sauté
pan and cook onions and garlic until soft, fragrant and
golden on the edges.

Add to the zucchini and carrots. Add the shredded cheese and 2 tablespoons of finely grated Italian cheese, such as Parmesan Reggiano or Locatelli Romano.

Add diced fresh herbs and oregano, a bit more salt, and ground pepper.

Beat the egg in a small bowl and pour into the mixture. Stir mixture until all the ingredients are completely blended. (If the batter seems too wet to form into cakes, you may add flour at this point, a teaspoon or two.)

Set the bowl in the refrigerator for 5 to 10 minutes.

Form the mixture in cakes: Wet hands, shape a handful of mixture into a small ball, about 1 inch or less wide. Place on the parchment paper and flatten to ½ inch high. The cake should be about 1½ to 2 inches wide.

When all the cakes are shaped, you may spray tops very lightly with cooking oil spray, or lightly brush with olive oil.

Bake on the middle rack of a preheated oven for 20 to 25 minutes. Test to see if cakes are toasted on top and crumbly on the edges. Take care not to overcook. They don't take very long. Sprinkle a pinch of sea salt over cakes before serving and even a bit more chopped fresh herbs if desired.

Serve with chilled Yogurt Dill Sauce. Recipe below.

*Note: If fresh vegetables are unavailable or you don't have time to shred, a bag of frozen vegetables (broccoli, cauliflower, and carrots) can be substituted for the shredded carrots and zucchini.

Microwave contents of 1 bag (about 12 ounces or 3 cups when cooked) in a large bowl. Drain out water completely. Grate in a food processor.

YOGURT DILL SAUCE

This quick sauce is the perfect light, tart topping for these zucchini cakes, but also goes well with grilled salmon and other dishes. No worries if you have some left over. Unlikely, since it is so tasty.

Ingredients:
½ cup plain Greek yogurt
2–3 tablespoons (plus extra for topping) chopped fresh dill
1 teaspoon chopped fresh mint
2–3 tablespoon white vinegar
1 teaspoon ground cumin
1 teaspoon sea salt
1 tablespoon fresh lemon juice or apple cider vinegar, optional

Combine all ingredients in a small bowl. If the mixture seems too thick (this depends on the brand and fat content of the yogurt you use), add a tablespoon or so of water or more white vinegar. A dash of fresh lemon juice or apple cider vinegar is a nice touch as well.

Chill sauce for 15 minutes.

Top with a sprinkle of chopped dill before serving along-side the cakes.